THE ONWARDS & UPWARDS GIRLS

Linda Mellor

This is fiction.

ISBN: 9798680996218

*The Onwards & Upwards Girls is dedicated
to the fiftysomething seekers of love,
life, and laughter. Never give up!*

*Also a special thank you to the good, the bad
and the ugly from online dating.*

THE ONWARDS & UPWARDS GIRLS

By

Linda Mellor

CHAPTER 1

'I have to go,' said Karen.

'Why so soon?'

'I have to get back. I have to see to animals, I am looking after them for friends.' Karen lied.

'Let me walk you to your car?'

She wanted to turn down his offer but it seemed mean. His dating profile had built up her hopes, and he didn't match up.

As they walked down the high street, Jeff jumped onto the road to avoid a puddle of water stretched across the pavement and was nearly hit by passing car. He checked his white baseball boots, then took the long way around a patch of grass.

'How about a meal this evening? I could follow you home, you see to your animals then I could drive you over to mine, and you could stay over for some fun?'

'No.' said Karen.

'Why not?'

'I'm not interested and I don't do one night stands.'

'That's a bit stuck up, isn't it!' said Jeff. 'You're on a dating site, so what's the problem?'

She stopped walking and looked at him.

'I'm not interested!'

'That was a waste of an afternoon!'

'Goodbye!' said Karen.

'Look, we're adults, it's only a bit of fun and I'll pay for your dinner, we could get fish and chips,' said Jeff. He reached out to grab Karen's arm.

'Don't touch me. Get off!'

'Come on.'

'Leave me alone!'

She pressed the key fob. The car doors unlocked. Jeff had turned and marched off in the opposite direction. Karen got into the car, and caught sight of the garage-bought, cellophane-wrapped carnations and chocolates on the back seat. She considered shouting after him, so she could return them, then thought better of it.

She took a couple of deep breaths.

Suddenly, a light-coloured estate car screeched to a halt next to her car and blocked her exit. It was Jeff. Karen pressed her central locking button inside the car, and locked all the doors.

He shouted something incomprehensible at her then attempted to drive off but lurched to a halt in the middle of the high street. He punched the steering wheel and continued to shout. Karen looked on. Finally, Jeff's car burst into life, and took off at speed down the road.

When Karen arrived home, she locked the door. As she changed into her comfy leggings and t-shirt she wondered if Jeff did this with every woman he met. Was dating always going to be a challenge? Karen looked at her reflection in the bathroom mirror. She was curious what sort of older woman she would turn into and how she would look. As she pondered a little longer, and looked closer into her blue eyes; her eyelids had more creases, surrounding lines and wrinkles extended outwards. Her eyebrows had thinned so much they no longer needed plucking. It gave her an odd feeling as she looked into her own eyes, was she searching for information or was it recognition.

At 52, Karen Knighton felt a deep-down acceptance of age and being happy in her own skin. Yes, there were things she would like to change but she could live with the scars and unevenness in her body. She was unafraid of her increasing years but didn't want to grow old on her own. Life was more fun if you shared it. She needed a man in her life and longed to feel that closeness and experience love again.

'Onwards and Upwards!' she smiled at her reflection then headed back downstairs to the kitchen.

Karen was determined to carry on dating, she kept positive a good man would be out there and they'd find one another.

Her 11 year marriage to Thomas had ended years before they separated and divorced. Her feelings for him had gradually dwindled when he refused to get help. He stopped working and started drinking. The depression gripped, paranoia took over and his online addiction became the centre of his life.

For years, Thomas had hid his addictions under the guise of searching for work. However, when Karen's part-time lecturing role ended, she began working full-time from home. Thomas stopped concealing his online life. He had done it for so long he no longer cared if Karen knew. In the afternoon, he slept for an hour or two, went to bed at 2 -3 am, and got up after ten. In the evening, he would take a bottles of wine, or cider from the fridge and head back his den to continue with his virtual life on his laptop.

One day, Thomas got a phone call from Legal Services in Wales telling him his son had been sentenced to three years in prison for a serious assault on his girlfriend, who had been five months pregnant and had suffered miscarriage. Thomas snapped out of his online life and drove down to Cardiff to see his son.

Ten days later, Thomas returned from Wales, determined to pull his life back together. Within months, he was offered a managerial role in a new book shop chain in St Andrews. Six months into the role, Thomas had booked his annual leave for a 5-day trip to Wales, on his own.

On the morning of the third day of Thomas's trip, Karen had awoken from a great night's sleep. She had forgotten about him. She got out of bed, walked across the room to the bathroom and saw her reflection in the mirror. As she studied her reflection, memories of her former self flooded back and she felt a powerful surge of emotion rise up through her body, and as it left her, she cried.

When Thomas returned from his trip on Tuesday morning, she told him she wanted a divorce, he acted as though nothing had happened, and went to work at the book shop.

That evening he arrived home from work, Karen said, 'we need to get the ball rolling with the legal stuff.'

Thomas looked puzzled.

'For what?'

'The divorce.' said Karen.

'Oh,'

'You still want to go ahead with it?'

'Thomas, what planet are you on?

'I thought you weren't serious.'

'We have been unhappy for years.'

'Look, I do not care. Do whatever you want but we need to get the separation underway, and find out how quickly we can divorce.'

Thomas pulled his phone out of his uniform pocket and started sending a text.

'Great! We are trying to sort out a divorce, and you start sending text messages.'

'It's about the shop.'

'I know you're having another affair. I want you to move out as soon as you can.

Distracted by his phone, 'eh, what did you say?'

'When can you move out?'

'Move out, what do you mean?'

'I don't want you living here. You are having an affair with one of your colleagues.'

'No, I'm not!'

'Thomas, Warren saw you in The Haunted Cellar in St Andrews having a cosy candlelit dinner on Sunday night, apparently you left with your arms around one another. You told me you were in Wales.'

The colour drained from Thomas's face. His phone buzzed in his hand, he slipped it into his pocket.

'Others have seen you around with her.

Within two weeks he had moved out. Karen felt relieved when Thomas drove away with the last of his belongings. He had left an envelope, addressed to her on the dresser.

She sat down at the kitchen table and opened the envelope and found an official-looking two-page letter. Thomas said he understood from their discussion on Tuesday 3rd May 2011, she wanted to divorce. It had been her decision to end the marriage, she hadn't consulted him, and it was forced upon him.

Then he waffled on about her increased book sales, the dates she was in the UK Fiction Book charts, when she had risen in popularity, and secured a new publishing deal. With all this taken into consideration, he should be party to some of her profits as he was married to her while this happened, and that he had sacrificed his career and family life to support her.

'I do NOT believe this!'

He asked for £50,000, in cash and stated he was within his rights to go to court to ask for spousal maintenance and/or part of her pension. He had become accustomed to a way of life with her, and that his expectation to continue with this lifestyle should not be ignored, and he was not being unreasonable.

Karen felt a huge abyss had opened up in front of her. She never imagined he would have resorted to cowardly letter writing.

If he had approached her, she would have sat down and worked something out. Yes, she had money in the bank, but she had money in the bank before she met him.

Karen had always bailed him out and never asked him to repay a penny. She had kept business and personal records of what she spent and where, and lodged them with her accountant.

Every holiday she paid for, each car she bought him, thousands of pounds of cash she had given him and the legal fees she settled while he battled in court with his second ex-wife over contact arrangements with their children.

Justine, Karen's lawyer, had advised her about protecting her assets. At the time, she winced at the thought of detailing all her personal expenses, including gifts she bought, and cash she had given to Thomas, but Justine insisted it would be to her benefit if she got into a routine.

Thomas's letter to Karen ended with an ultimatum. Karen's

ently the Police are taking it seriously now. I had a visit from them.'

'Oh my god, really?' said Karen.

'Yes, and, I have a date!' said Annie.

'That's....'

'Oh no, he's early! I'll have to go, the Farrier's pick-up is coming up the road. If all goes to plan I'll be free when he leaves.'

'Come over when you are finished, I will have the coffee on,' said Karen, 'see you later.'

Radio Four news filled the quiet corners of the kitchen. Karen had a good hour and a half to write before Annie would turn up. The Farrier worked fast but he was shooing Betty, a difficult Thoroughbred mare. Annie sedated the horse when she was due a visit from the Vet or Farrier, as it minimalized the stress and injury, to both horse and humans.

Karen looked forward to hearing Annie's news. She gazed out the kitchen window, and watched the birds on the feeder and a colourful cock pheasant sat on the nearby wall. As she ground coffee beans and filled the kettle, her mind drifted off with thoughts about dating, relationships, and marriage.

She paused and looked at the pictures on the front of the fridge before she opened the door. The pictures made her smile and re-minded her of the fun she had with her friends.

Karen sat down at the kitchen table with her notebook and pencil. She wrote quickly, and letting the words flow. This free-flowing style of writing helped her to get her feelings down on paper, and tapped into her intuitive thoughts. She was lost in the moment, and unaware of time passing, and had filled ten pages when a noise made her look up. It was Annie coming up the drive in her mucking-out gear and wellies, she dangled a headcollar from her wrist like women dangled designer handbags. She was talking on her phone, eyes down, and smiling.

Annie stopped at the gate, unlatched the metal lock, and swung it open, then closed it with her foot. She hung the headcollar on the post then walked over to the old stone doorstep, and used the edge to pull her feet out from her wellies. She peered into the kitchen window and waved to Karen.

Karen closed up her notebook satisfied she had made a great start on her lists and switched the kettle on. She could hear Annie trying to wind up her phone call.

'Okay, yes, that's great.'

'Yes, that works for me.'

'No, really, it is a good time.'

'Okay then, I shall see you at 3 o'clock in the café carpark.'

'Bye!'

Annie walked into the kitchen.

'What am I going to wear on my date this afternoon?'

Karen laughed. 'Go as you are. It's how you normally dress, and if he's the one for you, he'll like the Eau de horse you stink off!'

They laughed.

Annie took her coat off and hung it on the old coat stand in the small hallway between the main door and the kitchen.

'I can't believe it! Nothing happens for months and then, in the space of 24 hours it all descends!'

As Annie washed her hands in the utility room, she shouted through, 'the Police came to see me last night?'

She walked into the kitchen, 'there was a knock on the door at six-thirty last night, I got such a shock as my first thought was that something had happened to my horses. It was a policeman and woman, I asked them in because I didn't want them standing on the doorstep for everyone to see.'

'Wasn't their Police car parked outside your gate?'

'Oh Christ, you are right, so everyone knows I had yet another visit from the Police.'

'You haven't done anything wrong, have you?'

Annie looked startled and then faked a laugh.

'Oh no, of course I haven't.'

'Why worry then?'

'Well... err... you know what the village gossips are like.'

'What did they want?'

'They wanted more information about the flasher and asked if I could help with a description of what he looked like and what he was wearing, and, wait for it, did he have any distinguishing features. I couldn't help it, but I laughed.'

Karen smiled.

'I told them everything I could. About the red, white, and black or blue Confederate flag tattoo, on his left thigh.'

'At least you can laugh about it, years ago, most women would have been traumatised,' said Karen.

'They asked if I knew who it was? He had been seen at the other end of the village and had flashed at one of the elderly ladies living in the converted Mill. She had also identified a tattoo on his leg.'

'Eww, what a creep, imagine going around flashing your bits at women?'

'My next story is more positive. Remember that horsey people dating site you mentioned to me weeks ago? Well, I looked it up, and spent an entire evening reading through their pages, and I joined up!'

'Well done, I'm pleased you did, hopefully, you'll meet someone nice and live happily ever after.'

They both laughed.

'That reminds me, I hope you don't mind but I used one of the photos you took of me, you know the one of me looking sort of smart and smug after I won that dressage comp last summer?' said Annie.

Karen smiled, and said, 'I don't mind, if it brings a decent man into your life, then you are welcome to it! So, who is the hot date this afternoon?'

'He only lives 30 miles away, near Culross, and has a couple of horses, divorced, with two grown-up children, and a dog. He sounds nice. We have exchanged email addresses, so I also have proof he can write and spell,' said Annie.

'What's his name?'

'Donald,' replied Annie. 'I think he's semi-retired or does some sort of consultancy work.'

'He sounds pretty normal compared to the others.'

They laughed.

'I am happy to do normal, normal is good!' laughed Annie. 'I'm sick of the weirdos, the pervs, the odd balls who want to suck your toes. Oh god, that turns my stomach just thinking about it.'

Annie pulled a face, 'remember that ex-Navy submarine bloke I met at the dressage, great company, well-mannered, educated, loved horses. I was so hopeful. Then I slept with him, and each time he was naked, he called me his bitch, what the hell was that about?

Karen laughed.

'You should have asked him.'

'Not sure I wanted to know.'

Annie took a deep breath and sighed loudly.

'I need to make a magic wish for Mr Right, do you think the fairies can do the impossible?'

Karen laughed loudly, then looked at Annie.

'I had forgotten all about him, on god, remember his masturbation confession.'

There was a pause, and then 'the Halasana pose!' they said in unison.

'Eeww yuck, that was awful! He seemed so proud of his flexible body!'

Annie gagged, coughed, and laughed.

Tear ran down Karen's cheeks, she could hardly breathe. She laughed and wheezed as she tried to suck air into her lungs.

'I needed that. You can't beat a laughing fit for making you feel better. I'm putting the kettle on would you like another coffee?'

'Do you think I should? said Annie, still laughing, 'I may turn up for my afternoon date with Donald wired to the ceiling thanks to my morning caffeine intake.'

Karen nodded.

'Oh, go on, I'll have a weak one, thanks.'

'I didn't have to push hard to convince you.'

'Tell me more about this new stallion on the horizon?'

'Ha, ha! If only.

'Well, you never know.'

'He did say he had a mild heart attack five years ago. He blamed it on the stress of his divorce, so maybe there's no stallion potential.'

'You don't want a sexless relationship, Annie?'

'Hmm, most of my relationships end up sexless so maybe I should start that way. Sometimes, you just get bored of it, or rather, I get bored of them because it all gets predictable and nothing new happens. They seem to think once they're in a relationship they can lie back and do nothing.'

Annie paused.

'No, I'm too young for that to happen, maybe when I'm older but right now, I'm only 59, and maybe I'd like to try sex again with the right man.'

'Right man? Don't you mean any man?' said Karen.

They laughed.

'What is he like?'

'He's tall, about six foot, he looks medium build from his photos, has reddish, blond hair and looks like he is thinning on top, but he wears hats so it's difficult to see. When he described himself, he said he was an athletic build and a sort of blond version of George Clooney. I laughed when he said that, but he didn't say anything else so maybe he is genuine.'

'He looks fit and healthy, and he has a lovely smile.'

'Do you have a picture of him?'

'Not on my old horsey phone but I have a few on my tablet.'

'Where are you meeting?'

'The Farm shop outside St Andrews. I took your advice and arranged to meet over coffee. And as you say, it is long enough to get a look at him, get a sense of the sort of man he is.'

'I exchanged a couple of messages with a guy on the Date50 site,' said Karen.

'Oh, anything interesting?'

'No, but I did get the offer of a free haircut in his salon.'

'Isn't that a bit of an insult?'

'Ha, no I didn't think it was an insult just a bit weird. I mean, who'd want to go on a first date with a hairdresser? You'd look like a bedraggled mess when he washed your hair, and when he cuts your hair he'd ask you about dating and may get a bit carried away, and lob all your hair off.'

They laughed.

Annie picked up a biscuit, and nibbled around the edge, and looked deep in thought. 'I decided I needed to change my attitude towards dating. I thought it was all going to be a waste of time, and every man I met would not be right for me. I have set my standards higher, and I make sure we have common ground before we progress to the next stage.'

'Sounds like you are going into the dating with a good frame of mind.'

Annie replied, 'I am quite excited about meeting him but I have two dilemmas to sort out; what to wear and the best route to St Andrews?'

CHAPTER 3

They had been friends for a few years and had met when Karen and Thomas moved from Northumberland and rented Castone Stable Cottage. Annie had leased some good pasture land for her horses close by.

Over the months Karen and Annie friendship developed from brief chats at the horses' field to Karen inviting Annie in for coffee and some warmth one wintry morning.

In January 2015, after the divorce was settled, Karen bought a small farmhouse on the edge of Maryard, after a tip off from Annie. Annie lived in Upper Maryard and had heard the farmhouse was going on the market and told Karen.

Annie rarely spoke about her family but Karen had pieced together Annie had been born in Germany where her parents had been in the army. They were transferred to Scotland when Annie was five, and she had a younger brother. Karen wasn't entirely sure if Annie's parents or brother were dead or alive.

Annie was barely five feet tall, but her lack of height did not stop her from working with big horses. Over the years she had clocked up many trips to the hospital to mend her broken bones.

She lived in Wren cottage in Upper Maryard. Previously, she had lived on Fetterby Farm a few miles outside the village with her husband, Ron. The farm was a mixture of arable and cattle. Ron had a prize-winning herd of cows, and grew vegetables for local supermarkets. One winter, Ron was found dead in the bull pen. He had left everything to Annie, so, immediately after the reading of Ron's Will, she sold the farm, livestock, and machinery, bought Wren cottage, and moved in.

Annie had no-one in her life apart from her animals. They gave her a purpose, a routine, and a reason to get out of bed in the morning.

Karen felt sorry for Annie some of the time, she could see she was a kind-hearted and thoughtful person who had been full of life, but something had happened and turned her into a bitter woman with a hard exterior. Karen sensed Annie had lots of dark secrets. Mostly, she was good fun, and loved to laugh, on her bad days she was cold and standoffish.

'Why don't you wear something straightforward, classy, smart casual sort of outfit?' said Karen

Annie pulled a face.

'I don't want to look as though I tried too hard to impress him, it may make me look desperate.'

'Well, there you go, smart casual is the answer.

Annie got up from the table, picked up her battered old mobile and put it in her jodhpurs' pocket.

'Thanks for the coffee and a chat. I have a silk shirt that goes well with my dark trousers, that'll look presentable but casual enough.'

'Annie, do you want me to text or phone you five minutes into your date?'

'Oh yes please! My escape route from a bad date. I am meeting him at three o clock, and I will keep my phone in my pocket.'

'Good luck, and remember to relax and smile, and I will call you at 3.05.'

Annie had just over an hour to get ready before she drove over to St Andrews for her coffee date with Donald.

This was her first date since the disaster dates last year with the chemistry professor. Their first two dates had gone well, they had fun, but they were always cut short because Annie had to get the train back to Fife from Edinburgh to tend to her animals.

The professor told her he was doing a lecture in St Andrews and would see her afterwards, so she invited him to her house for a meal.

Quickly, he made himself at home, Annie offered him coffee.

'Have you anything stronger?'

Annie had wine chilling in the fridge, she poured two glasses and handed him one. She asked him about his lecture but he was reluctant to talk about it. Annie checked on the food and returned to find both glasses empty. The professor asked for more wine. Unsettled and unsure what to do, she made a comment about drinking and driving but he insisted on more wine. The table was set, and they sat down to eat. He ate the food like a pig in a trough, and shovelled most of the vegetables onto his plate. An entire bottle of wine had gone down his neck in less than an hour and he wanted more.

'You have to drive home tonight.'

'I can't, I have had too much to drink, I'll stay the night,' he said, matter-of-factly.

'But… but…but… we haven't talked about it!'

'We have now,' he replied.

'I have plans.' said Annie.

She tried to think of a way to get rid of him. She did not want him in her house, and had no interest in the drunken man sitting across the table from her, licking his plate.

'I only want to stay for one night and not for a month on full board. You told me you had a guest room, so I thought you were hinting I could spend the night with you.'

'There were no hints. I would prefer you did not stay here.'

'Well, lady, I have drunk too much and am over the limit for driving.'

'And since I am not going anywhere tonight, pour me another drink?'

Annie fumed. A prisoner in her own home, forced to have someone in her personal space. She did not feel safe. Home was her secure place where she shut the door on the outside world. He couldn't spend the night.

'I need to make up the bed for you.'

'Don't bother because I'll sleep with you.'

He looked across at her and grinned.

'No, you won't, I don't want to sleep with you!'

'I'll make it worth your while, consider it payment for dinner, bed and breakfast.'

'*BREAKFAST?*' Annie looked at him, fists clenched and showing her teeth

'I DON'T WANT BREAKFASSSST, I WANT DRINK?'

He banged the empty glass down on the table.

Annie walked into the kitchen searching for something. She saw bottles of whisky, port, and brandy by the cupboard, and thought she'd hide them. As she put the bottles in the cupboard, she discovered a bottle of cheap blended whisky at the back. She took it out, blew the dust off it before she unscrewed the top and stuck her nose closer and inhaled.

'Ooh, that's awful!' she said quietly.

She looked in the cupboard where she kept her spices and herbs, and grabbed the bottle of sleeping pills, took the top off and tipped three into her palm, she shook so much they fell onto the floor.

'Damn!'

She picked them up then wrapped them in a sheet of kitchen roll and took the rolling pin from the drawer and crushed them into a powder against the countertop. She filled an old glass with the blended whisky and mixed in the powdered sleeping tablets. She stopped for a moment and wondered if she was doing the right thing. Was three enough?

'Is that drink coming up soon? A man's dying through here!' shouted the professor.

'Bastard,' she muttered.

She went back to the cupboard and took out two more sleeping pills, crushed and stirred them into the glassful of whisky.

She caught sight of herself in the mirror, she looked wide-eyed and unhinged. It reminded her of the others.

Annie walked back into the sitting room and picked up the professor's empty wine glass.

'I'll get you a refill. Do you fancy something stronger?'

'Aye, I do, fill it up, wench!'

'Wench?' she spat back at him.

'Hurry up wench, a man needs his drink!'

Annie turned the heating thermostat up high. She hoped the combination of whisky, pills and heat would hasten his need to sleep.

She returned from the kitchen. 'Here, try this.' Annie watched him as he looked at the glass, and wondered why he hesitated.

She hoped he'd be out of it soon. Then in the morning when he wakes up, she'd kick him out.

He was slumped in the chair; his tie pulled away from his neck and his shirt buttons undone.

Annie screwed up her face and clenched her teeth, and cursed the stupidity of the situation she was locked into.

The professor downed the drink in one.

His eyes widened. 'What was that, it tasted stronger than the first wine?' His words were slurred.

'It's my homemade cocktail. Fancy another one?'

'Fill her up!'

'I'm going to the loo, I'll sort out a refill in two minutes.' Annie went out of the sitting room door then along the hallway and up the short staircase to the toilet. She wondered if she could tie him to the chair, so he couldn't move around the house when he woke up, find her in bed and rape her. She'd need to go out to the shed to find the rope. A good plan, it gave her hope, she thought.

Annie opened the sitting room door. He wasn't sitting at the table where she left him, she ran into the kitchen, he was not there either.

'What the hell?'

She looked on the floor, around the back of the sofa, behind the curtains, in the cupboard, the hallway and the kitchen. She ran upstairs, checked the rooms, under the beds, inside the bathroom, and behind the shower.

Annie ran downstairs, '*WHERE ARE YOU?*' She yelled.

Outside a car started up, the engine revved and pulled away at speed.

'Bastard!'

She watched the car lights disappear off into the distance then she checked all her windows and double-locked the doors. She was shaking and was not sure if it was with fear, stress, or relief.

Annie went into every room twice, and checked the cupboards. She knew she was being irrational, but it confirmed to her he was no longer in the house and that she was safe. She cleared the plates from the table, and blew out the candles. He had taken the bottle of the cheap whisky she'd left out on the kitchen counter. She poured herself a large Vodka and tonic before sitting down by the log burner.

Another dating disaster.

CHAPTER 4

Annie turned left out of the village, within 10 minutes she was on the A91 and headed to St Andrews. Today was a good day, she liked everything about Donald and he had horses. Her perfect man.

She had made good time as she turned across the A91 and onto the track up to the farm shop. Annie slowed down over the concrete speed humps then parked up by the main entrance.

She glanced around and looked for a man fitting Donald's description. She opened the window a couple of inches to get some air as she scanned every vehicle in the carpark. She reached up to the rear driving mirror and angled it so she could see her face. She tilted her head and lifted her chin and looked into the mirror then smoothed her hair down, ran her finger over her eyebrows, and straightened her earrings.

As she stretched her arm across into the passenger footwell to get her mobile from her bag someone tapped loudly on her window. Startled, she let out a short, high pitched squeal.

'Is that you Annie?' said a rotund man in a checked shirt and a green, padded Barbour waistcoat.

'It is me, Donald!'

Annie pressed the down button on her car window, 'Donald?'

The window opened two more inches.

Her face was screwed up with a look of disgust.

'Hello Annie, you look lovely!' He lurched forward and tried to fit his head into the gap of the open window.

She swerved away from the window.

'No, stay back!' yelled Annie.

'Come on, just a little kiss!'

Saliva gathered in the corners of Donald's mouth. He puckered up and moved in again and tried to get his head in the gap and into her car. The edge of the car window burst a huge blood blister on his chin. Annie's car window was smeared with blood.

Annie's phone rang. 'Hi Annie, it's Karen.'

She spoke quickly. 'Hi Karen, is everything okay?'

Karen laughed, 'there's an international wine crisis, if you do not return within the hour you will never see a glass of wine every again.'

Annie didn't reply.

'Annie, what is that sound, are you okay?'

Annie closed the car window but Donald knocked again, and again. He tried the door handle.

'Thanks for the call, Karen, I'm leaving now.'

Annie held up her phone, she pressed the button to open the window by an inch, she shouted through the gap.

'I have an emergency, I can't stay!'

'Come on Annie, we're here now, come out and give me a kiss and a cuddle.'

Annie felt the panic rising in her throat. She needed to stay calm. Frantic thoughts ran through her head about a stupid old man keeping her a prisoner in her own car.

'Go away, leave me alone!'

'Oh, come on, sweetie, let's talk?'

'BUGGER OFF!' yelled Annie.

She started her car, drove forward but the panic blinded her and she couldn't see her exit in amongst the parked cars. She braked then put the car into reverse, and turned the steering anti-clockwise, determined to get out of the parking space. Donald called out to her, but she didn't dare look. She straightened up the steering wheel, kept her eyes to the front, crunched the car into gear and sped off as quickly as the car would go, she changed gear and took off as she hit the speed bumps as she careered towards the exit.

She drove through the stone pillars at the exit before she stopped and looked in her rear-view mirror. Donald stood in the middle of the road on one leg waving at her. She indicated left and pulled out onto the main road.

Driving through Cupar she stopped at Tesco, and reverse parked at the back of the carpark, and watched all the cars coming in. Five minutes passed, then ten before she stopped shaking. She scanned the carpark but could not see anyone resembling a limping fat man.

She phoned Karen.

'You will not BELIEVE it!' said Annie.

'Are you okay?'

'Yes, I am okay a bit shaken up, but I am good. I am in the Tesco car park in Cupar, I am going to pick up some wine, do you need anything?'

'No, thanks. Are you sure you are okay?'

'Yes, I am, I'll be quick, then I'll drive back. I need a friend more than ever now, especially one I can drink wine with, are you free?'

'Of course, I am, is there anything I can do to help?'

'Yes, get the bottle opener and two glasses at the ready!'

'Drive carefully, see you shortly,' said Karen.

Annie looked like a startled animal as she whizzed around the aisles of Tesco picking up a large pizza, a cheesecake and two bottles of Chablis from the chilled wine cabinet. She raced back to her car, on high alert for signs of a green Barbour waistcoat and a checked shirt.

Back in Maryard, Karen met Annie at the front door.

'Now, don't say one word. Come in, sit down, and drink some wine. Take a deep breath and THEN tell me what happened.'

After large gulp of wine, 'you will not believe it. He was huge and looked like he slept in his clothes, with a big blood blister on his chin where he had cut himself shaving, his hair was all over the place, it was shoulder length and there wasn't much of it on top.' She took in a deep breath.

'Oh my god.'

'He looked nothing like his photos, maybe they were taken twenty years ago or more, but I saw nothing that made me think, oh look that's Donald.'

'The only thing that made me sure it was him was his voice.'

'Blokes like that should be done for misrepresentation or something in the trade descriptions act.'

'I did not get out of the car. Not once. I did not step foot in the carpark. I was sitting in the car when he crept up on me and gave me such a fright when he knocked on the window. I kept the car locked, thank god or he would have been in the car, he tried to fit his head in the gap of the open window to give me a kiss and his blister burst on the edge of the window.'

'You are joking.' said Karen, laughing.

'It's disgusting, I have his blood on my driver's window!'

'Awwwww, yuck.' Sounds like a murder scene.'

Annie looked puzzled, 'Murder, what do you mean?'

'You know, blood left behind, identify the victim, it was joke!'

'Ah yeah, yes!' Annie faked a laugh.

'How did you escape?' asked Karen.

'When you called and heard that sound, it was him knocking on the window trying to encourage me to get out of the car, so we could go have a kiss and cuddle.'

'He's keen.'

'Ha, well, I think I've given him a lasting memory of the date that never was because, I'm sure I ran over his foot in my panic to get away from him.'

Annie gulped down some more wine. 'I reversed, and drove over something I think was his foot. I think he cried out. When I reached the bottom of the road, I saw him in my mirror, he was standing in the middle of the carpark on one leg, and waving.'

'Has he tried to contact you?'

'He's called my number about twenty times.'

Annie left Karen's later that evening, she walked down the road happy, and consoled herself she had avoided a disastrous date. She was niggled about a wasted an afternoon getting dressed up and the cost of the fuel driving to and from St Andrews and, more importantly, she'd forgotten to eat cheesecake she'd left at Karen's.

Karen's phoned beeped.

'Morning! Thanks for last night, it was great fun and a perfectly timed dating debrief and much needed wine therapy.'

Karen replied 'Morning! Yes, it was fun, and we forgot about the cheesecake.'

Karen's phone rang.

'Hi Annie, how are you feeling?'

'I am okay, not quite bursting with energy yet but I'll get there. The horses are done so that's the first task of many.'

'Have you got much on today?' asked Annie.

'This morning is quiet, thank god. I am useless, all that wine we had has given me a fuzzy head and need a few more gallons of coffee to get me going. This afternoon I have a clay shooting lesson and a business catch up with Warren.'

Karen showered and dressed, and made her way downstairs to her office to check her work emails before she left.

She pulled on her thick hooded sweatshirt and searched for her gun cabinet keys. She opened the door under the stairs, flicked the light switch on and studied the two keys. The keys turned in the correct locks and the cabinet door creaked open and she took her 12-bore shotgun out from the cabinet, smiled at it, pushed the top lever, and broke the gun open. She locked up the cabinet and took her gun carefully out into the light. She placed her feet firmly on the ground, one slightly in front of the other and hip-width apart.

'The gun is empty,' she said out loud.

She closed her gun and mounted it into her shoulder and brought her cheek down on the stock. It felt wonderful. The gun fitted Karen perfectly. She pointed it through the kitchen and closed her left eye, focussed her right eye on a distant pigeon sitting in the tree. The smell of the gun instantly took her back to her childhood, and days when she went shooting with her mum and dad. As she moved the gun down and away from her face, she pushed the lever and broke it open, and the light caught the engraved plate. Karen eased it, barrels first, into the sheepskin and leather gun slip. She closed the gun, zipped, and buckled the slip and put it over her shoulder, she walked into the kitchen, grabbed her bag and her shooting vest from the kitchen chair.

By the time Karen arrived at the shooting ground, her head was clear and focussed on shooting well.

The clubhouse was busy.

The ground's shooting coaches huddled around a table, looking at a diagram and having a rather intense conversation.

Jane waved to Karen from the coffee machine at the back of the clubhouse.

'You look great!' said Jane. They hugged.

'So do you, so healthy and slim. What have you been doing?'

'I've started running again so it must be working if you have noticed a change. Find a table, I'll bring coffee over and we can have a catch up before Warren gets here, I think he is at his mum's.'

Karen sat down on the big red sofa at the back of the clubhouse, Jane brought the coffee over.

'How're things?'

'Not too bad, it has been steady in here and I am looking forward to my holiday next week.' said Jane

'A holiday! That's a great thing to look forward too, where are you going?'

'We're going to Turkey, a rural villa and meeting up with some of Lucy's friends. I think you met a few of them at our wedding?'

'How long are you going for?'

'Two blissful weeks of sun, private swimming pool, cocktails and lovely food. Check your Facebook page because I'll be posting up loads and loads of photos.'

They laughed.

'How's his lordship doing after last week's psycho episode?'

'Oh dear, it was bad, wasn't it? I thought she was going to do something really dreadful, and I'm glad he did not teach her how to shoot.'

'It was all caught on the CCTV, wasn't it?' asked Karen.

'Yes, it was. The full gory details.'

'All of it?' asked Karen.

She faked a surprised expression, lifted her eyebrows, and opened her eyes wide.

'Oooh yes, everything including when she peed in his Louis Vuitton overnight bag in the boot of his car. At first, I couldn't figure out what she was doing but then I saw a flash of her bum. It was so white compared to the rest of her orange tanned hide!' said Jane.

Karen snorted and laughed.

'Kaaaaren, my darling!' said Warren, loudly and dramatically.

Warren sat on the red leather sofa next to Karen and gave her a big hug and a kiss on the cheek.

'How the hell are you?'

'I'm great thank you, Warren, how are you?'

'Fantastic, and I am single once more, have you heard?'

'Yes, Jane was just telling me the damage had been captured on the CCTV. Are the police going to charge her?'

'I spoke to them this morning, and yes they are but I don't know with what and when. As long as they keep her away from here and from me, I'm happy.'

'What happened this time?'

Jane looked at Warren, 'tell Karen what happened.'

'I told her right from the start that I did not want anything serious, and I also said, as per your advice, I am not relationship material. But she pretended we did not have that conversation.'

'Uh huh.'

'I went home one afternoon after I gave a lady called Debora a shooting lesson, and took her with me. I made her one of my Avocado salads and she just sort of, well, sort of, told me she needed something meatier than a salad.'

Warren laughed

'Aww, that is so cheap!' said Karen, rolling her eyes, and laughing.

'So how did what's-her-name come into it?'

'Oh, Lauren, well, she saw my car on the drive, and thought she would surprise me by coming in through the patio doors by the kitchen.'

'Oh, don't tell me, you and Debora were at it in the kitchen?'

'Yup, guilty as charged.'

'Those freestanding workstations are just the right height.'

'You never change.'

Karen finished her coffee. 'Right, I am going to get my gun from the car and get organised to shoot. See you at the Down the Line stand?'

'I'll bring a card for the trap, have you got shells?'

'Damn it, no, I don't!' Karen shook her head in disbelief.' I can't believe I have forgotten them!'

'Don't worry, I'll grab a couple of boxes.'

Karen smiled. Thanks!'

'Why do you want to start on DTL?' asked Warren.

'I don't know, I just fancied it, and I haven't shot it in ages.'

Warren swiped his plastic card through the reader on top of the electronic trap control box and pressed the buttons to make the system deliver 50 clays.

'Okay, it is set up, so shoot when you are ready,' said Warren.

Karen put her earplugs in and leant her gun slip against her body as she unbuckled the leather straps and pulled the zip down to reveal her gun. As she took her gun out of the slip, she pushed the lever across, breaking the gun, and pulled it out of the slip in a steady and deliberate movement.

The gun was placed on the wooden bench by the stand, Karen tied her hair back and cleaned her shooting glasses then emptied a box of twenty-five cartridges into her waistcoat pocket. She picked up her gun and walked over to the first of five stands and got into position then looked out onto the grassy area.

Karen looked at her feet, raised her head up and looked out while filling her lungs then slowly released the air, she inhaled again and as she did so, she loaded two cartridges into her gun. Karen closed the gun, and put it into her shoulder, settled it in and brought her cheek down so she looked along the barrels and out. She imagined a clay target flying out from the trap, and shooting it.

Karen positioned her barrels and kept her eyes out in the area beyond the trap house and clicked off the safety.

'PULL!' she said, in a smooth, controlled voice.

The instant the orange clay flew out from the trap house some

16 yards in front of her, she was on it and fired. The clay exploded.

She returned to her position.

'PULL!'

Again, the clay few out but at a different angle, but Karen was on it, she fired and the clay broke.

She flicked the safety on, opened the gun, and the two spent cartridge shells ejected out. She reloaded.

'PULL!'

She called for ten targets and shot everyone.

'Well done!' said Warren, 'You are in the zone and shooting brilliantly.'

'Thanks, Warren, it feels so good to be shooting again, I have left it too long.'

'Yes, I know but you must make time for it otherwise it won't happen, and you will just fill your days with more work and no fun.'

'Oh, I don't know about no fun part, I have started dating again.'

'About time.' Said Warren.

'Oh, I know,' said Karen extending her words. 'I have tried but there hasn't been Mr Right or anyone vaguely near.

Karen moved to stand 2 and went through her routine but Warren stopped her as he could see she was rushing.

'Unload your gun, and step back off the stand.'

'Do some deep breathing to centre your mind and pull your focus back to where you need it.'

'Remember the visualisation techniques and believe in your ability to shoot all the targets.'

Karen followed Warren's instruction and shot four out of five targets, the last one she lost her concentration when she saw a pigeon fly overhead.

'Ha-ha, that will teach you to keep focussed, I saw what happened, your barrels followed your eyes and went upwards as you looked at the woody.'

After 50 targets, Karen was satisfied to have shot enough. 'You were shooting well, not much going wrong apart from the pigeon distraction and you looked a little tired towards the end.'

'Yes, I could really feel it, my strength isn't as good as it used to be. But I am happy with what I shot. At least I am back out shooting again, and I plan to attempt a weekly session.'

'If you can, that would be great, next week we can work on the other stands and see how you get on.

Warren's phone rang, he looked at the screen and frowned.

'Sorry, Karen, I need to take this.'

'Hi Mum, are you okay?'

'No, it's not a problem, I shall be over in 20 minutes.'

'Yes.'

'No.'

'Yes.'

'Do you need milk or anything else?'

'No.'

'Yes.'

'Yes.'

'What did you order on your tablet?'

'How MANY?'

'No, DON'T!'

'No.'

'Yes, mum.'

'Put the kettle on, I'm on my way.'

'Okay.'

'Bye!'

'Sorry Karen, I have to dash off to sort out my mum, she needs some help to lift some boxes, and if I don't get there, she'll start moving them herself,' said Warren. 'She has been ordering things online again. This is how she deals with the news my dad has married again.'

Warren gave Karen a big hug and kissed her on the cheek, 'you shot well today, and it is great to see you looking happy, my darling. Text me some dates for shooting next week, and let us have lunch or dinner afterwards so we can catch up on everything in and out of work? I have a few ideas for business I need to talk over with you, it should have happened today but there we are. Mothers! Let me know about next week, whatever suits?'

Karen locked her gun in her car boot and went back into the clubhouse and hoped to see Jane but there was no sign of her. The old shooting coaches were still huddled tightly over the same table, a few tables were taken by small groups making the most of the pensioners afternoon tea offer.

Karen returned home, cleaned her shotgun before she placed it back in the locked cabinet. She wondered about dating, and how long it would take before she met someone she'd like to get know more.

There was a tap on the kitchen door, 'hellllooooooo!'

'You've started early.' said Annie when she spotted two wine glasses on the kitchen table.

'Well, it is 6pm, and that means it's evening by my standards.'

They laughed, raise their glasses, 'Cheers!'

'Why is dating a challenge when you're in your fifties?

'I'm not sure,' said Annie. 'I would like to meet someone nice, I'm not asking for the impossible. Just meet a good man, take it slow and get to know him.'

'That's how I feel, I'm not looking for anything other than getting to know them and progressing on from there or not.'

'Men seem to be on the prowl for one-night stands. Have we both missed big changes in the world?'

Karen took out the bottle of white wine from the fridge, and topped up their glasses. 'We are in our fifties, we are not nineteen and sowing our wild oats.'

Annie shook her head, 'it's not as if we send out messages saying, I'm desperate and will have sex with you. It's quite the opposite.'

Karen took a mouthful of wine, 'oh, don't move!'

She quickly got up from the table, grabbed her car keys and went out the kitchen door to her car.

A short time later she returned, smiling as she locked the door behind her.

'These are from my dating disaster with Jeff, I'd stuck them in the car boot and forgot all about them.'

'Oh, lucky girl.' laughed Annie. 'The man has taste! Mmm, Milk Tray.'

'You can eat all the fancy choccies in the world but there will always be a place in your car boot for Milk Tray,' Karen laughed.

Annie sighed, and took a mouthful of wine.

'What's wrong?'

'Oh well, at least he was thoughtful, shame his faults were pretty overwhelming.'

'He rated himself very highly. I guess I've failed womankind by not recognising I was in the presence of a white baseball boot-wearing hunk who thought he could persuade me to sleep with him for the cost of a takeaway.'

'My first husband was a bit like that, he thought I should be privileged to be in his company, and when he wanted sex he would lie back and expect me to do everything. This was his way of allowing me to worship him and show my appreciation for the life he mistakenly thought he provided for us.'

'That is just so backwards, Annie.'

'I had a good career in toxicology, and earned much more than him.' said Annie. 'He was addicted to Viagra, and bought bulk boxes of them. Honestly, I don't know how many he took daily, but he had a permanent hard-on.' She snorted air out through her nostrils and sneered, 'bastard'.

'I didn't know you had two husbands, sorry, two ex-husbands.'

'Yes, my first marriage did not last long, within months of getting married everything changed. He started going out without me, coming home late, made arrangements, didn't include me. A boat turned up one day on the back of a trailer. The guy delivering it wanted me to sign for it. I thought he was going to ask for directions to the harbour. He told me he had sold it to the ex-husband for £15,000.'

'£15,000 is a lot of money to spend without discussing it with your spouse.'

'He was a dark character, and there were times when he frightened me with his rages. That Jeff you met sounds like him. Those rages came from nowhere and were a regular thing.

'Oh my god, don't tell me his name was Jeff?' asked Karen, with a horrified look on her face.

'It wasn't him,' said Annie confidently.

'Oh?'

'How are you so sure?'

'I was young, and I did not know what was going on. I thought I had a married a good man, and we had a great marriage, would have children, and live happily ever after, you know, a sort of modern day fairy tale. I genuinely believed that. Amazing, isn't it.' said Annie. She faked a laugh.

Karen smiled.

'I know you did not meet him because he disappeared after we had been married for 13 months. I reported him missing after a couple of days, and the Police found him dead in a burnout rural hotel on Arran or Bute, I can't remember which one. Initially, they thought he had died of smoke inhalation, but it turned out he had died after a fall, brought on by an overdose of Viagra.'

'Oh dear, I am sorry, it must have been a shock for you?'

Annie looked up from her glass.

'I was pleased. He was a pig. A male chauvinist pig.'

'You did not miss him then?'

'No, I didn't. It actually worked out well as the insurance pay-out gave me the chance to get my life in order, and basically, start again, and I didn't have all the aggro of a divorce.'

She dipped into the box of chocolates and selected the orange cream.

'Mmmm, these may be old fashioned but they're still delish.'

'I went from being unhappily married and to a merry widow with money.' Annie smiled.

Karen refilled their empty wine glasses, and said, 'Cheers, and here's to the girls.'

'Cheers!'

Annie left after they finished the wine and the top row from the box of chocolates. Karen settled in for a quiet night.

She flopped down onto the sofa, her mind went back to Annie talking about the death of her first husband and how cold and calculating she sounded and her delight when the insurance paid out.

'Damn, where's my phone?' She wandered into the kitchen, picked up her bag from the chair and found her phone in the side pocket. She flicked the kettle on and read through her phone messages.

There were five alerts from the dating site. She logged in, clicked on the profile photographs, and read the profile information.

'Hi, Tallladybooklover,

I found your profile this afternoon and was delighted to read we have many interests in common. I joined this website last week and have spent lots of time reading through many profiles, and it's been a struggle, so I was delighted to discover you as your profile is refreshing different, and I would like to know more about you?

I am a tall man, and a book lover, my name is Simon, I moved up to Fife two years ago but travel lots with my work. I work in the specialist software industry in the farming sector, in Technical Post-sales. I am single, having divorced just before I moved up to Fife. My ex-wife and I have an amicable relationship, and I still have some contact with my stepdaughters. I like to live life (not in a racy way!), I am positive, and reasonably outgoing but not a party animal, I think am too old for that at 59, but have no plans of growing old gracefully!

That is enough about me, and I hope my profile is of interest to you and I look forward to hearing from you.

Yours,

Simon.'

She re-read through Simon's profile information and looked at his photos. A new alert popped up saying there were lots of new profiles. Karen clicked on the link and viewed a list of profile pictures.

Each photo had a username, and a welcome phrase. Karen scrolled through the profiles with a sense of horror.

The first guy was age 51 and looked as though he was going to have a fight with the person taking his photo, the caption read, 'no drama queens or looneys'. The next one was also 51, from Edinburgh and his profile picture was taken from an unusual angle, looking down on his bald head, a showing off his football shirt. The next one had a huge earring in his left ear, he looked sort of lost, thought Karen. He was 49, 'Lliars, chaets, and nutters is that's all there is.' The next one was a 50-year-old from Glasgow, had no detail in his profile apart from one line, 'live life with no regrets live life as if you stole it.'

The next guy wore a flat cap, and thick coat but the photograph was taken in a house by a radiator. The next guy said, 'big handsome, sensitive guy' he was 56, and was wearing a big baggy t-shirt and had a coat hanger in the back of his photograph. The next guy had such a thick beard you couldn't see his mouth, but he was 'looking for that special lady.'

Another notification popped up.

'Hi, Tallladybooklover,

I read your profile with interest, you sound a confident, strong woman. I live local to you and need a woman to tell me what to do, anything, and I will do it. I get pleasure from being told to do things and from doing them and making you happy. You look like to sort of woman who could do that for me. Can we meet for a coffee to discuss a possible arrangement?

Yours,

Rick.'

'Hi, Rick,

No.

Yours,

Tallladybooklover.'

She laughed and blocked him.

Her Saturday night entertainment was complete. Dating must be a numbers game. The only potential dating candidate on the horizon was Simon. She would play it cool and reply to him tomorrow.

That night Karen slept well. She wanted to crack the online dating code.

'Did you have a peaceful evening after I left?' asked Annie.

'Yes, I did. In fact, my evening was a fun-filled event full of laughter How was yours?'

'Really?' said Annie, disregarding Karen's question.

'I made a cup of tea after you left and sat down to watch some rubbish on TV, but it was never switched on. I spent my Saturday night curled up on the sofa gawping at my phone and going through all the profiles of the potential partners and sat back in awe!'

'What? Seriously, lots of potential?' enquired Annie.

Karen laughed. 'Remind me to show you some of the hunks, you'll be drooling and desperate to sign up.'

'What was wrong with them?'

'It'd take too long to explain, you need to see it for yourself.'

Annie paused, and said, 'do you think you are maybe being a bit picky?'

Karen roared with laughter, 'just remember you asked that question when I show you the mug shots.'

Sunday mornings were relaxing, and Karen delighted in no fixed plans. She made a fresh pot of coffee and sat at her desk to reply to Simon. The spring-time sunshine stretched through the windows and illuminated parts of her office. Karen thought about new beginnings. The snowdrops in the garden, the energetic, mixed staccato chirps from the garden birds were all classic symbols of spring. There was renewed hope, and a deep-seated feeling of optimism within Karen.

'Hi, Simon,

Thank you very much for your message, it is lovely to hear from you. I have searched through many profiles on this dating site, so I share your frustrations.

Delighted to hear we have many things in common. My name is Karen, I'm tall, work in the publishing industry and love books.

I am also divorced. My ex-husband returned to south Wales, and I remained in Fife where I was born and lived for the first 20 years of my life. I moved to London and have lived in a number of lovely locations before returning to Fife two years ago. I am 52, with no children.

Oh yes! Life is most certainly for living, and also doing it with a positive attitude. Online dating is never dull, and there's such a variety of potential dates, many not so positive. Is it the same for men?

Best,

Karen.'

CHAPTER 5

As she looked out of her office window, a movement close to the woods caught Karen's eye. A fox sat on the edge of the woodland sunning itself. She picked up the binoculars from the window ledge to study it. The fox's thick fur coat looked a brilliant orangey-red in the sunlight. As Karen watched, the fox tilted its nose up to the sun as if to give thanks for the heat and light. Three cubs burst out from the cover of the woodland, play fighting with one another as their mother.

'For god's sake!' Karen reminded herself she should be out there with her camera. She grabbed her camera, pulled on her wellies at the back door, and put her camouflage jacket on. Slowly and quietly she opened the door, and closed it behind her, and did not stop to lock it. She cursed the noisy gravel underfoot as she made her way to the woods. The wind direction was in her favour and would not betray her and alert the fox, and the trees made a noise as they swayed in the breeze. She crouched low using the wall as cover, then the thick hawthorn hedge. She lent the long lens on the old gate and got herself into a comfortable position. She looked through the lens as the cubs wrestled in the long grass and their mother basked in the sunshine. Occasionally, she pushed them away from her when their rough play impinged on her relaxation.

Karen took a number of photos before the fox slipped back into the safety of the woodland with her cubs at heel.

As soon as she reached the house, she switched on her laptop, took the memory card out of her camera, and stuck it in the card reader.

Karen felt a twinge of excitement as she clicked on the folder of downloaded images.

'Yes!' She skimmed through the images, the vixen looked amazing basking in the sunlight, but one image stood out. It was a family scene, a proud mother watching over her offspring with an expression that oozed motherly love.

She tagged the image and opened her email to send it to her photo agency. The image would earn her a few hundred pounds if it was used, she also sent the digital file to her favourite printing firm to be made into a huge canvas for her office wall.

She sent the images to her various contacts, and checked her personal email. There it was a reply from Simon. He had responded to her email almost the instant he had received it.

'What do you want for the fox photo, Karen?' an email arrived from Tim at the newspaper picture agency.

Karen replied, 'Thanks Tim, where are you going to use it, and what size?'

Tim made Karen a good offer for the photograph, she created an invoice, and emailed it over with a user licence. She was happy it had made her money so quickly, and it was going to be in a good position in the national papers on Monday.

She felt happy her Sunday had started so well. She opened the email from Simon.

'Hi, Karen,

It was great to read your email, and I am delighted we have made contact. Without a doubt, we will have plenty to talk about. Would you like to join me for dinner next week? I am Scotland based all week but on the road, then I am away with work across Europe looking at some new software developments.

More about me, originally from Exeter, then my family moved to South-east London, near Greenwich as my Father was in the Navy, and took a land-based position. I got my MSC in Computer Science at Glasgow University, returned to work in the home counties. I met my first wife, we had a happy marriage for fifteen years and then parted, we have one son. I was in my forties and single, so I applied for an EMEA manager role thinking the travel would be fun. It is, but it can be a challenge with the flight delays. I am now a European Director and have a team of people working for me. At 59, I would love to travel less and am looking at my options. I met my second wife, and we married at Gretna Green six months after we met, crazy? Yes! Over the years, we just grew apart, we talked and made the decision to divorce. We are proud of the way we handled it. My two stepdaughters come up to spend the occasional weekend with me.

Married and divorced twice, no young children, no baggage, no issues (I hope!).

I like going out to the theatre and enjoy some classical music. I'm not religious, I enjoy reading a wide range of subjects and am rarely without a book or two, I do have a Kindle; it's a bonus when travelling and attempting to keep within the luggage allowance at the airport.

So, how about dinner? My diary tells me I am in Kinross, Dunkeld, then on Thursday I am travelling up to Aberdeen, and Friday I am in Inverness. Are you free on Monday, Tuesday, or Wednesday, otherwise I could do Saturday? Here is my number.

Yours,

Simon.'

Karen clicked on the photo attachments and studied them with interest. Simon looked handsome, he was tall, well built, and had dark hair. There was something about his physique that reminded her of a rugby player. Yes, he was someone she would like to meet and wondered what he sounded like. There was one photo of him lying in a bath or a hot tub that gave her a slight feeling of unease but thought he may have sent it to her to show her was in reasonably good condition with no additional plumage.

Sitting back in her chair, she tilted her head back, her eyes looked up at the ceiling of her office, and for a couple of moments, she imaged meeting Simon. He would smell nice, clean shaven and in a good quality shirt; one he had ironed himself. Casual trousers or trendy, designer denim, and a trendy Montblanc brown leather belt finished off with leather shoes or boots, highly polished and well cared for. He owns a number of tailored tweed jackets, and one will be his favourite. The more she thought about how he would look, the more interested she was. The late afternoon sun warmed the back of Karen's head and she drifted into a nap.

On Tuesday, Karen finished her interviews and headed back to her hotel. She wanted to look over her notes before meeting Simon for dinner in the pub on Atholl Street, Dunkeld.

After they had spoken on the phone on Sunday evening, and Karen was satisfied he was in the normal category, and proceeded to the next stage, so dinner was arranged for Tuesday at 18:30.

Karen showered, and put on her favourite cream coloured shirt with a green bird pattern running through it, and her black trousers. Years ago, Karen was proud of her figure and wore clothes to show it off. She kept fit and active and could look in the mirror and be happy with her reflection but nowadays, clothes helped cover up the insecurities she had about the way she looked. Black reigned supreme, green marginally edged in front of navy followed by red if she felt daring. Black made her feel smart and business-like. She put on her black jacket, stepped into her black leather heeled boots, and zipped them up. This gave her more height, she loved being tall, and at 5ft 11" her favourite boots added 3" to her height, she could comfortably walk in them. Had she thought about her exit already?

She stood in front of the hotel room mirror she felt all her body insecurities queue up to take a bow. She told herself to stop it, and looked into the mirror again and smiled, and encouraged positive thoughts to flow. It took a few moments, but it happened, and one after the other, the positive thoughts eroded the negatives ones, 'Onwards and Upwards,' she said.

She sprayed on some perfume, picked up her bag, and checked her phone. Simon had texted to say he had arrived. She replied, 'I am on my way, will be there in 5 minutes.'

The daylight had faded into dusk as Karen walked down Atholl street, she felt slightly nervous about the evening ahead, a meal was more than a coffee, and required lots of conversation. It could be hours and not minutes unless it was a complete disaster and they couldn't stand the sight of one another. She was less than 10 yards from the pub entrance.

'Hi, Karen!'

Simon greeted her with a firm handshake and a kiss on each cheek. His aftershave had a wonderful smell, and he was wearing more or less what she had seen in her vision.

'Hi Simon, how nice to meet you!'

'You look lovely,' said Simon. 'Here, let me.' He held the door open for her and ushered her in first.

'Do you want a drink in the bar or shall we go straight to our table?' he asked.

'Can we go to the table?' Karen felt her phone vibrate in her pocket, it was Annie doing their dating safety call.

The lighting was bright in the pub, he looked older than his photographs. His hair was thinner and greyer, and he walked with a limp. Simon's skin looked good, but he was not quite the same as the man in his photos, he had to be more than five years older. He was tall so he had been honest and accurate about his height.

The waitress sat them in a corner booth towards the back of the pub. The green exit sign by the door caught Karen's eye.

'A sparkling mineral water, please.' said Karen.

Simon ordered a local beer. 'Are you driving?'

'Yes, I am,' said Karen. Technically she would be driving tomorrow but she did not want him to know she was booked into a hotel around the corner.

'I'm driving but as I am having food I am going to allow myself a pint,' said Simon. 'Plus, I deserve it!'

He had a nice smile, and seemed relaxed in her company.

They chatted as they looked through the menu, Karen was relaxed and felt an attraction towards him.

'What do you fancy?' he asked with a grin.

Karen ignored his schoolboy attempt at flirting.

The waitress took their order.

Simon was good company, he was well-travelled and knowledgeable. He answered her questions and asked plenty of his own but never made her feel uncomfortable. Simon balanced the seat on its back legs as he spoke to her. The time flew.

Halfway through her coffee she looked at her watch, she had enjoyed Simon's company and the evening had been very easy going.

'May I have the bill?' Simon asked the waitress.

'Let me pay half?' said Karen.

'Absolutely not, this is on me, you can buy the next one if you wish.' he said.

Karen looked at him and smiled. Yes, she would see him again.

As the put their coats on, he left the waitress a generous tip then held the door open for Karen.

'Let me walk you to your car?'

'Thanks, but it's okay, I'm parked up just around the corner.'

'Thank you very much for a lovely evening. I really enjoyed your company, and hope we can ....'

Simon lurched forward, his teeth clashed on hers, and his mouth clasped tightly around her lips. His arm was around her waist as he pulled her towards him. His other hand was on the back of her head, and forced her into him.

Karen tried to pull back.

'Stop it!'

She pushed him further away, and tried to break his grip on her. 'Let me go!'

'I have been wanting to do that all night, but you were playing it so cool.'

Karen said in a raised voice, 'I was not playing it cool!'

He moved in on her again and pressed himself up against her. She could feel his erection.

'Get off me!'

'Give me space to breathe,' she pushed him away again.

'Don't tell me you didn't notice?'

'What the hell are you talking about?' said Karen.

She pulled her eyebrows together and glared at him.

'From the minute we met, I was excited, and was trying to show you in the pub.'

He lunged at her again.

'Get the hell off me!'

'Okay, okay!'

'I'm sorry, I'm sorry, I just got carried away.' Slowly, it began to dawn on him she was unhappy and angry at him.

'Goodnight!'

'Don't go!'

'GOODNIGHT!'

'Karen! Look, I am sorry, please forgive me!'

'Simon, goodnight, I need to go.'

'KAREN!' he called after her.

Karen walked confidently down Atholl Street and headed towards the bridge. She did not turn around or slow down. She heard him get in his car and hoped he would drive off. Karen quickened her pace, she took a right turn, and within 20 yards she arrived at the hotel front door. The reception desk was closed but the bar was busy. She took the stairs to her room on the first floor. Quickly, she opened her hotel room door, stepped inside, then locked it and made a bee-line for the mini-bar.

She poured the mini Vodka into the glass and pulled the ring pull on a tiny can of tonic, it hissed. She poured half the contents into the glass.

She bent down and unzipped her boots then kicked them off, grabbed the glass and sat in the chair by the window, she took a large drink, swallowed, and put her head back, and said, 'what the fuck!' to the room ceiling.

The River Tay flowed in front of the hotel, only a road and a narrow pavement separated the water from the building. She took another swig from the glass and finished the drink.

A red BMW drove slowly down the road. Her phone rang. She silenced it. She could see the car's computer screen lighting up in the interior of the BMW. It was him.

She opened another Vodka from the mini-bar, she tipped it into her glass followed by the remainder of the tonic.

The phone buzzed, and the notification light flashed.

It was 9 pm, Karen wished she was at home and not in a hotel room but she looked for the positives; she knew she was anonymous in the hotel, safe and unreachable.

Was this going to be a constant theme for dating in your 50s? Full of creeps that wanted a leg over or older men pretending to be younger and taller. Why couldn't they just be themselves?

The following morning, Karen listened to Simon's voicemail, it was full of 'I am sorry' and 'please forgive me', 'give me another chance', 'Can we meet again so I can apologise'.

She texted him. *'Simon, do not contact me again. Karen.'*

Karen went down for breakfast then settled into the lounge and waited. Her morning meeting was booked for 9am with Colin Blackthrone. He finally turned up at 9.25am and did not apologise for being late.

'Lucy recommended you, and she spoke very highly of your work,' said Colin.

He sat across the table from Karen in the hotel's coffee lounge. His dark dyed hair reminded Karen of a toilet brush, and it took on a purple tinge as the sunlight shone through it. His thinly plucked eyebrows did not match his hair colour. His small eyes and a crooked grin made him look shifty.

'I would like to write a book, mostly based on my life but I am no good at writing and wondered if you would like to be my ghost writer?'

'Tell me about the book, the story, the plot etcetera,' said Karen.

She picked up her coffee, sat back in her chair with her notebook open in her lap.

Colin sat back with his legs spread wide. 'Well, I have had an interesting life, and I think it would make good reading in a book. I joined the army, left after fifteen years and then went to work as a bodyguard, mostly for private, high profile clients.'

'Why do you think it will be an interesting read?', asked Karen.

'Doesn't everyone want to read about that sort of celeb, gossip stuff? I toured around in big limousines, flew in private jets, and was told to turn a blind eye to the drugs, tarts, and orgies. I had some action myself so that could be a couple of chapters.'

He raised a plucked eyebrow and his widened smirk revealed many missing teeth.

'I think it would make a great film, and I have some suggestions for the actors I would like to play the parts.'

'Who are you aiming it at, your target audience?'

The more Colin spoke the less interested she was.

'I think the ladies will love it. Don't you all love a big, handsome hero?' he asked.

He twitched his groin.

'Can you expand on that a little more?'

'Well, I'm a sort of everyday 007. You ladies love that?'

Karen wondered how quickly she could draw the meeting to a close. 'You said you were a bodyguard, is that right?'

'You ask a lot of questions, don't you?'

She looked straight at him. 'I need to understand what you want to include in your book.'

'How long were you a bodyguard? Give me some names of your most high profiles clients?'

'It was a few years ago,' said Colin, looking a little coy. 'Err... the most famous ones were the Crinkies, Maggie Smart, and Sylvester McCrory. Oh, and Duncan and Donald Younger, the tweed twins, they didn't do anything but fish all the time.'

'What other ones did you work for?' asked Karen, as she pointedly looked at her notes, and read out. 'The ones with the Limos, private jets, and the orgies?'

'Instead of making it about me, could you make it into a fiction story and I could describe the scenes to you and you could write them out in chapters. I would be the action hero. It could be like the Kevin Costner film from years ago but only a Scottish version.'

Colin fidgeted, beads of sweat ran out from under his dyed hair and down his forehead.

Karen looked at her watch, 'I am sorry Colin, I need to draw this meeting to a close as ....'

'You are going to write it for me, aren't you?'

'I need to go away and study my notes, and then give you a price, and look at a timetable.'

'Okay, that would be great. Remember this will make a great film, it could have great sex scenes, just like that 50 shades of Grey. Sex always sells, doesn't it?'

'I shall be in touch.'

CHAPTER 6

'*Hi, Tallladybooklover, So good to read your profile, and I do confess to enjoying your use of words with more than two syllables. The profiles I was matched with seem challenged by the English language. I have been on this dating site for a while and have yet to secure a date – that is, until today.*

Dear lady, do forgive my boldness but may I have the pleasure of your company for lunch next week?

Yours truly,

Jonathan G D Merrywell'

As she clicked on his profile, she liked what she read; tall, intelligent, confident, single man of 57, with a love of fine wine.

She sat back and smiled, and thought about the possibilities.

The next email from the dating website read:

'*Hi, Karen,*

I thought it was you when I saw your pictures, sorry, I did not know you were single. Anyway, what is a good-looking, intelligent woman like yourself doing on a dating site? I would have thought you would have had a queue of admirers.

It's been a busy time, the shooting season was hectic, the dogs were glad of a rest when it closed but I was happy to be out and managed to get a few days on the peg at Lower Inverscot. I worked the dogs on the home beat and even retrieved for the Prince and the newlyweds. It would be nice to catch up. I am now single, Debs and I split up in the New Year, she moved out and back to the USA.

Are you going to the Kelso Book Fair and Readfest at the weekend? I'm booked into a local hotel for three nights, if you are coming down how about a catch up over dinner?

Brian.'

Karen looked around her office for her diary, she reached over the desk and moved some notebooks, and found her diary, she had been so busy and had forgotten about the Book Fair.

It was in her diary though, so she had not double booked herself into something else. She replied to Brian, said she would love to catch up with him, and how sorry she was to hear about the split with Debs.

Within minutes her phone buzzed, it was a text from Brian, *'checking your number hasn't changed. Dinner Saturday evening?'*

'Hi Brian, yes to dinner on Saturday evening. I shall see you at the fair. KK'

Brian was speaking on both days of the fair. Karen looked forward to seeing him again. They had met on a charity clay shoot he had organised. The Alba Outdoors Field and Stream Magazine had commissioned Karen to write a feature about the day, and as the organiser, Brian was her main contact and a source of quotes. He was a nice man, and they had stayed in contact on and off since the clay shoot and had met up at the game fairs. Debs was a wildlife artist and looked like the identical twin of Chrissie Hynde from The Pretenders. Brian was tall, with a lived-in but subtly handsome face, dark brown eyes, and hair. He walked with a limp, an old injury from his days in the Fire Service. He had retired early and spent most of his time writing and talking about his first career, as a professional footballer. He did motivational talks and had written a number of best-seller books.

Karen wasn't surprised Brian and Debs had split up. Debs had talked non-stop about America and always grumbled about Scotland. Karen smiled when she recalled the spectacle at the Scone Game Fair two years ago, when everyone had enjoyed the generous hospitality of the Land Agents. Debs got drunk, and argued with Brian, she had whined, and moaned about everything.

She fell asleep by the Taxidermy in the corner of the tent. Unable to wake her, Brian gave her the fireman's lift to the car park.

Dinner with Brian would be good, and Karen looked forward to it.

'Hellooooo Karen!' Annie called out from the kitchen door.

'Oh my god, am I glad to see you. Let me get the wine out.'

'Ooh, sounds like we could be in for a wine-therapy evening?'

'You couldn't make this up. Get yourself a chair and make yourself comfortable, it could be a long night ahead.'

'First things first, have you eaten, or made any plans to eat?

'Nope, and no plans.'

'Great, fancy joining me for chilli and rice then?

'Yes, please, that sounds delicious.'

Karen took a bottle of Chablis out of the fridge and filled two glasses. She picked one up and stretched over the table and gave it to Annie.

Karen's phone rang.

'Hi, Bernie.'

'Yes, I am'

'How was your mini-break with Dave?'

'Oh, no.'

'Come over?'

'Yes, Annie is here, if you get over in the next hour you can join us for a chilli supper?'

'Great, see you soon.'

Karen put her phone down on the table.

'Bernie is coming over, she is on her way back from a few days away with her new boyfriend. I am guessing it wasn't a success.'

Bernie arrived 30 minutes later.

Karen poured her a glass of wine. Bernie said hello, went straight to the table, picked up the glass of wine, tilted her head back and downed it in one.

'The guy is a prick.' Bernie announced.

'Dave?'

'Yup, and he has been swiftly demoted to ex-boyfriend.'

She took a deep breath and smiled. 'How are you guys?'

'Great,' said Annie.

'I'm just back from a meeting and a date from hell in Dunkeld,' said Karen, 'Sit down and make yourself at home, I'll tell you all about it.'

'Great, I could really do with the entertainment. I have had two days away with Dave, it won't take me long to tell you about it.'

'Do you want to go first, my story is a two-parter.' laughed Karen.

'Are we sitting comfortably, ladies? Well, we went to a little hotel in the Lake District, it was supposed to be a romantic few days away.'

'How long have you been seeing him?' asked Annie.

'About three weeks, I met him through work. I was astonished when he came up and asked me out. You know the old-fashioned way. The way people used to do the dating thing. He told me he'd taken ages to build up the courage to speak to me and ask out. I was flattered.'

Karen opened the second bottle of wine and filled their glasses. She checked the pot of chilli warming on the hob.

'What happened then?'

'Right. He was not my usual type of guy, but I fancied him. I had never gone for a man with a tan before, but I guess there's a first time for everything. He had long legs, a great butt and muscular arms but not the over-developed body-builder type.'

'But ….?' Said Annie.

Karen asked, 'is that what they call a himbo, or arm candy?'

Annie fidgeted and was keen to hear what happened. 'Go on….'

'The sex was rubbish and his idea of a good read was a car manual or The Sun.'

They laughed.

'We had sex once before we went away, he said he was stressed. So, I suggested we go away. You know the sort of thing, change of air, change of scenery, it sort of invigorates you, doesn't it?'

'Hmm, yes, I'd love to get away for a dirty weekend.' said Annie.

'I thought it'd give us both a chance to explore the two of us as a couple.'

Bernie pulled a face. 'Sex involved me honouring his request to dress in stockings, suspenders, and heels. I had to parade up and down the hotel room, bend over in front of him so he could get an erection.

I felt like such an idiot while he lay on the bed grunting something that sounded like, 'Come on big boy, yes, big boy, you're coming out to play.'

Annie laughed, 'sounds familiar.'

Bernie carried on, 'then, suddenly he announced, it's time, come here. At this point, I was thinking yes, he'll pay some attention to me. But all he did was tell me to lie down. He clambered on top, and it lasted about…'

Bernie paused, looked up at the ceiling, and faked a thoughtful pose.

'Oh, now let me count up the minutes on one hand.'

Bernie held up one finger.

'I'll be generous and say the sex lasted one minute. There was no foreplay, the roll on and the roll-off probably consumed, I don't know, say 30 seconds.'

'A minute!' said Karen.

'You are kidding?' said Annie.

'Nope, that's what happened.'

'After sex, he had a shower, admired himself in the mirror for longer than it took to have sex, and got dressed. He told me he had worn women's underwear since he was a child because his mum dressed him in his older sister's clothing.'

Annie pulled a face, 'oh, that's weird.'

'He said he liked the feel, and the fit, then he asked to wear mine, but I said no way. I couldn't imagine being with a man, knowing he was wearing women's knickers.'

'He got a bit moody afterwards then said my knickers wouldn't fit him because my arse was so much bigger than his.'

'WHAAT!' gasped Annie.

They all laughed.

'So you chucked him?'

'Yup, I did. I had no option,' said Bernie.

She shook her head, raised her eyebrows.

'He had to go. His arse was smaller than mine.'

'That's a new one.' laughed Karen, 'and you don't have a big arse.'

'If he were arm candy he'd have to be great in bed and I could do a trade in my head, great sex but no discussions about Maslow's hierarchy of needs or the changing dynamic of the creative world. Yeah, I think I could live with that. Just call me shallow, girls.'

They laughed.

'What did he say?' asked Annie.

'He told me it was my fault we were having a horrible time, and that I was uptight.'

'Oh god, that's an unusual point of view.' laughed Karen.

'That was the last thing he said to me when we were standing outside Penrith Castle.'

'Really?'

Karen put three plates on the table, cutlery and napkins followed by two large bowls of chilli and rice.

'Help yourselves, ladies.'

'What was the journey home like?' asked Karen.

Bernie smiled, 'Oh, it was peaceful.'

'Awww, come on, what happened?'

'It was a peaceful journey back home in my car.'

'Yes, but what did you talk about?'

'Nothing'

Bernie laughed.

'I was on my own, I left him in Penrith. I lied, the last thing he said to me, was 'you are crap at sex.''

'So I calmly said fine, and walked back to the hotel. Packed my bag, paid for the room and checked out. I put my bag in the boot of the car and drove up the road, and here I am.'

'Oooh, that's funny.' said Annie.

'How will he get back?'

'I don't know, but that's not my problem. It's his.'

'Penrith has a good train service, and it is right opposite the Castle if I remember correctly.'

'I thought I'd do the decent thing and pay for the hotel because he had a train fare to buy.'

They laughed and ate.

'Come on, your turn, Karen, what happened on your date?'

She took a sip of wine and said, 'I thought I was having a good date last night in Dunkeld, but the guy turned out to be a perv intent on showing me his erection while we were eating dinner, then afterwards he tried to swallow me whole starting with my head.'

'His erection? Did he get it out at the table or something?'

'No, he rocked the chair back on the rear legs, I thought it was odd, and considered he was maybe nervous or something, you know, a bit fidgety?'

'Was it poking out of his trousers?'

They laughed.

'When we were outside he told me he hoped I'd seen he was

turned on while I ate my food.'

'What the hell goes on in their heads?'

'You'd only just met him for a first date dinner.'

'Yup, and we'd only gotten to the starters when he, apparently, wanted to show me he had an erection.'

'But......it must have been small because I noticed nothing.'

They laughed.

'I went back to my hotel, slept well thanks to the help of the minibar, and then interviewed a complete fantasist straight after breakfast the following morning. He told me he worked in the fast lane, with high profile celebrities and had seen a lot of life and had enjoyed wild sex parties. When I questioned him about who his high-profile celebs were, he.... wait for it... he told me, they were The Crinkies, and ex-doctor Who, and the Tweed Twins from Glasgow.'

They all laughed.

'I was so pleased to get home. The only excitement we have around here is the Maryard flasher.'

Bernie looked surprised, 'a flasher?'

'He's exposed himself to the local ladies,' said Karen.

'Someone must know who he is?' asked Bernie.

'Actually, I do know who the bloke is. Definitely. I'm 100% sure.' Annie looked serious.

'What do you mean?'

'Promise you won't say anything?'

Karen and Bernie looked at Annie.

Annie gulped a mouthful of wine.

'You have our confidence,' said Karen.

'Okay. I had a brief fling with him when I moved to the cottage. He used to do some seasonal work on the farm for Ron. He was a general handyman, you know the sort, can turn his hand to anything, fix broken things, move heavy furniture, and get your car started.

Bernie and Karen sat in silence.

'He offered to move a few things, help with the horses and the like.'

'And sex.' said Bernie.

Annie nervously laughed.

'If you had a fling with him, why on earth did he flash at you?' asked Bernie.

'He's got terrible eyesight, I think he didn't know it was me. After I had spoken to the police, it clicked, and I realised it was him. My eyesight isn't the best either and if I don't have my glasses on I can't see much.

Karen said, 'that makes flashing very risky indeed if he can't see that well he may have flashed at men.'

'Maybe that's his thrill.' said Bernie.

Annie nodded, 'he can't see any further than a few feet in front of his face, and I'm the same, especially if the light is poor.'

'How did the handyman become the Mellors of Maryard?' asked Bernie.

'I had just moved to the new cottage, and he was still married to that grumpy, old cow, Jenny. He had been helping me for a number of weeks, and one night he came over late, saying he'd seen something moving around in the garden. I had forgotten to tuck the hens in for the night. I was drinking wine, felt a bit lonely and offered him a drink and it just sort of started from there.'

Karen looked at Annie, her eyes wide, 'you never mentioned

this before?'

Annie kept her eye line down on the table, 'well, it's not the sort of thing you share over a cup of tea, is it?'

'I guess not,' said Karen.

Annie faked a laugh, and said, 'oh, by the way, see the perv that's frightened all the local women, his name is Terry, he's married to Jennifer Brownlee, and I had a fling with him a few years ago.'

'I guess it's not for broadcast on the village noticeboard.' said Bernie

They all laughed.

'What happened?' asked Karen.

'It fizzled out. After sex a few times, I came to my senses and stopped it.'

'What made you come to your senses?' Bernie's curious mind ticked away.

Annie laughed and looked a little embarrassed. 'He was a bit odd, a couple of times I found him peering in through the windows, it frightened the life out of me.

Karen screwed up her face, 'I think that's called being a stalker.'

'I asked him why he did it, he said he liked watching me and I was nothing like Jenny.'

'That is WEIRD.' said Bernie.

'What was he trying to do, justify it to you, Annie?'

'I've no idea but Jenny came to see me one day, I nearly fainted. She wanted to see if I had one of the horses up for sale. I took her up to the stables, and she asked me if I had seen much of her husband. The fling was finished months before, so I told her truthfully I had not seen him in months. Apparently, the village gossips told her I was having an affair with him.'

'Oh Christ, what did you do?' asked Bernie.

'I was tidying up the stable, so I didn't have to look at her. I took a deep breath, hesitated and tried to think but I didn't have to say anything because, suddenly, she said she knew he wouldn't have an affair with me out of respect for Ron.'

'Your husband?' asked Bernie.

'My dead ex-husband. The local gossips told her he had been seen lurking around, and people had told her his van was parked up on the outskirts of the village a lot.'

'The village gossips should be working for CID.' said Bernie.

'The funny thing is, when he used to come and see me, he'd park his van on the other side, pointing back into the village as if he were visiting another house. He knew how people around here gossiped.'

'Anyway, she didn't buy one of my horses. I almost felt sorry for her.'

'Maryard, despite its small size, has a hell of a lot going on.' said Karen.

Annie raised her glass. 'Agreed!'

'Maybe it's worthy of a book.' Bernie laughed.

'Maryard's Murder, mystery and madness.' said Annie.

Karen thought that was an odd title to come up with.

'Well, I wonder what will happen to him now? Surely the police will arrest him?'

Annie made a face and said nothing.

'Ladies, I have some more news to share.' said Karen.

'I have had three more potential dating emails, and one of them is from Brian, someone I know through clay shooting, and I am meeting him tomorrow for dinner.'

'You haven't been put off dating after what happened?' said Bernie.

'Oh no, if anything, it is making me more determined to carry on, and battle through the dross.'

'What about you?' asked Karen

'I think I am going to sign up with a dating website, so I'll be looking for recommendations and not your cast-offs,' laughed Bernie.'

'What about you, Annie?

'I'll stick to the horsey dating website for now but, all that nonsense with Worzel Gummidge the other day really shook me up.'

'You should give it another go.'

'I will keep looking through the dating site. If I don't, my life will revolve around shovelling horse shit morning, noon and night and repeat ad infinitum.'

Karen filled the kettle and ground some coffee beans.

Annie made a move to go home.

'Thanks for this evening, it was great fun and lovely to see you again, Bernie.'

Annie took her coat off the coat stand and pushed her feet into her wellies. She pulled a torch out of her pocket and stretched the elastic banding over her head and straightened the torch lens so it sat in the centre of her forehead.

'Thanks, Karen, nights gals!'

Karen yawned. 'I think Annie has the right idea, I am going to head to bed, I'm shattered. It's been two long days.'

'Hasn't it, and a few more miles.' said Bernie.

Karen picked up the glasses from the table, 'I'll finish up in here, you know where everything is so help yourself to whatever you need.'

'Thanks, are you having a lie-in tomorrow?

'No. I need to be up and out before 8 for the Book Fair in Kelso. You've got a key so if I don't see you in the morning, sleep well, make yourself at home, stay for the weekend and lock-up behind you. It's up to you.'

'Goodnight.'

CHAPTER 7

Karen liked to hear Bernie moving around the house, it was nice to have company again. Lying in bed, about to drop off to sleep, she wondered why Annie hadn't told her about the fling with the flasher before? But Annie was strange. She said strange things.

Bernie was still asleep when Karen left for her drive south to the Book Fair. The roads were quiet at 8 am on Saturday morning. As she turned onto the A68, she started to feel relaxed about the drive and excited by the Book Fair.

The weather was mild and dry, ideal for driving and Karen was grateful it was not snowing, otherwise the snow gates at Soutra would have been closed. There were large areas of snow in the verges and in the laybys as the road reached the highest point with a long swooping left-hand bend. The static wind turbines rose up and punctured the open landscape to the east. They reminded Karen of the 1982 Pink Floyd Film 'The Wall'. The forest on the left was work in progress and had been partially cleared. A new road snaked its way across the hill to give access to even more turbines. It had been such a scenic spot, wild, open, and bleak, and no doubt the peaceful, undisturbed habitat to many species of animal, bird, and plant life.

A car on the other side of the road flashed its lights. A second car did the same. She checked her speed and looked ahead and saw a camera van in the distance, parked up on the grass, just off the road on the left-hand side. Her eyes momentarily dropped down again to glance at the speedo to double check.

Just before 10 am Karen arrived at the outskirts of the town. She drove down Kelso's main street and followed the one-way system around the back of the main shopping area and down Abbey Row. At the Abbey, she turned right onto the cobbled street hoping to find parking.

The Book Fair and Readingfest was in its 10th year and brought people into town for the weekend from all over the UK. Numerous tents and stalls lined the pavements and filled the entire market square. An official-looking girl in a luminous orange jacket flagged her down.

'Hi, can you tell me where I should park?' asked Karen.

'Are you here for the Book Fair?'

'Yes, I am.'

'Okay, keep left, drive up the road 100 metres, take a left at the end of the shops and follow the signs.'

'Thank you,' said Karen.

As she drove up the road she saw a man crossing a few yards in front of her, it was Brian. She honked her car horn, and he jumped in fright, and quickly turned around and was about to give Karen some verbal abuse then he recognised her.

'You gave me such a fright!'

'Sorry Brian, how are you?'

'Great, I'm in a rush as I'm preparing for my first talk at 11 am. Why don't you come over and find me in the North Tent?'

'Okay I will do, I'd better go park the car, see you shortly.'

As Brian walked away from Karen's car, he shouted, 'I shall leave a pass with the door steward.'

'Thank you very much!'

'Bye gorgeous,' said Brian.

Karen drove up the road towards the parking and looked for the left turn. She was smiling, she felt good and was pleased she had driven down to Kelso.

It was too early to check into the hotel, so she left her bag in the car boot, and walked back into town taking the scenic river-bank route along the Tweed. Floors Castle looked magnificent in the mid-morning light, surrounded by acres of bright yellow daffodils, and mature trees.

Not much had changed in Kelso since her visit last year, she crossed the road over the cobbles towards the big north tent. There were two smartly dressed Stewards on the main door.

'Hi, I'm Karen Knighton, Brian McArthur has left a pass for me.'

'Good morning Mrs Knighton, thank you, will you sign here,' said the young Steward.

She smiled, 'I'm Ms and not Mrs,' said Karen as she signed the visitor's book.

'Sorry, my mistake Ms Knighton. Here is your pass.'

Karen opened the envelope and took out the guest pass. She unravelled the long lanyard and hung it around her neck.

'Ms Knighton, may I ask you a question?'

She looked up.

'Yes, of course.'

'Are you Karen Knighton, the author?'

'Yes, I am.'

She smiled.

'I love your books on the Scottish Countryside and your magazine work, I never miss your Alba Outdoor Life column.'

'Aww, thanks, and great to know they're appreciated.'

'Can you sign my programme for me, and would you pose for a selfie?'

He went red, and spluttered, 'I completely understand if you don't want to but if you don't ask you don't get.'

'Happy to do both.' said Karen.

'What is your name?'

'Daaaaaavid Sssssoutar.'

She signed David the Steward's programme and posed for a selfie with him then headed over to the main aisle towards the coffee lounge.

'Karen, over here, my darling.'

Brian gave her a big hug and kissed her on the cheek.

'Everyone, this is the famous Karen Knighton, author, columnist and damn fine photographer.'

Karen smiled at the small group, and one by one she shook everyone's hand as they introduced themselves.

'Brian!' A voice from the stage called over to the group. *'You are on in fifteen minutes!'*

'Thank you, I'm coming over now.' replied Brian.

He turned to Karen. 'Make yourself comfortable, there is one row of seats either side of the stage for special guests, so pick a seat. He pointed to the coffee bar on the left. 'Excellent Americanos and bacon rolls over there.'

'Thanks, Brian, go do your stuff, I'll settle myself in.'

Karen got herself a coffee and a bacon roll. She had felt empty and remembered breakfast had been a long time ago. She ate the roll as quickly as she could and took her coffee with her to the front row. The tent filled up, there had to be over 150 seats lined up in front of the stage. She sat on the left-hand side, opened up her jacket and loosened her scarf around her neck, and made herself comfortable. She wondered if Bernie was still asleep and stifled a yawn.

'Hi Karen, lovely to see you here.' said a female voice enthusiastically on Karen's right.

It was one of the staff from the Alba Field and Stream office, Karen quickly scanned for her name badge.

'Hi Jasmine, how are you getting on?

'Great thanks, what a turnout!'

'We have a stand directly in front of the hotel, pop in and say hello if you can.'

'LADIES AND GENTLEMEN, MAY I HAVE YOUR ATTENTION PLEASE!' said the announcer on the stage.

'I'd better go sit down, see you later.'

Jasmine disappeared into the rows of seats.

'I would like to welcome you to the 10th Annual Book Fair and ReadingFest.'

For an hour Brian talked about writing books, self-belief and how important it was to be positive about life. He was an engaging speaker and knew his stuff. The audience listened, laughed, and gave him a lengthy applause when he finished.

Afterwards, Brian signed books, chatted to people, and posed for selfies. Karen mingled and chatted to lots of different people. She felt an arm around her waist. 'How are you getting on? Are you enjoying yourself?' asked Brian.

'It's great to be back down here again, I had forgotten what it is like to be in amongst book lovers.'

'You are looking great.'

'Thanks, Brian, and you are looking well, and very happy.'

'It's been tough, but we move on, don't we.'

'Yes, we do, and life is for living and not enduring.'

A waiter interrupted them with a tray-full of tall, slender flutes of champagne.

'Not for me, thanks. said Brian, 'I'll save myself for later. I have two more talks to do this afternoon then I'm finished after the book signing, hopefully, it won't drag on much further than 5 pm.'

'You are very busy.' said Karen.

'I'm being paid well for it.'

Brian paused, and looked at Karen.

'Would you like to be my special guest and take part in my last afternoon talk?'

'Oh, I'm not sure! I am totally unprepared.'

'It's okay, I would like to invite you up onto the stage to talk about the importance of getting outdoors and not being stuck at a desk all day. I think everyone could benefit from this. It's just a short talk about what you love about the outdoors and nature. You can do it.'

'Nothing like putting me on the spot.'

'Call it singing for your supper.'

Brian laughed.

'It's very straightforward and you know the subject matter inside out.'

Karen began to think she could do it.

'How long would I be on stage with you?'

Brian shrugged, 'ten minutes, it'll be a casual chat between us if you get stuck for something to say you can bounce it back to me. It's easy.'

'Okay, I'll do it.'

'Great!'

'Brian, you are on in ten minutes,' said the voice from the stage once more.

'That guest pass will get you into all of the tents, so feel free to use it to explore.'

'What time are you on stage for your last talk?'

'3.30pm, so why don't you come back here for 3.20pm?'

'Okay, that works for me.'

'Do you fancy an early dinner? I have a floating booking for the little Italian around the corner on the Horsemarket. The food is great, service is excellent, and it is cosy.'

'An early dinner suits me.'

'Sounds like a plan.'

Brian leant forward and kissed her on the cheek. In the fleeting moment, the faint smell of his aftershave stirred a warm flow through her body.

Karen visited all the tents, when she checked her phone, it was 3.05pm, so she made her way over to the North Tent.

David the Steward was standing at the entrance of the North tent, he welcomed Karen with a huge smile.

'Good afternoon, Ms Knighton, how lovely to see you again.'

'Thanks, David.'

She walked to the left-hand side of the tent and stopped at the coffee bar and bought a bottle of mineral water. Brian appeared behind her, 'Are you enjoying yourself?' he asked.

'Yes, I am loving it.'

It had been ages since Karen had been out at an event and enjoyed herself and had something to look forward to. Brian was good company and attentive, she felt happy around him.

'I am back on shortly, get yourself a seat near the steps onto the stage. I will talk for a little while then after I have explored creativity, and why it is important to stay inspired, I'll introduce you. Come up on stage. Easy!'

'Excellent, looking forward to it, and a little nervous,' said Karen.

Brian leaned over into her personal space and gave her a hug. His nose brushed passed her hair, and he whispered.

'You will be fabulous.'

The smell of his aftershave made her draw a breath in, the scent lingered in her nostrils. As he slowly withdrew from the hug, he placed a light kiss on the cheek. Karen let out a breath, tilted her head back slightly and looked up at Brian. His eyes met hers, and a fleeting, powerful surge of excitement ran down her body, deep inside her then down the backs of her thighs. Her eyes widened and sparkled with mischief.

Brian's late afternoon talk was popular, every seat was taken, people squatted in the aisles, sat on the stools by the coffee bar and stood at the back of the tent.

Thirty minutes in, Brian looked over to Karen.

'I would like to introduce Karen Knighton, Author and Photographer.'

Karen was surprised when she heard Brian introduce her halfway through his talk, she wasn't expecting to be on so early. She should have twigged why he looked at her. The audience gave Karen a round of applause. She carefully navigated her way up the steps, reminding herself to pick up her feet, and onto the stage. She joined Brian and talked about walking, being in the moment and seeking out the details. Brian finished the talk off and thanked Karen for joining him. The audience gave them a standing ovation. Brian's book signing lasted until 6.15pm. His book had sold well, and two publishers asked to meet with Karen, and one woman asked if she would like to join the Scottish Author Speaking Circuit. She left her card and said she would be in contact next week to arrange a meeting to discuss the format and the fees.

'Wow, what a finale.' said Karen.

'Oh, it's not finished yet, the night is young, my darling!'

'Come on, let us have a proper Saturday night out on the town.' said Brian. 'It is my treat, no arguments.'

Karen sat by the coffee bar and waited for Brian. He was finalising his plans for the following day. As she watched, she inwardly acknowledged an attraction to him, and felt the pull of his magnetism. He was charismatic, warm, and engaging. He took care of his appearance; a well-made shirt and colourful chinos fitted his tall, slim frame, and being an ex-pro-footballer, he had kept himself fit over the years, he legs looked strong, his buttocks looked firm and muscular. He had elegant hands with clean, manicured nails, his skin was moisturised, and hair trimmed. His tan leather brogues were polished and clean, he had an air of warmth and confidence.

Brian and Karen walked across the cobbled streets towards the Italian restaurant.

'They know me, and the food is always excellent in here,' said Brian. He opened the door for Karen and placed his hand on the small of her back.

'Buona sera Madam!'

'Buona sera signore!'

Brian ordered a bottle of champagne.

'Don't get me drunk, I have to drive tomorrow.'

'Don't worry, you can work it off, and be my stage guest tomorrow again.'

They talked, and caught up, Karen told him about Thomas.

'He was never going to be good enough for you. So, let us raise a glass to the people of the past and long may they stay there.'

'Cheers!' they said in unison.

'Oh god, I need to slow down, I feel the champagne going to my head and making me feel a little squiffy.' said Karen.

'Squiffy?' laughed Brian.

'Yes, squiffy.'

Brian said, I love the food here, but find it hard to resist mussels, they go so well with champagne, actually, everything goes well with champagne.'

'I love seafood. On the east coast, we get plenty of fresh fish...'

Brian cut her off, 'oh, don't worry about that, this is fresh,' and continued to tuck into the decreasing mound of mussels.

'I couldn't believe it when I saw your profile. How is the dating scene going for you?'

'So many men are dishonest about themselves or what they are looking for.'

'It's the same on my side. Their profiles state single or separated but they are not. All they're looking for is sex while their husbands are away on business.'

'Really?'

'I thought it would be my chance to get back out on the dating scene and enjoy myself again. I had felt sorry for myself when Debs left, and traded me in for a young stud, it doesn't do much for a man's fragile ego.'

'I have spoken to a few nice women, but they were at the other end of the country.'

Brian was a Glasgow boy, born and bred. He played for one of the two big football teams in his twenties and has dined out on his football career ever since. When he was dropped from the team he left the sport and signed up for the Fire Service where he stayed for nineteen years. He was badly injured in a building fire, could not return to work, and started to write about his life.

'I got interested in one woman who was bright, attractive, successful, and bold. We emailed, we chatted, we met.'

'That sounded promising.' said Karen.

'Hmmm, more champagne?' Brian filled Karen's glass and then his own.

He pulled a face. 'We met for lunch, she turned up in a spanking new Range Rover, the private plate did not tally with her name. She looked great although I did note she was a little older than her carefully taken photos, she was fun, a great conversationalist and witty, and had read all my books – always good for one's ego, don't you think?'

They both laughed.

'It was all going well, then, by God, she blew my socks off! She told me she was married and was looking for a virile man for no-strings sex-on-tap-sort-of-arrangement.'

'Not your thing?' Karen laughed.

'Honestly, I did not like what she had in mind.' Brian took a long swig out of his champagne glass

'I like sex, but the thought of turning up for lunch at 1 pm then swiftly after dessert I'd be expected to have an erection, complete a performance then showered, dressed and back in the car by 4.30pm, it's not quite the afternoon delight I'd like.'

Karen laughed.

They finished their coffee at the restaurant. 'I need to go up to the car park to get my bag from my car.'

'Where are you booked into?'

'The Cross Swords at the town square.'

'Oooh, me too! I'll settle up here and take a walk with you to the car and carry your bag.'

Brian reached over and took Karen's hand, turned it palm downwards, pulled it towards him and kissed it.

'Take my arm, you can keep me upright,' joked Brian, as they gingerly walked across the cobbles, and up onto the pavement heading towards the river. Kelso was peaceful, and the waning moon turned the river and surrounding landscape into beautiful shades of blue.

As Karen retrieved her bag from the boot of her car, Brian noticed a bottle of brandy. 'You've come prepared to offer me a nightcap?' as he took out the bottle and held it up to the moonlight.

'It's been in there for ages, it was a present from the publisher at Christmas I think,' said Karen.

'Is that a no then?'

'A no to what?'

'Offering me a nightcap?'

Brian stepped into Karen's personal space, tilted his head downwards, and in a quiet, low voice, said. 'I was suggesting you invite me to your room for a nightcap.' Brian kissed Karen on the lips, softly and gently. She closed her eyes, and let her lips linger on his. Brian held Karen's bag in his right hand and the bottle of brandy in the left, she had her bag in her right and car keys in the left. They stayed together held by the kiss for minutes.

'Okay, I hereby officially invite you to my palatial room for a nightcap,' said Karen with a big smile.

'I accept your kind invitation with great pleasure,' replied Brian.

She giggled.

'I'll be serving alcohol, I'll need proof you are over eighteen.'

They turned left up to the steps into the hotel reception and looked through the glass doors into the bar to see crowds of people, mostly from the book fair. Someone waved. Karen recognised David the door steward, she smiled and walked to the reception desk.

They checked in. Karen was on the first floor and Brian was on the 4th floor. They walked up the wide carpeted staircase, turned right and found room number 12.

As she took her coat off, Brian touched her on the shoulder, she turned around and he gently walked her backwards two steps so her back was against the wall by the door and kissed her.

He pressed his body up against hers as his left hand cradled the back of her head. He moved in and kissed her, she felt his right hand tough the small of her back and gently pulling her into his body. His kiss was slow, soft, and considered. She felt the firmness of his shoulders and back as she put her arms around him and kissed him back.

His right hand opened wide across her back, she could feel the warmth of his touch and the heat from his body. His left hand gently moved across her neck, along her jawline, down her throat and onto her breasts.

'You feel amazing.' he said.

'Mmmm, and so do you,' as her hand slid down and caressed his bum. It was muscular and as firm as she had hoped.

'What do you want to do next?'

She felt his breath against her skin, she turned her head, and responded with a wicked grin. 'Shall I pour you a brandy?'

He took off his jacket, and tie, and loosened the top three buttons of his shirt, undid his cufflinks, and put them on the table. He sat down on one of the chairs and watched Karen pour the drinks.

'A nightcap.' Karen leaned over him, he looked down her top as her breasts were about to spill out inches from his face. She stood up and smiled.

'I don't want another nightcap.'

'Oh, what do you want?

Brian smiled. Karen bent down, and lightly kissed his forehead and worked her way down his nose, she encircled his lips with her tongue and pushed her lips onto his mouth. He kissed her back.

Brian kissed her deeply and put his hand inside her top making contact with her skin. She moved her hand down across his chest, over his belt. He was solid and upright.

'Shall we move over to the bed?' suggested Karen, as she squeezed him.

He could barely speak, as she walked him over to the bed. She knew she was doing the right thing and would have no regrets in the morning. She was empowered, aroused, and wanted sex and tonight, Brian was the man.

'Give me two minutes, I need to go to the loo,' said Brian.

Brian did an awkward jog to the bathroom. The door slammed shut, altering the relaxed atmosphere.

The toilet was flushed a few times, and five minutes passed.

'Are you okay?' called out Karen.

'I'll be out shortly!' replied Brian.

His voice sounded odd as if he were in a hurry or stressed. Another five minutes passed. Karen heard Brian moving about.

'Brian, are you sure you are okay?'

The bathroom door opened, Brian stood in the doorway, hanging onto the door frame, he looked pale and discomposed.

'I'm sorry Karen, I am feeling very ill, I think those mussels were off. I'm so ....sorry...I..'

Before he finished his sentence, he stepped backwards and slammed the door shut.

It was another half an hour before Brian opened the bathroom door again, he was sweating, and pale.

'I'm so sorry.'

'Don't worry, can I get you something? Water? Tea?'

'No, I'm okay, I think it is passing now.'

'Come and lie down, just rest.'

'Oh no....' Brian slammed the door shut, he was violently sick again.

Karen felt disappointed. Their night of passion was now a distant memory, eradicated by the unpleasant smells wafting from the en-suite bathroom into the bedroom. She got up from the bed, unzipped her overnight bag, and she rummaged through her toiletries, She found a body spray and gave it a few squirts into the room hoping it would mask the smell.

It was 11 pm, and Brian was still in the bathroom.

'Brian, how are you doing?'

She didn't get a reply. She knocked on the door, said his name, and still no reply. She opened the door and found Brian asleep on the floor with his head resting on the wall next to the loo.

'Brian?'

'Uh, oh, sorry Karen,'

'Let's get you up. I need to use the loo.'

Brian got himself to his feet, he was unsteady.

'Do you want to go to your room?'

'That would be a good idea, just let me sit down and drink some water then I'll make a move.'

Karen left him sitting on the chair by the desk with a bottle of water while she used the loo. The bathroom was a mess.

'How are you feeling now?'

Karen barely had the opportunity to finish her sentence when Brian got up and ran to the bathroom.

She fell asleep on the bed and woke up to the sounds of Brian being sick, she looked at her phone, it was 2.15am. She slipped herself under the duvet and went back to sleep. The next time she looked at her phone it was 6 am, and she could hear the shower running. Brian opened the bathroom door.

'Karen, I am so, so, sorry and I am deeply embarrassed. I can't believe how violently ill I was last night. I'm sorry it ruined our evening.'

'Stop apologising, it's okay, these things happen.'

'Can I make it up to you? How about a dinner next week? I shall cook, come over and spend the weekend at the farm?'

'That sounds like a good idea.' Karen tried to fake some enthusiasm, but she was shattered.

'I am going to go up to my room to tidy myself up, shall we meet for breakfast at 8 am? I am not sure I will be able to eat anything, but I would like to try some coffee.'

'Yes, great, see you downstairs at eight.'

Brian had tidied up the bathroom, it was spotless, and you would never have known it had been the scene of carnage hours before. She filled the bath and threw in all the hotel toiletries, so the water would smell nice and fill her nostrils with a pleasant aroma and help her to relax and forget about her sleepless night.

CHAPTER 8

Three women sat with Brian. Karen recognised them from the Book Fair. She walked over to Brian's table.

'Good morning, Karen, how are you today?' asked Brian.

'Good morning, Brian, I am well, thank you?' She smirked but it went unnoticed.

The women ignored Karen.

'Oh Brian, can we get you some coffee, and you can tell us all about your next book?' said one, and touched him on the shoulder. The women fawned over him, the mingling scent of their perfumes created a rather heady mix, Karen wondered if this would turn Brian green about the gills again.

He was in his element and loving the attention.

'Brian, could you autograph your book for me?'

'Yes certainly, let me find my pen.'

Suddenly, there were high pitched howls of laughter. As Brian had pulled a pen out of his pocket a condom packet fell onto the table.

'Oooh Brian, can we start with an autograph first?' laughed the smaller woman. Brian reached over, grabbed her hand, and kissed the back of it.

'Your wish is my command,' said Brian to his admirer.

Karen laughed, not so much at the funny scene, more at Brian for being such an ass. She couldn't listen to anymore of his schmoozing.

'Enjoy your breakfast, see you later,' said Karen.

He did not acknowledge her.

She walked over to a table on the far side by a window, ordered breakfast and made some notes. The loud, shrill cackling from the women, now having breakfast with Brian, annoyed other guests. The waiter delivered Karen's breakfast on a beautiful white china plate, the small pork sausages reminded her that having sex with Brian was not all that an attractive thought.

Karen took the stealth approach to the exit to avoid Brian and his fan club. She packed her bag, checked out at the hotel reception. The sound of Brian and his harem could still be heard in the breakfast room.

The receptionist asked, 'I hope your breakfast wasn't disturbed by the loud group on table 7?'

'No not really, it was amusing watching them, nothing like people watching when you are having breakfast.' Karen smiled.

She walked over the cobbled street and in between the trade stands as they were getting ready to open for the final day of the Book Fair. She bought three notebooks and some pencils. It was a lovely spring morning, and the riverbank looked beautiful lined with daffodils and snowdrops. She sat on one of the wooden benches overlooking the water, and placed her bag next to her, she took three or four deep breaths, closed her eyes, and raised her face up to the sun, and listened to the sounds of the river and the birds. She stretched her legs out straight and smiled. It felt good to be outdoors.

She opened her eyes and looked out across the river, the tranquil scene reminded her of an oil painting.

Karen picked up her bag and headed up to the car park. Her phone rang. She ignored it. She started the car and drove the back route out of Kelso along Roxburgh street and onto Edinburgh Road.

Two hours later, she made her way through the Sunday traffic, to arrive back at Maryard. It felt good to be home. Bernie's car had gone. She slung her bag into her bedroom. She went downstairs to her office, and as she sat down at her desk, her phone rang.

'Hi Brian, how are you?'

'Hi, Karen, where are you? I searched all over for you.'

I left Kelso after breakfast.'

'What? You're not in Kelso?'

'No, I am back home.'

'Oh, but I wanted you to be my guest on stage again this afternoon.'

'Did you?'

'Look, I am really sorry about last night….'

'Will you come over to the farm next weekend?'

'I am not sure. Can I get back to you about it?'

'I would love to see you and make up for everything.'

'Okay, I'll be in contact. I need to go, I have just arrived back home, and it's been a long drive. I hope the rest of the Book Fair goes well for you.'

'Thanks Karen and speak to you soon. Call me,' said Brian.

He did not sound convinced Karen would contact him, and he was right, she wasn't convinced either.

Karen made coffee and checked her emails, there were four messages from the dating website. Only one sounded as though he had any potential.

She logged onto the dating site, and clicked on Jonathan's profile. He was a gold star member, looked normal in his photos, tall with dark hair, he liked reading, clay shooting, photography, and cooking.

'Okay, Jonathan G D Merrywell,' she said out loud, 'let's see how we get on.'

'Hi, Jonathan,

Thank you very much for your message. Isn't the dating scene a challenge?

I joined a few weeks ago and have had two dates with no plans to investigate them any further. Have you had much joy?

Karen'

Four lengthy emails later, and a lunch date was arranged for Tuesday.

Karen refilled her coffee mug, scooped up the Sunday papers and put them down on the table by the sofa. She turned the heating thermostat up and flopped down on to the sofa. She bundled two large cushions on top of one another, sat down, and curled her legs up underneath her. The hours skipped by as she read through large sections of the papers. As she flicked through the pages of the Literary Guide, a photograph caught her eye. "Ex-football star launches next best-seller on National tour". She read the review of his book and tried hard to get rid of the images of Brian asleep on the bathroom floor in her hotel room with his face folded up against the tiled wall by the loo.

Karen dozed off.

CHAPTER 9

On Tuesday morning, Karen got up at 5 am, and shut herself away in her office, and only surfaced to grind more coffee beans and eat a bowl of cereal about 7.30am. It had been a good day to write and the words flowed. She wanted to give herself enough time to get ready for her 1pm lunch date without having to rush.

A big part of her really wanted to go on a date and find a nice man, and a smaller part of her could not be bothered with the hassle.

It was a fine day for a drive to St Andrews. She parked up in a space close to the restaurant, then pulled her bag up from the passenger footwell and rummaged around to find her lip-gloss.

The glass-encased modern building of the restaurant stood out on the Bruce embankment.

'Hi Jonathan, I've arrived, have parked in the public carpark.'

His reply was instant.

'Hi, Karen, what sort of car are you in? I'm already here, and parked up.'

Karen opened the door of her car, got out, and looked around.

'Hi, Karen!'

A male voice from three cars up from her.

'Hi, Jonathan!'

On the first impression, he looked nice, but she noticed he was not as tall as his profile height.

'Gosh, you're a tall lady.' he said. Karen smiled.

Jonathan had booked a table next to the huge window. The vista stretched for miles beyond the West Sands and out across the mouth of the River Tay towards Carnoustie on the hazy horizon.

As they settled in, Karen heard her phone buzz, it was Annie's dating safety text. Jonathan was attentive, polite, and interesting. They got on well, she enjoyed his company. He was a management consultant for a big firm in Dundee and lived in Balmullo, not far from St Andrews, separated from his second wife and they had one daughter.

Karen checked the time on her phone when Jonathan went to the toilet and felt a little pang of disappointment when she knew she would have to leave. She could have sat and chatted with him all afternoon.

'What a breath of fresh air meeting you,' said Jonathan.

Karen smiled, 'I was going to say the same to you.'

'I would love to see you again. Would you be agreeable to that?'

'Yes, I'd love to see you again.'

'Can I tempt you over to my place for roast duck and plum sauce?'

Karen smiled, and replied, 'Thank you, that would be lovely.'

The goodbye was natural, he walked her to her car, kissed her on the cheek, and opened her car door.

By the time Karen had reached home, Jonathan had sent her two text messages, the first one thanked her for her company, and the second invited her to dinner at his place on Friday night. She had a warm feeling about Jonathan, she was flattered by his interest in her and felt genuinely pleased she had met him.

'Hi Jonathan, thank you very much for a lovely lunch, I really enjoyed meeting you, the time flew. Yes, we have a date, Friday is perfect. Shall I bring dessert?'

'Can't wait to see you again, here's my address: Seaview House, Lucklot Road, Balmullo, KY16. Bring yourself, I have dinner organised, see you at 6.45pm?'

There was a missed call and a voicemail message from Brian.

She sat back in her chair, listened to the message, and pondered on her weekend in Kelso and meeting Brian again. She recalled the way he discarded her at breakfast in favour of his adoring female fans. She reasoned if she were keen to see him again she would have felt interested and excited. They were going to have sex but maybe that ship had sailed. His call helped her make the decision not to see him that weekend.

Picking up her phone, she replied to Jonathan.

'Wonderful, looking forward to it, see you at 6.45pm on Friday.'

He replied within seconds.

'Have a great week, J x'

It had been a long day with her early start, she switched off her office machines, and was walking up the steps from the office into the kitchen when her phone rang.

'Hi Karen, it's Brian.'

She tried to sound neutral. 'Hi Brian, how are you getting on?'

'I could be better if you would agree to come up to the farm this weekend?'

'Sorry Brian, I don't think so.'

'Honestly, Karen, I think it is something we should explore, no pressure, just me and you, good food and fine wine. I would really like to make it up to you, I'm so sorry and I am deeply embarrassed by Saturday night. I could hardly look at you on Sunday morning.'

Brian grovelled and eventually won Karen over with his honesty. She agreed to drive over to his farm on Saturday afternoon for dinner and spend the night in his guest room. No strings. No promises. No expectations.

Karen got in her car to drive to Jonathan's house in Balmullo. It wasn't that far away, only 20 miles north of Maryard.

In Balmullo, the houses were modern, with showy, polished BMWs sitting on the driveways. She counted five houses on her right and pulled onto the half-moon shaped driveway of Seaview House. Jonathan opened the door before she had a chance to ring the bell, he greeted her with a big hug. He invited her in, took her coat, and asked if she wanted a tour of the house. She declined. It felt a bit awkward being given a tour of a man's house when she had only had lunch with him. The house would give away his secrets and overload her with information too quickly, and maybe he had an awful bedroom or a weird hobby room. Jonathan took her into the kitchen, it was modern, clean, and sterile, with a 'guess where the appliances are hidden' style.

Two black Labradors greeted her and she made a fuss of them. 'What's their names?'

'Hattie on your left and Freddie, both great gundogs.'

'What would you like to drink, wine, tea, coffee, port?'

'Tea would be great, thanks.'

'Hattie, Freddie, beds!' said Jonathan.

'Are you sure I can't tempt you to some wine, I have some great wines in my cellar.'

'When I'm driving I don't even sniff at wine.'

Karen felt comfortable around Jonathan, he multi-tasked well. He looked after her, cooked and talked about his daughter. There were lots of photos on the wall of her. When Jonathan's back was turned Karen counted the photographs. There were fifteen pictures of his daughter hanging in the kitchen.

When Karen tried to change the subject he pulled it back to 'Chloe this' and 'Chloe that'. Chloe was amazing at everything, she was talented, beautiful, gifted and a daddy's girl. Karen was bored of listening to stories about Chloe. He had been an interesting lunch date and had traversed plenty of subjects but, in his home, he only talked about his daughter. He hadn't mentioned her once over lunch.

'What are your plans for the weekend?' Karen asked.

'Oh, I usually spend the weekend with Chloe, she's such fun company.' He stopped and looked thoughtful. Karen wondered if he had had a small epiphany and realised he wasn't the best host in the world to a prospective new girlfriend.

'Why don't you join us tomorrow for a walk along the West Sands and lunch in town?'

Without pausing, Karen replied, 'I have a busy day tomorrow.'

As they had coffee, Jonathan continued to gush endlessly about Chloe, and said, 'I do everything for her, buy her whatever she wants, take her places, pick her up, organise her night's out.'

Then he said. 'It's important she likes you, Karen. Once you've met, and she tells me she likes you, then we can get onto a more serious footing.'

Karen did not say anything.

'May I use your bathroom?'

'Of course, out that door,' said Jonathan, pointing to the door discreetly nestled in between the large cupboards, or was it a fridge. 'Turn right, and go down the hall, it's the last door on the left, you'll know you've reached it because there's a huge professional photo of me and Chloe on the wall next to the door. I'm sure you'll love it.'

Karen left the kitchen and counted all the Chloe pictures on the wall along the hallway. Ten pictures. There it was. By the bathroom door on the left was a huge professional studio shot of Jonathan and Chloe, they looked more like lovers than father and daughter.

Karen let out a snort when she walked into the bathroom, it was as modern and sterile as the kitchen and decorated in pictures of Chloe.

She said, 'yuck,' as she looked around the bathroom walls covered in pictures of a teenager. Karen sniggered when she thought of drawing a moustache and blackening some teeth out.

Karen found her way back to the kitchen. 'Jonathan, thank you so much for the lovely meal, the food was delicious. I really must make a move.'

'Oh, I'm sorry you are leaving so soon. I was just about to text Chloe to see if she wanted to pop around to meet you.'

'No really, no need. I have to go. It looks like rain. I do not like being on the road late when it is dark.'

Karen was waffling. She wanted to leave, get in her car and drive back home.

'But it's only 8.30 pm, Chloe and her mum live next door, they both want to meet you...'

Karen's eyes widened. 'Err, no. It has been a long day and I love my beauty sleep and I need to wash my hair.'

'That's a shame, I am sure Chloe and Cherrie will be disappointed.'

She patted the dogs' heads and said goodbye to them. Karen looked at Jonathan, gave him a fake smile, leant forward, kissed him on the cheek, turned on her heels, and headed for the front door. She pressed her car fob, the doors unlocked, she jumped in, started the engine, and pulled away sending the loose gravel flying out behind her and landing on the porch steps. At the end of the drive, she hesitated briefly to put her seat belt on and glanced in the rear-view mirror and saw two large bare patches she'd created in his gravel. He stood on the porch, cheerily waving.

'Oh dear, oh dear, oh dear.'

As Karen was about to pull onto her drive she saw Annie walking down the road. She flashed her headlights. Annie waved.

'Hi Karen, anywhere nice tonight?'

'Yes, and no. Do you fancy a glass of wine?'

Annie and Karen parked themselves around the kitchen table and drank wine while they caught up on Karen's Friday night dating adventure.

'Oh god, look, he's texted me.'

'Read it out..!'

'Dearest Karen, I loved having you over tonight, and it was a joy to cook for you. It was such a disappointment for Chloe, Cherrie, and me you did not stay longer. They really wanted to meet you. How about that lunch and a walk tomorrow with us in St As?'

'Thank you, Jonathan, I have decided I do not wish to see you again. I hope you, Cherrie and Chloe live happily ever after, Karen.'

'Are you going to send it?'

Karen smiled. 'It's gone. Delivered. Sent and no doubt it'll be read by Chloe and Cherrie. Do I care? NOPE!'

It was 11.30pm when Annie left, Karen locked the doors, and headed to bed feeling happy, tired and a little disappointed.

CHAPTER 10

Brian lived outside the tiny village of Harrietfield, 10 miles north-west of Perth. He had a small farm which had belonged to the Lorgannie Hill Estate many years ago but had been sold off when the old Laird died. He wrote his books from his office on the farm in the converted kennel block.

It was Karen's first visit to the farm. As she drove up the hill beyond the village she saw the red sign 'Author's Block House' on the right and turned up the potholed track. She gingerly picked her way around the potholes, steering as best she could to avoid them. Brian waited at the front door and opened her car door, helped her out and gave her a full body contact hug. Karen noted how well the bodies fitted together.

'It's great to see you Karen, and welcome to Author's Block House.'

She was pleased to see him, his warmth relaxed her.

He carried Karen's bags into the house and went into the kitchen, it looked lived in and loved, with a big solid wood table in the centre.

'I love your Aga,' said Karen.

'It's older than me,' said Brian, 'and we've both got our quirks.'

'I've had this one so long it's part of the family.'

Two champagne glasses sat on the table, and Brian produced a bottle of champagne from the fridge. In a few swift movements, the bottle was opened, glasses charged, and one was in Karen's hand.

'Cheers, and here's to a relaxing Saturday and great company.'

'Cheers!' replied Karen, as they delicately chinked the crystal flutes together.

Brian's house was comfortable and tastefully decorated. 'Did Debs do the decorating?'

'Yes, she did, do you like it?'

'It's different, and I guess that's her American influence, but it all flows. Are you happy living with it even though she has gone?'

'Sorry, that's a very personal question, Brian.'

'Oh no, don't worry. Honestly, I haven't thought about it or her. I guess I have moved on.'

Downstairs was open plan, with lots of wooden beams. There were no photographs or paintings of Debs, there were no altars or obvious coupledom trinkets just pictures of Brian, his gun-dogs, and Brian fishing, and more of his animals. A large central staircase flowed up into a small upper hall, Brian took Karen's bags into the guest suite, it was a comfy room with far-reaching views over the fields to the east and towards the River Tay. Karen had hoped he would have taken her back downstairs, but he insisted on showing her his bedroom and the other guest room. His bedroom had a huge bed with a bold dark wooden bed frame and headboard.

'Do you like it?' he asked.

'Yes, it's very unusual.'

The bottle of champagne was finished and another one appeared and Karen's glass was filled. They sat on the sofa, and

Brian gave her another apology. A mischievous glint twinkled in his pale blue eyes.

Karen double-checked and looked directly into his eyes. Yes, there it was. Their gaze lengthened, she felt her mouth stretch into a smile, she lifted her chin up a fraction as though she was offering herself. She wanted him to be bold, rise to the challenge she had just set.

He did not break their eye contact as he slowly leaned into her, she could feel the heat of his body and scent of his aftershave. 'Tonight, we have some catching up to do, and I've just shown you where it will happen.'

His lips contacted with hers, and she felt that familiar clench of her muscles. And in that instant, the dynamic between them had been turned up full. Last weekend she thought it had been lost forever but he had reconnected them and brought her back to an erotic place where they had met before. She was full of hope.

The champagne made them feel light-headed and full of fun. It felt good. 'Tonight, is all about you,' said Brian. 'You will be my sole focus.'

Karen smiled.

'I am going to cook for you. I want you to relax, pick some music and drink champagne while I attend to a few things in the kitchen.'

'Thank you, that's very kind of you. Are you sure I can't help....?'

'Not a thing, now do as I ask.'

Karen felt a shudder travel up her spine from her core. Brian leant across and kissed her deeply but then pulled away unexpectedly.

Game on.

Brian sounded busy in the kitchen, as an array of wonderful smells wafted through to the sitting area. The warmth of the house comforted her. Classical music played softly in the background as Karen stretched out on the sofa and drifted off. She was awoken by Brian touching her hair.

He leant over her and whispered in her ear. 'I'm pleased you dozed off, it means you'll have plenty of energy for the late night I have planned for you.'

He kissed her lightly.

'Come through to the kitchen, your dinner is about to be served.'

Brian had prepared a three-course meal and printed a menu.

'Impressive, and I'm flattered.'

Karen read the menu: a homemade game terrine to start, followed by venison wellington, blackberry sauce and vegetables and finished with individual lemon meringue pies.

'I had no idea you could cook so well, Brian, your food is amazing.'

'I wanted to train as a chef when I was at school, but a talent scout picked me out and that started my football career. Can't complain though, I played for Scotland, travelled the world, and I have a great pension. If I had gone down the chef route, it would have been a completely different ending.'

After the meal, Brian instructed Karen to take herself to the sofa. A clatter of dishes later, and he appeared at the foot of the sofa with a cheese board, crackers, port, and cognac.

Karen nibbled a cracker with cheese, sipped port and wondered how he was going to start the next phase of the evening, or would she be the one to move it along?

He must have read her mind. He took the glass from her hand, put it down on the table and touched her lips with his. They kissed, and slowly they slipped down the sofa. Karen loved kissing Brian because he kissed her with such care and passion, and never overdid it. He waited for her to respond before he kissed her deeper and for longer. The care he took made her feel relaxed, and she wanted more. She hoped he would be a kind and considerate lover.

Her hands moved down his neck and across his shoulders as they lay together on the sofa. He held her tightly to him, it made her feel safe, wanted, and small.

It was 2 am when Karen was woken up by a numb feeling down the right-hand side of her body, she was cold and stiff. Brian was asleep next to her, with his face resting on his folded-up arm.

'Brian, wake up!'

He didn't stir.

'Brian, WAKE UP!'

Nothing.

She extracted herself from the sofa and put her hand on his shoulder and gave him a gentle shake.

'Brian, wake UP!'

He mumbled a few times, and the last words he said were: 'I'm coming Debs, I love you babes.'

Karen went upstairs to her room, she brushed her teeth and got into her nightwear, her faded 1983 Whitesnake tour t-shirt and went to bed feeling frustrated, and stiff. Some hours later she was woken up by the sound of the cockerel in the courtyard. At first, she wondered where she was, her mouth was dry and her head a little fuzzy.

She got out of bed, went to the loo then pulled on her trousers. She went downstairs barefoot and saw Brian still fast asleep on the sofa. She left him sleeping and padded through the kitchen and filled the kettle with water and put it on the hot plate of the Aga. The early morning sun was streamed in through the window.

She heard Brian moving around on the sofa, and groaning.

'God, my head hurts.'

'Morning Brian.'

He looked around, surprised by the voice coming from the kitchen.

'*OH NO, oh no, oh no….*'

'Karen, I am so sorry. I don't believe it I'm so sorry!'

She tried to sound generous, 'We both must have been tired.'

'Tea?'

'Yes, please.'

Brian washed his face in the downstairs loo, he reappeared looking less like he had slept on the sofa. Karen put the teapot, cups, and milk jug onto the kitchen table. Brian walked up behind her. 'We have unfinished business.'

And before she could answer, he put his arms around her waist, and then up to her breasts, gently massaging them. The previous night's seduction was still warm, unfinished, stored, and unused, his touch had switched her back on in an instant. She turned around, and they kissed deeply. She felt the pressure building, and her muscles tighten as she ran her fingers through his hair as she picked up the faint aroma of his aftershave. His hand was inside her t-shirt teasing her, and she could feel his erection pressed up against her.

He undid the button of her trousers, then pulled the zip down, slowly, and deliberately. He slid his hand inside the back of her trousers and down her right buttock, his erection twitched when he discovered she wasn't wearing any knickers. He pushed her trousers down without losing the rhythm of the kissing. Their body movements flowed, they were tuned in to one another. She felt the cold edge of the kitchen table against her bum, as he slid his hand down and massaged her rhythmically.

'Shall we...?'

He cut her off. 'Ssshhh...'

He slowly turned her around, giving her enough time to shuffle her feet with her trousers at her ankles, and gently bent her over the kitchen table, she heard the sound of a condom packet being opened. The few seconds it took for him to put it on made her want to cry out in frustration at the loss of his touch. She didn't want to wait any longer. She felt the heat of him against her as he eased inside her. She closed her eyes, tilted her head back and let out a gasp. She slid her hands out across the width of the table and held on to the edge as he pushed inside her, then drew back away from her so slowly, and then back into her.

Suddenly he shuddered and let out a sound, it was a mix between a groan and a panicky cry, swiftly followed by, 'I'm sorry. I'm so sorry.'

So much for it being all about her.

'It's okay' she said. She lied.

'It's been so long, I lost my self-control.'

Karen stood up, bent down, grabbed her trousers, and pulled them back on. Brian apologised again.

'Shall I pour the tea?' said Karen, and started laughing.

Brian faked a laugh.

CHAPTER 11

K aren left Brian's after breakfast. On the way home she drove back to Maryard in silence, and thought about her time with Brian. There were things she liked about him but ....

As she arrived in Maryard her phone rang.

'Hi, Bernie.'

'How's your diary looking for Friday or Saturday night? Guess who's flying in from Paris?'

'Oh, Is Faye coming over?'

'Yes, I've just had a WhatsApp catch-up with her, she has a meeting with a new gallery the following week, but she wanted to spend some time in Fife before heading down to London.'

'That'd be great, I haven't seen her in ages.'

'Shall we go for Friday night, that'll give us Saturday and Sunday to recover.' They laughed but knew it was true, recovery always took longer when you are over fifty.

'What do you fancy eating, and where?'

'That's a challenge, I don't know. Any suggestions?'

'I'll need to have a search and see what inspires.'

'Let's talk in the next day or so and firm up plans?'

Karen had planned an easy Sunday of doing nothing much. It was one of those days when she felt the loneliness. She made a cup of tea and rummaged around the kitchen cupboards. The champagne from the night before left her with a craving for something sweet.

'Ah, Jaffa cakes!' She took the box, and her tea through to her office desk so she could read her emails.

'I have a date tonight!' said Annie, in a text message.

'Who's the lucky man?' asked Karen.

'Are you in?'

'Yup, come over, the door is open, and I'll get the kettle on.'

'Great, I'm at the far side of the field, and heading over now.'

Ten minutes later, 'Hellooooo!' came a voice from the kitchen doorway.

'Hi Annie, come on in, grab a seat, coffee is brewing. How are you?'

'Excited, and this one has been thoroughly vetted. His name is Craig, and he is a widower. I have spoken to him a few times on the phone, and he's coming down to take me to dinner tonight at Balbirnie House.'

'Very nice, what are you going to wear?'

'I have it all planned. He is picking me up at 6.45pm and driving us there.'

'Is he local?'

'Not really, he's from Stirling.'

'Sounds keen, and so do you.'

'His wife died last year and he feels ready to start dating again.

He's some type of the consultant in the oil industry and loves his horses.' Annie got her phone out and showed Karen some pictures of Craig.

'He looks tall.'

'He is 6ft 5. We're going to look odd together, but I don't mind.'

'Shall I call you as usual?' said Karen.

'Yes please, although I have broken my own rules, and have agreed to him picking me up at the house because he sounded so nice, thoughtful and kind.'

'Well, as long as you are sure, and you feel safe.'

'I've done it now, he has my address.'

Annie looked worried.

'Do you think I've done the wrong thing?'

'Only you will know if you are comfortable with him or not. Look, if it helps, I could be at the house with you when he arrives?'

'Karen, you always have great ideas, thank you. I feel such an idiot, I don't know why I agreed to it. Actually, I do. I had this romantic hope he'd be great, and we'd ride off into the sunset on our horses, ha bloody ha!'

Karen rang the doorbell at Wren cottage, and heard a distant call of, 'come in!'

'You look great.' said Karen.

Annie was distracted, she walked over to the window. 'Oh bugger, he's here already.'

'Go meet him and bring him in.'

Annie walked down the hallway, and stopped to take a look in the mirror at herself before she opened the front door.

A high pitched male voice said, 'Hi Annie, how lovely to finally meet you.'

'Hi, Craig, come in!'

Karen waited in the kitchen as the two sets of footsteps made their way up the hall.

'Craig, I'd like you to meet my friend Karen.'

Craig lurched forward with so much enthusiasm he startled Karen. He was tall and his clothes hung from his shoulder blades. His dark brown thick hair sat on top of his head like a mushroom cap and when he turned he had a huge bald area at the back that looked like a monk's hairstyle.

'Hi Karen!' he squeaked.

'Lovely to meet you, Craig.'

Annie smiled. Karen wondered if she had seen his hair.

'Can I get the book, Annie?' Annie looked at Karen blankly.

'The bird watching book…?'

'Oh yes, sorry, I was miles away.'

'Nice to meet you, Craig, have a lovely meal.' Karen made her way down the hall, Annie gave her a book and the thumbs up.

'He's okay, thanks for being here though, it means a lot.'

Craig he held Annie's coat while she put it on, he opened doors, he gave her his hand when she got into his car, and even handed her the seat belt strap. He had a goofy appearance, emphasized by his two prominent front teeth, and when he smiled, his eyes opened up wide giving him a sort maniacal expression.

During their meal he talked continuously about his dead wife. How wonderful she was, they were childhood sweethearts, everyone loved her, and her family was his family. Annie ate and listened.

When the meal was finished they moved swiftly onto coffee at his insistence. When Craig got up to go to the gents, Annie got her first glimpse of his large round bald patch. The light bounced off it. He walked with big lolloping strides, bending deeply at the knee.

When he returned from the gents, Annie didn't bother to look up, she was worn out by the dead-wife chat.

'I'm sorry I will have to go soon,' said Craig, 'it is a long drive back home.'

'It was a lovely evening Craig, thank you.'

'I shall drop you off at home and thank you very much for your company.'

Craig pulled up at Annie's house, he quickly got out and around the car to open Annie's door. As she stepped out, he opened the back door, and produced a beautiful bouquet.

'Thank you for your company evening, these are for you.'

'Oh, my goodness, thank you, they're gorgeous.'

'It was nice to meet you, but I am really sorry, I can't see you again.'

'Oh, okay.' Annie was puzzled. Surely that should have been her line.

'Can't?' she said in a raised voice.

'You see, Carol follows me everywhere, she even guided me to pick your flowers. I saw her in the mirror when I went to the toilet, she told me off because she doesn't think you are good enough for me, and I have to listen to her.'

'What the fuck, Craig!'

'You've bored me shitless talking about her all evening, and now you are telling me her ghost follows you around and casts judgement on your dates?'

'You need therapy, I recommend shock therapy because you are seriously fucked up! Goodnight, Craig!'

Annie gripped the bouquet, and stomped off in the direction of her front door. She opened the door, stepped inside, and closed it loudly behind her. She locked the door and put the chain across.

She kicked her shoes off.

'Fucking prick!'

She heard the sound of his car disappearing into the distance. She dumped her coat and flowers on the chair and went straight to the kitchen and grabbed a glass and a bottle of gin. She filled half of her glass with gin and looked in the fridge for tonic. The fridge had a few tired vegetables, a couple of jars, a bottle of tonic, and a carton of fresh orange.

Annie grabbed the tonic and shook it up then poured it into her glass. She took a swig of the gin and flat tonic and made room for some orange. She poured the orange in and filled the glass to the brim. She took a deep breath, put the glass to her lips and knocked it back then poured another and took it to the sitting room. She sat down, switched on her tablet, and logged into Facebook.

Alex, one of the men she had been chatting with on the dating site had sent her a Facebook friend request. She clicked accept and opened Messenger. The page took an age to load. She checked the router on the bookcase, the lights flashed green. As she turned around, she tripped over her shoes and cursed her own stupidity for leaving them there. She sat back in her chair, took a long swig of her gin, and lifted her tablet up. She blinked a few times and looked at a picture of a man sitting in front of a mirror, naked and shaved from the waist down. The accompanying message read, 'my nick-name is horse, if you fancy a ride, call me...'

CHAPTER 12

At 4.30am, Karen got out of bed determined to have a full day at the office. Her week was a mixture of writing deadlines, one or two meetings, and her annual mammogram. She looked forward to going to a local Am Dram production of Jesus Christ Superstar with Annie that evening.

When she stopped for a break, she logged in to the dating site to read a very long and interesting message from Liam. He described himself as a rock star. She wasn't sure if he was sincere about his looks or it was his humour. Karen thought he may have potential, but she would have to wait to see him as he was on a 'Rock of Ages' tour with a number of other bands from the 1970s in the USA. He had sent her a couple of clips of him on stage, and 15 photos. The pictures looked dated.

She googled him. Liam Prendergast had a number of hits in the 1970s, and had more than ten albums to his name but his career had taken a nose-dive. She read through his profile, and went from feeling optimistic to less so when she read 68 year-old Liam was the father of nine children, and three of the girls were under ten.

She checked her phone.

'Morning Karen, how are you? I hope you had a good drive back home yesterday. I enjoyed spending time with you, it was nice having you visit the farm, come back soon. Brian xx'

Karen realised she hadn't thought much about Brian after spending a night at his Farm. '*Morning Brian, I am very well, thank you. I had an easy drive and thank you for making me feel so welcome. KKxx*

It was just after midday when Karen came out of her office. She stood in the kitchen and pondered on what to make for lunch. She saw a small figure in the distance with a wheelbarrow and decided she'd put her wellies on and take a walk across the fields to see Annie.

The raw northeast wind blew across the fields, it was 6 degrees but felt much lower. Karen walked with her hands in the pockets of her padded jacket, as she worked her way around the muddy area and thick gorse of the rough ground towards the horse fields. She loved the wind blowing through her hair, it was a sensation she associated with feeling free and being positive about life. Annie waved, and turned her wheelbarrow in the direction of the gate.

'Hi Annie, how are you?'

'Tired but looking forward to tonight.'

'How did it go with, what was his name?'

'Craig, and I won't be seeing him again.'

Annie parked the wheelbarrow full of horse dung a few yards from the gate.

'The positives; he gave me a bouquet of flowers.' She paused, 'he talked nonstop about his dead wife. Apparently, she was still with him and said I wasn't good enough for him. He dropped me off, gave me the flowers, ones she'd picked, of course, and disappeared off into the night after I told him he had bored me shitless and he needed shock therapy because he was so fucked up.'

'Wow, what an awful experience, are you okay?'

'Yeah, I'm fine but I need a fuckwit detector app for my dating profile.'

The wind whipped across the open fields and reminded Karen her warm house waited for her. 'I'll leave you to it. See you tonight, I'll pick you up at 7 pm?'

'I'd better get on and finish clearing up, if it stays dry, I'm hoping to go out for a hack.'

Karen felt spots of rain blowing through on the wind and quickened her pace back to the house. She pulled off her wellies, made a coffee and watched Annie working in the distant field. The rain turned heavier.

She read her emails.

'Hello, Tallladybooklover,

A fellow book lover! How nice to meet/find you, I read your profile with great interest and wondered if you would like to meet for lunch in town or thereabouts? My name is Alexander, I'm a retired consultant.

I lost my second wife two years ago and have a son and a daughter, both have busy careers. I got myself out into the modern dating world recently and have had a one or two nice dates with ladies but there wasn't that real connection. I enjoy company, love conversation, some theatre, and reading. I keep fit with a walking club and have a wide circle of friends.

I have a flat in Edinburgh and a place down in the borders but feel I just rattle around them on my own. I started dating hoping to meet a like-minded lady I could share my life with.

How about that lunch?

Yours sincerely,

Alexander.'

She sat back in her chair at the kitchen table and wondered if Alexander had any potential. She looked through his profile, there were group pictures of walkers up in the hills, two photos of a hat-wearing male on the deck of a boat and a side profile taken on a seaside pier. He was 6ft 1', and everything he said in his email was reflected in his profile. He had moved swiftly but also explained his reasons for dating. They were similar to hers, and on balance, why were people dating if they didn't want to meet a like-minded person of the opposite sex?

'Hi, Alexander,

Thank you very much for your message, it was lovely to hear from you.

Lunch in town sounds great! Would you like to call me, so we can make plans for where and when?

Karen.'

The small theatre was four miles away in the next village, it had a bigger population than Maryard and a train station. Karen drove them to the theatre, and as they turned left into lower Main Street, Annie said, 'oh god, look at all the cars, it's going to be busy.'

Karen pulled a face, 'not to worry.'

Annie sounded anxious, 'where are you going to park?'

'I don't know, keep your eyes open for a space on the road, we'll never get into the car park.'

They found a space on the far end of Main Street. As Karen reversed her car into the parking space, Annie fiddled with her bag zip, her hands looked taught and her expression was tense as she looked down the street.

'Are you okay?'

'Yes, I'm fine, it's just the thought of meeting any locals and Ron's family.'

Karen looked across at Annie. 'It's been years though?'

'Yes, but I don't think they'll ever get over it.'

As they walked back down main street towards the theatre, Annie looked through the groups of people and scanned the faces to see if she recognised anyone.

'Oh, they're all here' said Annie, as she tried to shield herself from view.

'Ignore them.' said Karen. 'Shall we find out seats?'

'Yes, I've got the tickets here, we're in row G-R, at the end, let me see.' Karen looked in her bag for her wallet and found the tickets. 'G-R 13 and 14.'

A man and a woman sat in their seats.

'I'm sorry, you are in the wrong seats, these are the ones we have booked,' said Karen.

The stench of stale booze reached her nostrils before the words reached her ears. 'Yeah, we booked 'em as well,' said the man.

He didn't have many teeth, and the ones he did have were rotten and discoloured. In his right ear, he wore a thick gold ring. His wife was tiny. She had a haunted expression in her heavily black-lined eyes. Her painted on black eyebrows reached up in bizarre high arches above her eyes. Her black dyed hair had two-inch-long grey roots growing out of her scalp, she sported a nose ring, an eyebrow piercing on the far side of her right arch and a small stud above her lip. Her outfit matched his, only it was ten sizes smaller.

'What's your seat number on your ticket?' asked Annie.

'G-L 13 and 14!' said the man as he dipped his hand into his stained grey jogging trousers and produced a scrunched-up pair of tickets.

'You're in the wrong seats!' said Annie, 'this is row G-R, your row is over the other side.'

He turned to his wife and waved the tickets in her face. She flinched. 'This is your fault ya stupid cow, you sat here.' They got up from the seat and pushed passed Annie.

The wife muttered, 'Ya money grabbin' murdering slag!'

'What did you say?'

The woman turned her head, she curled her lip. 'Ya money grabbin' slag, you deserved nothing, you should be locked up,' and quickly walked away.

'What was that about?'

Annie pulled a face, her eyes narrowed as she stretched her lips over her teeth into a snarl.

'The locals have always accused me of taking Ron's money.'

'Oh.'

'Why do they think it's anything to do with them?'

Annie sat down and looked in her handbag.

'Hi, Karen.'

Karen looked up and saw a face she recognised but couldn't recall the name.

'Hi!' Karen smiled.

'It's David. We met at the Kelso Book Fair the other week.'

'Ah, yes, hello! What brings you up here?'

'My mum lives in the village. That's her over there.' David pointed at an elderly woman dressed in a fur coat and a wrapped, turban style hat.

'That's nice.'

'LADIES AND GENTLEMEN, PLEASE TAKE YOUR SEATS!'

'I'd better go, nice to see you again.' David returned to his seat.

'Oh, he's keen.' said Annie. 'Want a swig?'

Annie had her hand on a small hip flask sitting in the opening of her handbag, 'I always keep it handy.'

'No thanks, I'd better not, I'm driving.'

Annie took two big swigs from her hip flask.

The show started when the cast made their way up to the stage from the back of the hall, through the audience, it was a full-on, energetic performance. The couple sitting to the left of Annie acted out some of the scenes and mimed along to the songs.

At the interval Karen stood up, 'I'm going to the ladies, are you coming?'

'I'm fine thanks, I'll stay put.' Annie watched as Karen walked down the aisle next to the theatre wall towards the stage, she pushed one of the double doors open and disappeared.

'What a nerve you've got turning up here.'

Annie looked up, a snarl already formed on her face. 'Oh, fuck off Vicky, and leave me alone.'

'You took all my dad's money ya money grabbing, murdering bitch.'

'Get over it, and he never liked you anyway.'

Ron's eldest daughter stood in the gap between the chairs in front of Annie's row. Each time she spoke, spittle shot out from her pumped-up lips. Her blue football top stretched tightly across her braless chest. Her large, rounded stomach divided her breasts so much they lay either side it and almost under her armpits.

'You stole that money, and Fetterby was never yours to sell!' her face was distorted, and her voice had gotten louder as she spat the words out.

'Fuck off! Leave me alone or I'll call the police.' snarled Annie.

The girl's right fist flew out towards Annie's face, and made contact, it knocked her and the chair backwards.

Annie got up and flew at the girl, grabbed handfuls of her long hair, and pulled her head down hard on the row of seats.

Annie screamed, 'You fat, ugly, troll how fucking dare you!' as she smashed the daughter's head down repeatedly on the backs of the seats.

Karen pushed open one side of the double door and walked back into the auditorium. The shouting and swearing startled her. She ran up to the large group of people and saw Annie and the girl fighting amongst a tangle of theatre chairs. David was in the middle, he grabbed a hold of Annie and two older men were tried to grab a hold of Ron's daughter, but she fought them as much as she fought with Annie.

The women were separated, blood poured out of the daughter's nose and head and her eye was swollen. Annie had a bloodied lip. They screamed at one another. David grabbed Annie around the waist, her arms flailed around and her fist caught him on the cheek. He picked her up and off her feet and took her away from the centre of the crowd.

He looked across at Karen. 'I'll take her outside.'

Karen was stunned and couldn't think straight.

'Yes.... yes, do that.' She picked up Annie's bag, searched under the seats, and tried to gather up the contents strewn across the floor, she saw the hip flask and put it back inside the bag. Under one of the seats she spotted a hoof pick and a large swiss army knife. They clinked together as she grabbed them. As she looked around for more of Annie's handbag contents, an older man walked up to her.

In a broad Fife accent, he said, 'dae yersell aw faver aund hae nothin' ta dae with thon evil ane.'

'What?'

'That yin murdered Ron and took aw his money. The same treatment as her furst hubbie.'

'I highly doubt that.' said Karen.

'Tack ma wird for it, a ken.'

'okay, yes, you know.'

'Am Ron's twin brither, aund yeah, I do ken whatt she did ta him.'

Karen tucked Annie's bag under her arm, and left the theatre by the main entrance. She stood on the steps of the building and scanned the car park then she heard Annie's voice. David sat with his arm around her on the brick wall boundary to the right of the Theatre building.

'Are you okay, Annie?'

'Yes, I'm fine, just a bit shaken up. Did you get my bag?' Karen handed Annie her bag, 'I picked everything I could see up.'

'Thanks for doing that.'

'Shall I take you to the hospital to get checked out?'

'No! I'm alright, really, I'm alright.'

Annie reached into her handbag and pulled out her hipflask, unscrewed the top, tipped her back and emptied the entire contents down her neck.

'Phew.' she exhaled.

'Who attacked you?'

'Ron's daughter.'

'You know her? Shouldn't you report it to the police?' said David.

'No, not tonight, I will contact them tomorrow.'

'Look, I can phone them now and they can meet you at your house?'

'No, it's fine. Karen, I'm sorry but can you take me home?' Annie stood up but was very unsteady on her feet. David moved quickly and helped her get her balance.

'Wait here, I'll bring the car down.'

Karen pulled up in her car. As Annie sat in the passenger seat, Karen leaned over, 'thanks David, I'll get Annie home.'

'If you need any help just shout,' he said.

'You should get your face looked at, I think you have some battle injuries,' said Karen.

'I'm fine, do you need help at the house?' asked David.

Annie looked up at David. 'Thank you very much for your help, I'm sorry I hit you.'

Annie's bottom lip and left-hand side of her face looked sore.

David gave Karen a piece of paper. 'Here's my number if you need anything call me.'

In the time it had taken to get back to the house, Annie's lip had swollen up and distorted her words, 'I'm shorry about tonight, Karen. Vicky punched me. I just shaw red, snapped, and hit out.'

'Don't worry about it, as long as you are okay?' Karen parked up, got out of the car quickly and opened the passenger door for Annie. 'Take my arm.'

'I'm okay, really, I am,' insisted Annie.

'Okay, I'll wait until I see you go inside, do you need anything?'

'I am okay, really, I am. I've had worse.'

Karen stood by the car, and watched Annie walk up the path. She put her key in the lock and opened the door, she turned and gave her a half-hearted wave before she closed the door.

Back at home, Karen poured a large Vodka and tonic, sat in her office, and stared at the screen of her laptop. The night's events had shaken her up. Her mind drifted back to Ron's twin and what he had said to her about Annie.

Her left breast ached. The vodka helped bring her back down to earth, but she knew she'd not fall asleep right away if she went to bed. There were two emails, another lengthy one from Liam and the other from Alexander.

'Hi, Karen,

I am so pleased you replied and have agreed to lunch. I am sorry, but it is better I don't call you as I get tongue-tied and it embarrasses me greatly. I will be okay once I've met you, but would you mind if we just stuck to communicating via email instead?

Are you free on Thursday this week? I understand if it's too short notice, but I'll be in town early for a meeting, it will finish midday, and I'll be free for lunch. The Duke's Room on George street is a favourite of mine; the food is excellent. I can book a table for 12.30.

Yours sincerely,

Alexander.'

Karen studied her diary, she had a meeting with Warren at the clay shooting ground on Wednesday morning followed by her annual Mammogram appointment at the Queen Anne Hospital, and Friday night she was meeting up with Bernie and Faye.

'Hi Alexander,

Thursday would be great, I look forward to lunch with you at 12.30.

Karen.'

Liam's reply was entertaining but full of examples of people telling him how wonderful and talented he was. He spoke about his commitment to work, world tours and how, despite being a great catch, his love life had suffered. His writing tickled her, but she couldn't be sure if he was laughing at himself.

It was late, she felt sleepy, so decided to reply to him in the morning. There were two more unread emails connected with the dating website but she consigned them to Tuesday's list of things to do.

On Tuesday after breakfast, she called Bernie.

'Have you found anywhere for Friday night?'

'Nope, struggling. There's a couple of places in Kirkcaldy but I haven't tried them so they're in the unknown category. Remember that place we tried a few years ago, and we all had a lasting reminder of how bad it was.'

'How about coming up here? Spend the night so no-one has to drive, and I could order in a takeaway from Pale Jade. I have eaten there a couple of times and it's always been a great and the food is fab. What do you think?'

'That sounds great.'

'I'll get it all organised, just bring yourselves.'

'That's it sorted. I'll call Faye, she'll love that idea, especially since she's been traipsing around the globe a hell of a lot recently.'

'I was going to ask you how the love life is going but don't tell me, we'll catch-up on Friday night.'

'I will guarantee you a laugh when I tell you some of the things that have happened recently. Shall I ask Annie over? She's had a tough time with a few dating horrors and hasn't been out much.'

'Yes, great idea, four is a better number than three unless you are in bed.'

CHAPTER 13

Karen drove to the shooting ground on Wednesday morning to meet with Warren then, drove to the Queen Anne hospital afterwards.

The huge revolving hospital doorway rotated slowly as Karen stepped in and walked anti-clockwise into the building, she passed the main reception on her right, walked down the corridor, through the doors into the consultants waiting room area. The strip lighting in the ceiling was gloomy, the walls and seats in the waiting area looked tired and uninspiring, with an awkwardly mounted flat screen TV blaring in a corner. People stared at their phones. It was a place of bad news. She followed the curve of the wall out through double doors and onto a long corridor leading to an area with huge windows.

Briefly, natural light flooded before it was replaced by strip lighting. Karen pressed the square metal panel to open the doors into the Radiology department, she walked down the slope, and towards the reception desk on the left. A grumpy woman asked for her name, date of birth and address. She printed off two long labels and handed them to Karen and directed her to the waiting room at the bottom of the corridor on the left. Karen made eye contact with her and gave her a big smile.

'Thank you so much!'

It was warm in the mammogram clinic waiting area. The seats

were more comfortable, but a TV blared out its banal tripe of daytime programmes.

Karen sat down and looked into her handbag. A female voice called out, 'Karen Knighton.'

Karen stood up, smiled. 'That's me.'

She was delighted to see the radiologist was Lyndsay, she always welcomed people with a smile. 'Hello there, how are you getting on?' she asked.

She opened the door to the x-ray room and showed Karen in. 'Time flies.'

The woman spoke and laughed as if they had known each other for years. A mammogram was an annual event for Karen, and an appointment she liked to tick off as done.

'That's you done.'

'Thanks, it goes so quickly.' Karen put her bra and shirt back on, pulled her coat on and slung her bag over her shoulder. 'Thanks for that, and hopefully, I won't see you until next year.'

The women said goodbye, and Karen reversed her journey back to the car at the far end of the car park.

On Thursday, Karen woke up early thinking about her lunch date in Edinburgh, she didn't feel excited about the lunch and decided to cancel.

It was just after ten o'clock when her phone rang, a call from an unknown number.

'Hello, Karen Knighton.'

'Hi Karen, it's Drew, we haven't spoken in years.'

'Oh my god, hello Drew, how are you getting on?'

'I am well, how are you?'

'Good, really good...'

'Is it okay to speak right now?' asked Drew.

'Yes, of course, how are ....?'

'Look, I have some bad news. My mum died yesterday.'

'Oh Drew, I am so sorry to hear this.'

'Thank you. It was totally unexpected, we are all in shock and I am sorry breaking it to you so suddenly on the phone like this.'

'Don't worry about that. I am so sorry. I know people always say it, but if there is anything I can do, please just ask.'

'Thank you, Karen. It's all a learning experience, you have to make appointments these days with funeral directors and the like but I'm trying to do what I can, but my Dad is in pieces, and so is Lizzie.'

'How are you, I haven't seen you in years?'

It wasn't the phone conversation Karen wanted to take over with her life story update. 'It must be at least twenty years. Doesn't time fly? You must have so much to organise, Drew?'

'You are right, there's a lot to organise, and you don't know how much there is until it happens. I can't seem to think straight about anything and you kind of go through the motions. Hopefully, we should know more tomorrow about the arrangements. Could you let your parents know about my mum?'

'Yes, of course.'

'Do you know where Faye and Bernie are these days?'

'Bernie is still in Kirkcaldy and...'

'Her mum's place, Jute house?'

'Yes, she is, and Faye spends most of her time in Paris, she has a studio there. She's coming up to Fife this weekend. I'll see them on Friday night.'

'Do you have Bernie's number, I don't appear to have the right one for her?'

Karen replied, 'I'll call her and let her know.'

Karen and Drew had known one another since primary school. Drew's family had relocated to Fife from Thurso when his dad moved with his job. Big Drew was a gamekeeper and Betty, his wife, used to do the catering for the shooting parties and the anglers. They moved to the Fable estate on the outskirts of Kirk-caldy. Drew and his sister went to the same school as Karen and her younger brother, Steve.

When Drew married Beth, Karen went to their wedding but over the years, different locations and life got in the way and they had lost touch but hearing his voice again closed the gap. There was a curiosity, so many years had grown between them; what had they done with their lives and how had life treated them. Drew and Beth had a daughter before they married, and adopted a son. Karen was given vague updates over the years when her mum met Betty and Big Drew but her mum's partiality to the brandy meant her ability to relay their news was seldom accur-ate.

Karen saved Drew's number then she called Bernie. 'Hi Bernie, give me a call back when you get this message.'

Karen spent the rest of Thursday in her office, it was time well spent as she had been productive. She felt satisfied she had made the right decision to cancel lunch, and made no future plans to see Alexander.

She took a large heavy crystal glass from the cupboard, put three ice-cubes into the glass, then took the Stolichnaya from the freezer and poured an inch into the glass. She opened the tonic water she found inside the cupboard and poured it over the ice and Vodka, the ice crackled and rose to the surface. The bubbles tickled her nose when she lifted the glass to her mouth. She took one long drink as her phone rang.

'How did you get on at the hospital?'

'Great thanks, all went to plan and now I have to wait for the results.'

'How long do you have to wait?'

'Anything up to 14 days but if there's an issue the dreaded letter arrives within a week.'

'Fingers are crossed.'

'How are you?'

'Not bad,' said Bernie. 'I had a couple of screen tests for fronting some documentary work but it's hard to share their excitement when you're as long in the tooth as I am. The girl, and I do say a girl with accuracy, that interviewed me looked like she was still at school, and no prizes for guessing she was blonde with big knockers.'

'Some things never change, do they? I called earlier as I have some news, and it's not good. Drew phoned me.'

'Drew?'

'Remember Drew, Big Drew, Betty, and Lizzie from Fable?'

There was a long pause before Bernie answered. 'Yes, of course.'

'He called to tell me Betty died suddenly yesterday in the Vic. She had gone in complaining of a severe headache, turns out it was a blood clot on the brain, and within an hour or so of going into the Vic she slipped into an unconscious state and died.'

'Oh no, I'm sorry to hear that. What a shock. Was he okay?'

'I think he is coping but there's so much to organise. Drew said he had tried to contact you but he thought he didn't have the right number for you.'

'Oh, really? He mentioned me?'

There was another pause.

'I said I'd call you and I'd pass the sad news on.'

'I'll need to send a card and flowers,' said Bernie.

'Why don't we all get together and do it from the three of us? Afterall, we were all at school together.'

'Yes, that's a good idea. I'll let Faye know the news and I'll organise some flowers to be delivered. On a cheerier note, Faye loves the idea of heading over to yours. I'm going to pick her up at Kirkcaldy station at 5 pm, so we'll just drive up to yours via a stop off at Morrisons for some supplies.'

'I'm looking forward to seeing her, and us all being together again. It's been a while and I could do with a laugh.'

'What's that noise? Are you are drinking?'

'Yes, it's been a strange day, and it was a shock getting that call from Drew. It makes you think and also realise time moves so fast.'

'Are you okay?'

'Thanks Bernie, I am good, just overthinking, as per usual I can't wait for tomorrow, it'll be the tonic I need.'

'You're right, it'll do us all the world of good. See you tomorrow.'

Karen lit two candles, and relaxed in the bath for an hour, determined to distract her thoughts and pamper herself. Afterwards she stretched out on the sofa and had thought about an early night when her phone rang again.

'Hi Brian, how are you?'

'Great thanks, how are you getting on, good week?'

'Oh, so-so but I had a call this morning from an old school friend to tell me his mum had died suddenly.'

'I am sorry to hear that, it must have been a shock.'

'Yes, he sounded shocked.'

'Sorry, I meant it must have been a shock for you?'

'Yes, it was. When he called and said who he was, I thought it was great to hear from him after so many years but it wasn't a catch-up call. I guess you get two jolts, the pleasant surprise of hearing from an old school friend, then the shock of hearing his mother has died. Bittersweet, I guess.'

'I hope you are okay, and if you need to talk about it, you know I am here for you,' said Brian.

'Thanks, that's very kind.'

'What are you up to tomorrow?'

'I've a busy day ahead as I have the girls coming over for a catch-up, why?'

'How about Saturday?'

'I'll no doubt be nursing a hangover.'

'How about I come down and take you out for a nice meal somewhere to ease away your hangover in the evening?'

'Okay, thanks, that'd be nice.'

'I'll find somewhere local, and text you when I'm on my way. Probably aim to get to you about 7 pm, is that okay?'

Karen laughed, 'great, but be prepared, I may be a little lacklustre.'

She felt a new, genuine warmth had grown between them. He had been very supportive after she'd told him about Drew's call about his mum's death. He was keen to see more of her. He had considered she may be feeling fragile and would take care of her. A good man. Perhaps.

CHAPTER 14

Karen's phone buzzed.

'It was great to speak to you yesterday; just sorry it was the wrong sort of circumstances. We've just heard the funeral is likely to be next week, I'll let you know the details when they are confirmed. I hope you managed to get in touch with Bernie? Drewxx'

Bernie and Faye turned up in Bernie's car.

'What a vista!' said Faye, as she walked back to the end of the drive to look at the view across the fields.

Faye let out a squeal when she saw Karen, and ran towards her and hugged her tightly. 'It's been too long, far too long!'

Bernie opened up a cooler box from her car and produced a bottle of champagne. 'Let's start the right way, where do you keep your flutes?'

Karen pointed at the dresser by the door. Bernie popped the champagne open. Bernie, Faye, and Karen stood in the kitchen and raised their glasses and gently clinked them together in a pyramid shape as though they were performing an ancient ritual to summon the devil from the depths.

They were about to refill their glasses when there was a knock at the kitchen door.

'Helloooooo!' called Annie from the doorway.

Karen introduced her to Faye, and Bernie poured her a glass of champagne, 'you'll need to catch up, we're one glass ahead.'

Annie said, 'cheers, ladies!'

She smirked and downed it in one, 'no bother, I'm ready.'

They laughed.

By the time the takeaway arrived at 8 pm they had almost finished their third bottle.

'Art exhibitions are never dull,' said Faye. 'A guy appeared at my latest one. He picked up my catalogue, unbuttoned his coat, dropped at his feet and calmly walked through my exhibition with the catalogue covering his bits. He kissed my hand, introduced himself as my greatest art lover and then danced around my paintings like the male lead from the Dance of the Matadors.'

'Wow, that must have been some sight?' said Bernie.

'I have to say, he knew his ballet, he moved beautifully.'

Bernie laughed. 'I meant his naked form must have been some sight!'

'Oh yes, very pleasing.' They laughed.

'Afterwards, some of the press accused me of staging it.'

'And had you?' asked Karen.

She faked an angelic look and turned her eyes skywards. 'Let me adjust my halo.'

'You always said all publicity is good publicity.'

They laughed.

'You are so lucky living in France, it's beats Maryard hands down. I wish I'd done something more exciting with my life,' said Annie. 'Thinking about it, you've all done exciting things with you lives. I worked in labs then moved on to shovelling horse dung from one side of the field to the other.'

Until Karen moved into the area, Annie did not have many friends. She retired early from her career as a pharmaceutical toxicologist, and filled her life with animals. The weeks would become months of no human contact. She forgot what it was like to enjoy conversation and relax amongst friends. Online shopping was her lifeline, and meant she could avoid going out in public.

Old Christmas cards sent to her in years gone by were brought out from storage in mid-December and displayed on the mantlepiece. Her family had lived in Dundee. She rarely spoke about them or any relations.

'Look at your wonderful horses, I'd love to be around horses each day,' said Faye.

The girls were merry, the mood was light, fun and filled with laughter as they shared tales about their dating disasters.

Annie said, 'I killed my first ex-husband, you know. I swapped his medication for concentrated doses of Viagra, blood thinners and mixed them with aspirin. He was found dead in a hotel which had been raised to the ground by a massive fire.'

'You murdered him?' asked Bernie.

'Yup, I did. He was a monster,' said Annie. 'The official investigation recorded he had fallen down a flight of stairs trying to escape the fire possibly due to the blurred vision caused by a drugs cocktail. He suffered massive internal bleeding and his charred priapism was still apparent on the mortician's slab.' She laughed.

The girls discreetly looked at one another, Faye and Karen stayed quiet. Bernie asked. 'Didn't the drugs in his system make the police suspicious?'

'Not really, he'd always taken them so that made it easy. I used to enjoy making up the drug cocktails and seeing how they worked on him,' said Annie. 'I made the Viagra so strong he had an erection for two days and had to go to A &E and confess to being a wanker.' She laughed.

Annie was so drunk she didn't notice Faye, Karen and Bernie had not laughed along with her.

'It was a fitting end to the cheat and I dealt with my parents, Dougie, Ron and …..ooops!' Annie knocked over her empty glass. 'Sozzy, whaaat was I zaying?'

Karen got up from the table and picked up the empty glass, 'who wants coffee?'

It was 1.30am when they finished the pot of coffee. Annie yawned, and said she felt sleepy. She got up from the table, and muttered incomprehensibly as though talking to someone over her shoulder. She balanced on one foot and skilfully pulled her wellies, put her coat on, then stretched her torch headband over her head.

'Goodnight, ladies, thanks for a brilliant night and loads of laughs. Night, night!' Said Annie.

'Will she be okay?' asked Bernie.

Karen nodded. The three girls sat silently at the table and looked at one another.

Karen said, 'Okay, let's not talk about this tonight. I need my beauty sleep.'

'I need as much as I can get, wake me up on Sunday.'

They laughed, as Bernie and Faye headed upstairs. Karen was going to follow them after she locked the doors but wanted to check her email. She promised herself she wouldn't reply to anything, just read.

There was a lengthy email from Liam, the gist of it was a date with him towards the end of next week as he was coming back to Scotland early due to tour date cancellation. Karen went upstairs happy, she found herself thinking of Liam. She looked forward to meeting him to find out if he was like.

As Karen got into bed her mind switched back to the evening with the girls, and wondered if she had just been implicated in some sort of murder confession. The tiredness and alcohol mixture fuzzed up her brain. She got herself comfortable, stretched out diagonally across the bed, and dropped off to sleep.

CHAPTER 15

It was 8 am on Saturday morning when Karen got out of bed and went down to the kitchen. She filled the kettle and picked up some of the debris from the night before. By the time the kettle had boiled, she had cleared the kitchen table of empty glasses, thrown all the napkins in the bin and wiped the table. She ground some coffee beans, and counted out loud as she scooped the coffee from the grinder into the pot and filled it with boiled water. She felt tired, slow, and fuzzy after last night's champagne and wine consumption.

Karen looked out from the kitchen window, and sure enough, Annie was pushing her wheelbarrow over the fields, shovelling horse dung and tending to her horses. Up until that moment, Karen had forgotten about last night's confession and now lots of questions rattled around in her head. The whole thing was surreal, and thinking made her head hurt all the more.

'Wow, that was some night in, and this is some hangover,' said Faye as she pressed her index fingers into her temples.

'Someone stop the throbbing pain.'

Karen took a box of paracetamol out of the drawer and slid them across the table in Faye's direction, she went to the sink, ran the cold tap, and filled two glasses.

'Here, join me, take two.'

'Cheers!' said Faye, and smiled.

Karen looked at her, shook her head and laughed.

'How did you sleep?'

'In truth, I don't know, I was in an alcohol-induced coma.' Faye laughed.

'Is Bernie awake?'

'I don't think so. I heard your coffee grinder, I can pick out that sound in a war zone and know there's fresh coffee not that far away.'

Faye looked around the kitchen. 'I don't recall it being this tidy last night.'

Karen smiled, 'amazing what you can do with a fuzzy head on a promise of strong coffee.'

'I feel like nibbling on something, are there any spicy eggplant and coconut leftovers?'

'I can't remember, have a look in the fridge?'

Karen poured the coffee, and looked at Faye. 'What do you think of Annie's confessions last night?'

'Hell, I don't know. Was she making it up or had we listened to a murder confession? If she hadn't been so drunk we could have found out what happened her parents, Ron and others...?'

'Up until last night, she never spoke much about her ex-husbands. If she did talk about them she was very matter of fact about their deaths and how she benefited financially.'

'Do you think she has murdered more than one?'

'Her old career as a pharmaceutical toxicologist fits, she knows her stuff about drugs and chemicals. She rarely calls a vet out to her animals because she treats them herself with drugs. I have heard her say she sedates her horses if they're acting up or when the blacksmith is due.'

'It sounds as though she has had a tough life, Karen, but how many of us would turn to murder? I have met a few idiots in my time but I walked away and didn't murder them despite having pleasing thoughts about doing so.'

'I find it interesting we haven't said nah, she wouldn't do such a thing, she's not capable.'

'What if she has decided to go after the stepdaughter who attacked her at the local theatre on Monday and bumps her off?'

'She drugged that professor, if he had crashed his car and killed himself, and possibly others on the road, that would bump her kill rate up to serial killer status.'

'Christ, it is making my head spin.'

'Drink your coffee, I'm going to take one up to Bernie, and a side order of paracetamol.'

Karen took a mug of coffee and two tablets upstairs.

Karen opened the bedroom door, and shouted, 'MORNING!'

Bernie was lying face down on the bed and groaned.

'Why do I have to drink so much?'

'Because we forced you into it. Don't worry, it was fun, we all drank loads and it's not as if we do it every night.'

'Gawd, you are cheery this morning.'

'I'm faking it.'

Bernie sat up, 'what's the tally on the local murders today? I've had some wild nights with the girls but listening to murder confessions is a new one on me. She's not related to Ruth Ellis, is she?

'Drink your coffee and pop a couple of pills down your neck and get your carcass down to the kitchen. I'll do us some breakfast once I've normalised my blood levels and flushed them through with three gallons of coffee.'

Bernie stretched and yawned, 'do you have a menu and I'll put my order in?'

They laughed.

Karen loved having the girls in the house, it was a nice feeling hearing them moving around. She shouted down to Faye, 'I'm having a quick shower, I'll be down in fifteen minutes, help yourself to whatever you want.'

Karen stood under the shower and washed off yesterday's makeup, and rubbed a handful of shampoo through her hair. She hoped the shower would speed up her recovery. It was a sociable weekend, she felt happy she had something else to look forward to later that day. It reminded her of having a boyfriend and going out on a Saturday night. She wrapped her hair in a towel, dried herself off, put on a pair of navy leggings, a vest top, and her favourite hoodie.

The smell of the Cucumber skin cleanser dolloped onto cotton wool reminded her of being a teenager, and her first forays into makeup and how embarrassed she felt about having thick, frizzy brown hair, and how she envied the girls with even complexions, and thick dark eyelashes.

Teenage magazines were the only source of entertainment, and advice in the 1970s. They'd 'bust the myths about boys' or share a reader's true experience. The stories were illustrated by photographs with speech bubbles, 'how to do your make-up or 'deal with fuzz' guides, horoscopes, letters page, and the 'Dear Cathy and Claire' problem page.

The weekly magazines like Jackie, My Guy, Oh Boy, and Fab208 cost less than 10 pence. Karen remembered the images of small-breasted wholesome looking girls with pale blue eyeshadow wearing multicoloured knitted tank tops, brushed denim high-waisted jeans with wide bottoms and platform shoes. The magazines promoted pop stars like David Cassidy, The Osmonds and the Bay City Rollers, and each week you'd get a 'sizzling' centrefold pin up to tear-out and stick on your bedroom wall. At Christmas time everyone asked for annuals and owned one pair of favourite boots or shoes, made from black or brown leather or suede. When the soles and heels wore down, they were repaired in Timpsons or at a Cobbler on the high street. You were bereft without your favourite shoes, but somehow you survived three or four days without them consoled by another year or two's wear.

She rubbed moisturiser into her skin, ran a brown pencil through her brows, some black eyeliner on the tops of her lids and covered her lashes with two coats of mascara. She unwrapped the towel from her hair and ran her fingers through it, sprayed on Coco Chanel, smiled at her reflection, and said, 'Onwards and Upwards!' and headed back downstairs.

'I think you're on the verge of falling in love, you know,' said Faye.

'What makes you say that?

'Well, you have a sparkle in your eyes and you smile differently when you talk about him. He does sound like a good guy and look at the things you have in common.'

'Really?'

'Yup, really. I think that's great, he gives you hope and there's definite potential there.'

'I hope so, in the last couple of days I have allowed myself to like him a little bit more.'

'He must be the man for you because he is tall.'

They laughed.

'Is Bernie alive?'

'Well, she moved, spoke and drank her coffee.'

Karen's phone rang. 'Damn, where is it?'

Her eyes scanned across all the surfaces in the kitchen as she walked towards the sound. She got to her office desk and picked up her phone just as the call went to voicemail.

Brian had called. How nice, he had called to see if she had survived a night of girly chat, food, and gallons of wine. She didn't bother listening to the voicemail, instead she called him back.

'Hi Brian, we were just talking about you. We're up, drinking coffee.'

'Yes, it was great, and feeling sort of human but breakfast and more coffee will get us sorted out.'

'Oh.'

Karen sat down at her desk.

'Really?'

'Are you serious?'

'Today?'

'Why?'

'For how long?'

'What can I say. I think you are mad.'

'No.'

'All you seem to do is apologise to me.'

'No, don't bother.'

'Goodbye.'

Karen put her phone back down on her desk, and looked out of the window.

Faye called through from the kitchen. 'Is everything okay,

Karen?'

Karen picked her phone up, and walked back into the kitchen.

'Guess who that was?' She took a deep breath. 'It was Brian. He's not coming to see me this evening because he is flying off to the USA to be with his ex-girlfriend. She's been injured in a car crash which also killed her new partner. Brian is the only person she knows who could help her.'

'Oh, that's crap.'

'Sorry, Karen. To hell with him, if he's gullible enough to drop everything when she shouts then they're welcome to each other.'

Bernie came downstairs looking very fragile. Karen told her about the call from Brian.

'He has missed his chance with you. Let him get on with it and you carry on with your life.'

Karen took another deep breath and pulled a face. 'You're right, I'm not going to dwell on it, anyway, I have other potential dates coming up.'

'That's the right approach!' said Faye.

'Onwards and upwards, girls. Some breakfast?'

As Karen cooked breakfast, the postman pushed four letters into the post box by the kitchen door, Bernie stepped outside in her PJs to get some fresh air and retrieve the post.

'Here's your post, Karen.' She put the letters on the dresser and complained of the cold and pulled Karen's woollen shawl over her shoulders.

Looking at the view she said, 'is that our local serial killer out in the fields already?'

'I said to Faye I really don't know what to think. I feel as though she has shared a burden, but she doesn't appear to be burdened by it. *AND,* we all seem to believe her, isn't that odd?'

Bernie tried to speak but coughed, and rubbed her throat and pulled a face. 'Why do I have a sore throat?'

'Don't you remember?'

'Oh my god, it's just come back to me, yesss! The singing!'

'It was a brilliant laugh, and I don't understand how I can't remember what I did last week yet I can sing the words to a song I haven't heard in forty years.'

'I'm going to update my tunes for the car with some of the classics you played last night, what was the name of the one I went to bed singing?'

'Substitute, I think. I'll go look it up.'

Faye said, 'it's the menopause, we all had good recall for everything. I get so forgetful I can't even finish a sentence. Last week I was doing an interview for one of the radio Arts programmes, they asked me questions, and I totally lost my thread and had to ask them to repeat it. They could have asked me my name and I'd have forgotten that as well. It's like my brain just turns to mush and I'm robbed of my power of speech.'

'I can relate to that, some days are worse than others, and there's no warning, is there?' said Karen. 'I end up sounding as though I'm new to the English language.'

Bernie laughed, and said, 'there were times when I slurred my words but that's due to drinking gallons of wine.'

'Here it is, it's a band called Clout, a 1978 classic.'

They sat at the kitchen table and nursed their hangovers with bacon, croissants, maple syrup and coffee.

Karen's phone flashed. 'It's an email from Brian, he's said sorry at least ten times.

'I think I'm feeling sort of normal. I managed to string a couple of sentences together,' announced Bernie. 'Time for a shower, if I'm not back down in 15 mins please send a search party.'

Karen walked over to the dresser and picked up her post. She flicked through the envelopes: bank statements, a local pizza delivery menu and a brown envelope from the NHS.

'Oh no, I know this is NOT going to be good news.'

'Why do you say that you haven't even opened it up?' said Faye.

'It's from the hospital.'

Karen looked up. 'It's arrived too quickly after the mammogram. If everything comes back okay the letter usually arrives in 7 to 10 days.'

'Come and sit down over here.'

'I'm okay,' said Karen. She opened the envelope.

'I have an appointment with the consultant next week in Dunfermline.'

'Could it be anything else?'

'I can't see how it could be anything else, Faye. I went for a mammogram, and now I have to see the consultant. He's not going to be delivering the all-clear for me. This is what happened in 2011.'

CHAPTER 16

It had been years since Karen had visited the Crematorium. Bernie reminded her it may have been Clodagh's funeral. The drab 1950s building sat low surrounded by trees and rhododendrons.

For once Karen and Bernie blended into the crowd. Everyone stood outside and sheltered from the rain under the covered entrance.

At 11.08, the hearse appeared and parked on the side road up from the Crem, followed closely by the black stretched limo. Big Drew in his kilt got out of the car first, Drew, Beth and other family members followed.

The family walked towards the entrance and a Crem official asked everyone to follow on. As more than a hundred-people filed in not a word was said, they stayed in their small groups and sat together on the lines of chairs. The interior padded doors overlaid with stretched PVC and dark brown raised knobs resembled big chocolate buttons. It reminded them of Kirkcaldy High School in the 1970s.

'I feel like an adult in a harsh, lonely world,' whispered Karen.

Betty's coffin was on view, surrounded by colourful flowers. The Celebrant introduced himself, then talked about Betty's life with humorous anecdotes and made everyone laugh. He read a poem Betty always loved, then guided everyone to spend some time reflecting on their own memories of Betty while some of her favourite Scottish music played in the background. The double side doors opened, and as the music continues to play everyone left to meet the family. Karen and Bernie joined the queue to pay their respects. They hugged and chatted to Big Drew, Drew, and Lizzie.

'My parents send their deepest condolences and they are sorry they were unable to make it.'

'Thanks, Karen,' said Big Drew. 'I hope you girls are coming over to the golf club for a cup of tea and sandwich?'

After a brief chat, Karen and Bernie moved towards the exit doors close to the carpark. Karen noticed Drew's wife, Beth, had detached herself from the family group and talked to a younger couple.

'That was a nice tribute, I don't think I've ever been to a funeral and laughed so much,' said Bernie.

'I feel sad she is no longer around but that service accurately reflected who she was and her humour. Your mum's funeral is still my favourite.'

'It was amazing, wasn't it? My mind wandered and I thought about her. I still miss her exuberance.'

Karen pulled a face and rubbed her left breast.

'Are you okay?'

'Yes, just a dull ache. I think I'm going to take a couple of paracetamol before we go in.'

'You must be worried about tomorrow?'

'I am, it's not an easy thing to put to the back of your mind.'

It was a short drive along Dunnikier Way. They turned left by their old school. 'It looks so dated?'

'Yuck, it looks tatty with the faded paintwork.'

'Can't say I have fond memories of the place, remember that pervy old assistant Rector who was a stand-in PE teacher? He lined up against the wall of the swimming pool and tell us to straighten our backs and stick of chests out. Then he'd walk up and down ogling at us.'

'Yeah, I remember what a dirty bastard he was. He'd be put away these days. Far too many of his sort got away with it. You're right, no fond memories of the place.'

The golf club car park was busy when they arrived.

'It's a day of memories, that golf course reminds me of the cross-country runs we had to do.'

'Oh yes, into the woods and around the perimeter of the golf course. Faye was a great runner, but I hated it.'

Most of the clubhouse tables were taken as Karen and Bernie made their way in. Drew waved and beckoned them over to a table near to the family group. He hugged them tightly.

The room was a mass of black clothing and grey hair, and no one had bought a drink from the bar.

When Karen returned from the bar, she overheard Drew complimenting Bernie. 'I'm pleased it went smoothly, Betty would have been laughing along with us.' said Big Drew. 'It was a very fitting send off,' replied Karen. As they chatted, Karen caught saw Beth standing away from the family area, she watched Bernie and Drew like a hawk.

'Bernie here is your wine.'

'Cheers Karen, it'll go down well.'

'It'd better go, I need to do a short speech before the food comes out, take a seat here ladies.' Drew pointed to the table at the end of the family group of tables. Karen and Bernie sat down, sipped their drinks, and looked towards the bar where Drew stood, he tapped the side of a glass with a spoon, the clubhouse fell silent in an instant.

Drew thanked everyone for coming and said Betty would have been chuffed to see them, he shared a couple of personal memories of his mum as staff worked at the back of room filling a long table with sandwiches, quiche, and sausage rolls, tea and coffee pots. Towards the end of Drew's speech, the oldies got on their marks. When he finished on a round of applause, all the oldies vaulted up from their seats and made an unceremonious stampede to the food table.

Bernie looked across the room, 'wonder if the plague of locusts have cleared the table?'

She got up from the table and walked over to see what had been left. The large refreshments table was littered in used napkins, empty trays, and a squashed slice of quiche and some discarded sandwiches. As Bernie was about to walk away, the kitchen doors opened, and a waitress brought in two large trays of food, Bernie moved quickly before a second feeding frenzy commenced, she picked up a plate, and two napkins. She put a couple of sausage rolls, two egg and cress sandwiches, and some crisps on a plate.

'Have a nibble.'

'Mmm, don't mind if I do.' said Karen.

'Don't eat them all.'

Bernie smiled.

'Shall we head off after this?'

'Yes, that'd be good timing. We've done our bit and I don't fancy hanging around.'

'Drew seemed really pleased to see us?' He is in good shape, has kept his looks and his hair.'

Bernie looked out across the room. 'Yes, he has.'

As they stood up to leave Drew appeared at their table. 'Here's my card,' and handed a card to both of them.

'Stay in touch. It would be good to catch-up.'

'You've got a fucking nerve turning up here!' hissed Beth. She stood next to Drew and stared at Bernie.

'I was invited by your husband.' Said Bernie without missing a beat. She looked at Drew. 'My sincere condolences to you and your family.'

Bernie picked up her coat from the back of the chair and pulled it on. She ignored Beth, looked at Drew and smiled. 'I'll speak to you soon.'

Beth was about to lurch forward when Drew grabbed her by the arm and held onto her. 'Get a grip of yourself!'

'She's got no right to be here!'

'Yes, she damn well has! She is one of my oldest friends, our families knew one another. Get over it.'

'She still shouldn't be here!' spat Beth, her eyes were wide, and her face distorted by anger.

'You are going to embarrass me and my family at my mum's funeral.'

Beth burst into tears and ran to the ladies toilets.

'What the hell was that about?' asked Karen as they opened the car doors.

'Remember when Drew asked you for my phone number last week? Well, he didn't have my number because I changed it a few years back after our brief affair.'

'Affair?'

'Yup, a very brief one..'

'You never mentioned it before.'

'There isn't really much to say, it was short-lived, only lasted a few weeks. It was around the time when Thomas moved out, you had your hands full so I didn't want to say anything to you because it was over as quickly as it started.'

'Drew had split up from Beth, and we met by chance in Morrisons Supermarket of all places. He was staying at Mitch's place just off the high street while he was away working on a contract in Germany. We met for a drink and it just sort of went from here. We got on well, had a good laugh and great sex a few times.'

Bernie smiled as if she recalled the good parts.

'So, what happened?' asked Karen.

'He was keen. We would go out for a meal or drinks but when he made himself unavailable to Beth, she got wind something was up, and asked him if he was seeing another woman, he said he was.'

'Sounds like the classic female trait, I don't want him, but I don't want anyone else to have him, doesn't it?'

'Did he tell her he was seeing you?'

'No but someone did, and I never found out who it was.'

'What happened? You stopped seeing him?'

Bernie said, 'Beth followed him to Jute house one evening and spied on us. Ironically, he joked about being followed.'

'Bloody hell!'

'He was getting dressed after we'd had sex and picked up his phone, there were loads of missed calls from her.'

'They had a big pow-wow, and then got back together.'

'She has blamed me ever since. We had an affair, if you can call it that, technically he was married but going through a separation instigated by her. She had asked him to move out, so he did. They had also talked about a divorce. The he and I went out a few times.'

'I see what you mean, it's not really an affair, is it?'

'He told me they had separated and on the way to a divorce so I guess it really isn't. After they got back together I never saw him again but she sent me threatening messages. It got really tedious, so I changed my number.'

Karen pulled up at Jute house. 'Well, she obviously still harbours a grudge and sees you as a threat to her marriage.'

'Yes, I guess she does,' said Bernie. 'I don't think she is very happy. But, I'd really like to see Drew again, just to catch up and see how he is doing.'

'Perhaps that's not wise…' Karen screwed up her face.

'I'm not interested in him, he is old news, been there and done that.'

'You mean, done him.'

They laughed.

'Thanks for today, and I'm glad we were there together especially in light of what happened.' said Bernie.

'Me too.'

'What time is your appointment tomorrow?'

'I see the consultant at 9.45am.'

'Do you want me to come with you for some moral support?'

'Thanks, but I'll be okay, I know the system and what to expect so it won't be a shock.'

'Give me a call when you get back home though.'

'Yes, I will do.'

The following day, Karen found a space in the distant corner of the hospital carpark and took the outdoor route to the main reception. The receptionist pointed her heavily tattooed arm to the right and told Karen to take a seat on the yellow chairs and wait to be called.

The waiting area was boring and dull with the obligatory flat screen TV mounted high up on the wall with the volume turned up. She looked around at other people in the waiting area. A middle-aged, stoney-faced nurse called out names from a list on her clipboard, Karen was one of them. She told everyone to follow her to the next waiting room. Everyone filed in behind her like sheep. The nurse didn't smile once. Karen considered the values of nursing, a caring profession after all, and how a smile, even if a nurse didn't mean it, would make the difference to how someone felt. No one wants to go to hospital, a smile could offer a little comfort in the cold, lonely world of hospital appointments and bad news.

The chairs were arranged around the perimeter of a small area with red doors into various consultancy rooms. Each door had a number, and on the left was the flat screen TV mounted high on the grey coloured wall, with the sound muted. The area was drab and devoid of natural light.

Karen sat down, pulled a book out of her handbag, and tried to read but the light was poor. She delved around in the bottom of her bag and found her glasses. Each woman in the waiting area had her partner, husband or boyfriend with her, Karen was the odd one out.

One of the doors opened, a name was called, and then another. Karen tried to read but was distracted by the comings and goings and wondered what news she would have to face when it was her turn.

Ten minutes later, the consultant she'd been under previously, appeared from the corridor, and walked towards the room directly opposite her. The nurse looked across at Karen.

'Would you like to come in?' she said.

The room had one metal framed window. The walls were painted a light grey shade. On one side there was a sink, and a curtained-off bed with two plastic chairs squeezed up against the wall near the head of the bed. On the other side of the room were various stainless-steel storage units. The consultant, Keith Oldham, sat at the old wooden desk by the window and greeted Karen. It was awkward. No smiles. He had to deliver news. The nurse sat on the chair towards the back of the room near the door.

'I am afraid the cancer has come back,' said Keith Oldham. 'We have taken a detailed look at the Mammogram.'

'Okay, tell me about what you have found?' said Karen.

It was in the left breast, like before, and also in an area close to the previous site. 'We have found it early. It is still at the cell stage.'

'That's a big positive?'

'Yes, it is.'

'I will need a lumpectomy?'

'Yes. I would also recommend a course of radiotherapy afterwards.'

'How big an area will you have to cut out?'

'Similar to the last time, maybe two centimetres by three centimetres.

Karen took a deep breath, 'okay.'

The nurse quickly chimed in.

'Look, Karen, don't feel under pressure to make any decisions today. You will be in shock, and you need time to take it in, go home and discuss it with Thomas.'

Karen screwed her face up. 'Discuss it with Thomas?'

The nurse's touchy-feely personal approach had failed. 'Thomas and I divorced years ago.'

'Oh, I'm so sorry, I didn't mean to, I'm so, so, sorry…'

'It's okay.'

'What happens next?' Karen looked at the consultant.

'Take a couple of days to think about it then get in contact with Jean or the other breast-care nurse on duty.'

'How soon can you do the operation?'

Keith Oldman opened his desk diary, and flicked three or four pages.

'I can give you a date as early as a week today.'

'Okay, thank you. I will need to think about it and look at my workload.'

'Of course, take as much time as you would like. It will be done in this hospital, and you won't be kept in overnight – given if it all goes to plan.'

'Do you have someone at home?'

'No, but I can organise that without delay.'

'You'll also need someone to drive you home.'

'That's not a problem. Regarding the radiotherapy treatment, has anything changed, any developments over the last five years?'

'No, there have been no significant developments or changes in treatment. You will require a course of radiotherapy in the form of a small daily dose over a period of 30 days at the Western General in Edinburgh. Once your body has healed then we would look at breast reconstruction, plastic surgery and skin grafts.'

'Okay, I am quite sure I will refuse the radiotherapy treatment again, but I would like to consider my options and come back to you.'

'Of course.'

The nurse gave Karen a breast care leaflet and asked her to call her if she needed anything. Karen left the hospital via the main entrance. The cool spring air on her skin woke up her senses as it travelled in through her nostrils and warmed up as it arrived in her lungs. She took a deep breath and tried to think but couldn't form any clear thoughts. As she walked to the far car park she noticed the vibrant yellow of the daffodils growing in the beds lining the pathway.

'Hello, Karen! Twice in 24 hours!' said Big Drew.

'How are you?'

'Not bad, actually I feel better than I expected because of the great turnout yesterday.'

'I'm pleased Bernie and I could be there.'

'Are you okay?'

'Yes, great thanks,' she lied. She wasn't going to share her health problems in a hospital car park with a man who'd just buried his wife.

'Sorry, I'd better run, my appointment is for 10.35am and I don't know where I've to report to.'

'Go in the main entrance, you'll see the big revolving door, and the main reception will be facing you.'

'Thanks, Karen.' Big Drew lent forward and kissed her on the cheek. 'Take care of yourself.'

Karen reached her car, opened the door, got into the driver's seat, took a deep breath, and stared out at the view over the rough wasteland.

She pulled a face, 'here we go again.' She wasn't sure how she felt, she hadn't reacted to the news, she hadn't cried but felt tired. She started the car, left the hospital car park, and turned right down the hill towards Halbeath Road. She queued behind a long line of cars. Slowly, she edged closer to the traffic lights. The eleven o'clock news came on the radio, she pressed the volume down button on the steering wheel. She wanted to drive back to Maryard in silence.

Parking the car in the driveway and finding her house keys in her bag made her realise she was operating on auto-pilot. She was conscious of the drive home and had driven safely, but it felt like a distant memory. All she wanted to do was to go home, lock the doors, wrap up warm and sleep until she woke up.

Her phone buzzed. The kettle had boiled, she made a cup of tea and took it upstairs to her bedroom. She closed the curtains, took her shoes off, lay down on the bed, and pulled the throw over her body. She had two sips of tea then fell deeply asleep.

Her head was filled with nonsensical images from the dreams. Freud said dreams were the road to the unconscious and Karen's had travelled miles and worked overtime. She woke up confused; what day was it, what was the time? Suddenly she recalled why she had slept during a working day.

She felt exhausted. She knew what was coming, and how it'd drain her life battery but she'd get through it. That evening, she called Bernie. 'I need to think about it all, so I've decided not to tell anyone else until I've made up my mind.'

'Sounds like a good approach,' said Bernie. 'If it's what you want to do then it is good for you.'

'I'm not ready to tell others, it sounds odd, but their concern clouds my thoughts and I don't have the energy to expend on explanations.'

'That makes sense but as your friend, I reserve the right to contact you and ask how you are doing.'

'You know me better than anyone, and you don't fuss.'

'Have you heard from Annie?'

'Yes, I phoned her to see how she was on Sunday night. She said she had a great time but got so drunk and couldn't remember the last few hours or her walk home.'

'You've got to be joking?'

'Nope.. She remembered the food, then the meringue, and the chocolates rotating anti-clockwise around the table with the port. She said her mind was blank after that.'

'Christ! That's unreal.'

'I asked her if she remembered us all singing?'

'She must have remembered us singing.'

'Nope, nothing.'

'Oh my god, she hasn't remembered her murder confessions then?'

'I don't think so.'

'That surely can't be right? I'll have to ask her about it the next time I see her.'

Over the next few days, Karen tried to focus on her work but often stopped, distracted by her thoughts, and about going back to the hospital. She had deadlines to consider, her work plans and goals were going to be interrupted over the next couple of months.

CHAPTER 17

On Friday, she looked forward to meeting Liam that evening.

Liam lived in Stanley, Perthshire, his house overlooked the River Tay. Karen imagined it would be decorated with lots of band memorabilia, old guitars mounted on every wall with American state flags, signed pictures and record discs. They had spoken on the phone, he sounded pleasant enough with subtle Glaswegian tones but had a tendency to use Americanisms. He said he'd forgotten his diary and it was in the trunk of his car, and he felt tired when they deplaned at Edinburgh Airport, so he picked up a take-out on the way home. Liam said he liked to eat before 6.30pm, and as he was rehearsing with his band early on Saturday morning for a forthcoming gig and suggested they meet for an early dinner on Friday, at the new Harvester near Kinross.

Karen drove into the Harvester car park at 5.50pm, picked a space, reversed into it and looked around.

She texted Liam. 'I've arrived and in a dark blue Merc.'

After 5 minutes her phone buzzed. 'am late 10 minz.'

She felt that familiar twinge of disappointment. For twenty minutes, she watched the cars come into the carpark. Eventually, Liam arrived in a silver Freelander. He parked up but missed the parking bay outline so his car look like it had been abandoned after a police chase.

Karen looked at her makeup in the rear-view mirror and took a deep breath. She got out of her, each movement she made increased her disappointment levels. Still, she was here and would see it through. As she walked across the carpark her phone rang. Liam sat in the driver seat of his car. She stood six feet from him when she answered her phone. 'Hi, Liam.'

'Yes,'

'Look to your right, you'll see me.'

He dropped his phone in his lap and took off his thick dark-rimmed glasses. He looked to his left, then in front and, finally, to his right. As he got out of his car, her disappointment surged.

'Hi, Karen.' As Liam moved towards her, she couldn't quell her dissatisfaction. He looked a lot older than his profile pictures and a quick calculation confirmed he was not even close to six feet tall.

Karen smiled. 'Hi, Liam, nice to meet you.' She lied.

Liam looked her up and down as though he was judging a prized cow in a farm show. 'You're a tall lady!' he said.

She replied, 'you're shorter than I expected!' He didn't react.

They shook hands, and she kept her distance, but his aftershave grabbed Karen by the throat.

'This is for you,' he said. Karen unfolded a t-shirt, it was Liam on the front playing his guitar. 'I could autograph it for you later on.'

'Err, thanks,' Karen smiled.

Liam had a head of sandy coloured hair, it was thick and straight, and reminded Karen of a sable brush. He wore one of his own tour-t-shirts from 1977, faded jeans and tan cowboy boots that clopped as he walked. He was a strange shape; it looked like he was hiding something underneath his t-shirt, his arms were skinny, and he wore numerous rings and bracelets. He hung a load of keys from his belt, which sagged loosely around his narrow hips. Karen wondered if it was a type of distraction. His aftershave was rank. He walked with a sort of short step shuffle as though he was trying to keep his buttocks clenched together. He had a limp.

Without missing a beat, he talked about his jet lag, his globe-trotting, rock star lifestyle and his favourite subject. Himself. He told Karen he had only just started dating online. 'I'd rather meet someone like you, sort of ordinary, and who doesn't have a career. It's important you understand my lifestyle and fit in, in the background.'

He nodded as though he was congratulating himself. 'I don't need these,' he said. He pointed at his hearing aids. 'I forget I'm wearing them, but if it's busy it makes sure I can hear you. It's just like being on stage.'

Karen smiled, not really believing him.

The waitress had shown them to a small table towards the back of the eating area, much to Karen's relief. 'Is it normally this busy?' asked Karen.

'We do half price weekday food deals, so it brings everyone in before 6.30 pm, after that, it's quiet,' replied the waitress. 'Looks like you've made it just in time.'

Liam chattered continuously as they looked through the menu. The unnatural indoor light was less forgiving than the fading dusk light in the car park. Karen wondered if he had lied about his age as well.

Karen smiled at the waitress and hoped Liam would stop talking long enough so she could order a drink. Liam talked over her, and ordered himself a drink. The waitress looked at Karen and smiled back, it was a silent acknowledgement between women, invisible to men.

As they waited for their food, Liam talked about himself. He was his own favourite subject. During the meal, he continually looked around the restaurant as if he expected to see someone. 'Do you know this place well?' asked Karen, trying to fathom out who or what he was looking for.

'No, I've never been here before....'

The waitress returned with their food, she smiled at Karen then at Liam.

'You see, the thing is, being a rock star, I tend to get recognised everywhere I go. Did you see the way the waitress smiled, it's because she recognised me, and don't be surprised if she asks for a selfie or an autograph?'

Karen nodded.

'You'll need to prepare yourself when you are out with me, all my fans come first.' Liam's eyes constantly scanned the room as though pleading for someone to recognise him. No one did. No one looked. No one spoke.

Karen listened as Liam applauded his own achievements. When the waitress brought coffee to their table, she asked Karen if she was planning to write more books.

'Yes, there's one in the pipeline and its due out later this year.'

'I love your work, and I enjoyed your talk with Brian McArthur at the Book Fair in Kelso.'

'Thank you, it was good fun, and I was very nervous and totally unprepared.'

'You were a natural, you should do more especially around here.'

'Aww, thanks, you are too kind'

'Lovely to see you, I'll leave you to enjoy your coffee.' The woman gave Karen a knowing smile before she walked away. Liam looked unhappy he had been ignored. 'You could have introduced her to me, maybe she didn't recognise me?'

'Why would I introduce you to her? I don't know her. She recognised me through my work.'

'I think she was too shy to speak directly to me so she spoke to you. It often happens, you know.'

'Yes, I can imagine.'

'I will leave her my autograph on this napkin.' Liam opened his jacket, pulled out a large marker pen and scrawled his name on the used napkin.

'Okay, it was an interesting experience meeting you but I am going home now.'

'It was great fun, Carol, I really enjoyed our evening, you are perfect company for my high profile.'

'My name is Karen.'

'Anyway, come and see me play at the Edinburgh Playhouse next month?'

Karen said, 'shall we go Dutch?'

'Yeah, okay,' said Liam. He looked disappointed, she wasn't sure if it was due to the waitress failing to recognise him or if he expected her to pay for the privilege of his company? The waitress returned to the table, they paid separately, Karen left a tip. Liam didn't but smugly pushed the napkin into her hand.

Karen purposely walked faster in the hope no-one would think they were together. 'Right babes, it was a fun evening and nice to meet you, let's do it again? I think we have a good thing going on between us. Come to see me play at the Playhouse next month, the tickets are only £45 a head.'

'Thanks, Larry but no, I don't think so.' She faked a smile, turned, and quickly walked away.

CHAPTER 18

Saturday morning, Karen got up, padded down the kitchen in her bare feet and made a cup of tea. As the kettle boiled, she her mind wandered, she wished she had a partner to make a cup of tea for as well. Bad news made her more aware of the gaps in her life and the loneliness.

She sat at her desk, sipped tea, and enjoyed the view over to the woodland. Her mind wandered back to the bad news, she couldn't believe she had to deal with cancer for the third time in her life. She felt vulnerable. The disease hindered her life again.

she felt a massive relief as tears fell onto her cheeks and dripped off her chin. She detested feeling so weak, and insecure. The disease commanded attention, with its own agenda.

She tried to turn her dark, irrational thoughts into positive ones but she couldn't. Thoughts churned around and spat out her worst fears; the cancer had spread and had infested other parts of her body and her life was about to be cut short. She tried to tell herself she was being silly, but the thoughts taunted her and lingered. If she had a partner, he would say positive words, make encouraging plans for the future, and give her endless hugs. She wanted someone to tell her it'll be alright.

Her phone rang, she looked at the clock before she answered it, it was 10 o'clock.

'Morning Bernie.' she wiped the tears from her cheeks and tried hard to sound upbeat.

'Good morning to you, how are you?'

'I'm good, just thinking about last night's crap date.'

'Oh no, not another one? Who did you see last night?

'A rock star.'

'What? A Rockstar?'

'I met him for dinner at that new harvester near Kinross, and my disappointment started in the carpark.'

'Oh no!'

'He was about 5ft 9 with his 3 inch Cuban heel cowboy boots on. He looked a decade or so older than his photos on his dating profile.'

'Oh Christ, nothing like an honest representation.'

'I spoke more words to the waitress than I did to him.'

'Was he quiet?'

'Nope, he never stopped talking about his favourite subject all night.'

'What was that?'

'Himself!'

They laughed.

'Yup, he talked constantly about himself. The biggest reaction I got from him was when the waitress asked me if I was writing a new book, he was miffed she didn't recognise him and that I didn't introduce him.'

'Is he a famous rock star?'

'Err. Nope. Google him. Liam Prendergast. I had never heard of him.'

'I will do but that name doesn't mean anything to me either.'

'Then to finish the evening off, he said, 'let's do it again, and asked me if I wanted to go to his next gig at the Playhouse and pay £45 a ticket. His pièce de résistance, he called me Carol. So I called him Larry.'

'That's hysterical!'

'Honestly, I walked as fast as I could and was about to break into a trot when we left the pub, so people couldn't see the two of us together.'

'Haha!'

'He had a strange walk and a limp, I had the agility advantage when legging it out to the car park.'

Bernie laughed.

'That's a fair and accurate summary of my Friday evening.'

'How you are feeling?'

Suddenly Karen stood up, 'I must go, there's a knock at the door, I'll call you straight back.'

Karen grabbed the woollen shawl hanging on the back of her office door and flung it over her shoulders as she walked through the kitchen to the door.

'Karen Knighton?' asked the woman.

'Yes, that's me.'

'These are for you,' said the woman as she handed over the bouquet.

'Thank you very much'.

Closing the door, Karen stuck her nose into the bouquet: a wonderful sweet smell from white roses and purple freesia filled her nostrils. The colours lifted her spirits and sung to her. She opened the envelope, it read, *'Dear Karen, I miss you so much, please, please forgive me. I will be back from the USA next week and really want to talk to you about the future. Love Brian.'*

Tears filled her eyes, and ran down her cheeks, again. She wiped them away with the back of her hand. She felt confused, why was she crying? She didn't know if she wanted Brian or not. She had been so annoyed at him for disappearing but somehow his kindness touched her.

Karen called Bernie back, 'Sorry I had to dash off like that. I just had a huge bouquet of white roses and purple freesia delivered.'

'Oh, how lovely! Who were they from?'

'Guess?'

'They're not from the rock star so they must be from .... Brian!'

Karen smiled. 'Well done. They've really picked me up because I was having a cry to myself before you phoned.'

'Do you want me to come over?'

'No, I'm okay. Honestly, I am. Anyway, crying is supposed to be good for you.'

There was a concern in Bernie's voice, 'yeah, I guess it is, but you will tell me if you are not okay?'

'Feeling the way I do it is to be expected, suppose it's just my way of digesting the news and thinking about the future.'

'Promise you'll call or text me if you want to talk?'

'Yes, I will, I promise.'

On Sunday morning Karen woke up at 5 o' clock, made a pot of tea and sat at the kitchen table and wrote in her diary.

'I think about the future, I am strong and positive, but I get reminded I have no magical powers, a disease is a disease. It's there and I need

medical help to rid me of it. I hate cancer. I hate it has invaded me three times. I worry about my future and hope all the cancer is detected. My life and living it are important to me. I hate feeling weak. Sometimes I feel as though I want to shut myself away from everything. Random acts of kindness, mindfulness and thoughtfulness bring me back. I am shattered. I don't want to cry but it's hard not to. I go for a walk and hope it readjusts my state of mind, but when I see happy older couples, they make me cry. It makes me feel lonely and sad. I want the chance to grow old. I feel weak and pathetic. I don't know what to do, I need to pull myself up and get on with it. Is this what it feels like to be depressed and down? All the battles and having to face cancer are very draining on my life battery. I need to go to a place most people don't know about to draw on life reserves. I worry mine are depleted. Three times! Three damn times!! Why me? I don't understand why it must be me again. I try to lead my life in positivity and surround myself with kind and loving people. Am I guilty? Am I to blame?

I need to sort myself out, build my strength against this wave of weakness and fight it square on with optimism and positivity. I want to stop crying. Writing this is making me cry. I wish I could stop worrying. Where the hell has my confidence gone? I shouldn't be like this. I need to make a list of people and things I am thankful for. Cancer seems to be everywhere, I must keep upbeat. It's hard. I feel so raw.'

It was 10 o'clock, and a safe time to call her mum. Karen thought she'll be out of bed, and hopefully drinking only coffee.

'Hi Mum, how are you getting on?'

'Karen, I'm good. Just give me a minute to sit down. I've just been out in the garden.' She lied.

Karen could hear her mum's footsteps as she walked across the room and rested the phone down on the table. Karen recognised the chink of a crystal, and the glugging sound of brandy being poured from the decanter into a glass. There was a pause, and then footsteps back to the phone.

'Are you keeping busy?'

'Mum, I have some news.'

She heard her mum taking a drink. 'What sort of news?'

'I've been told the breast cancer has returned. It's been detected early.'

'Oh dear, keep strong and positive. You'll be fine.'

'Thanks.' She detested that word, 'fine'. It was so lazy, so mediocre, and so impersonal.

'You're such a strong girl, you cope with everything and you'll be back to normal. She took another drink. Why don't you pop over for a visit during the week?'

'I'm hoping to get the operation done.'

'Okay, let me know what happens and keep your chin up.'

Karen heard the clink of ice against the glass as her mum took another drink. 'I will do, bye mum.'

Karen let out a long breath of exasperation. Brandy was Margaret's priority in life, and Karen wasn't surprised by her mum's reaction, but she lived in hope that maybe, she'd astound her with some caring, motherly support sans brandy.

CHAPTER 19

By Monday morning Karen had made up her mind, she phoned Jean the breast-care nurse and told her she wanted to go ahead with the lumpectomy and would be free as soon as they could fit her in. Jean called her back to say the pre-op checks appointment would be organised in a phone call within 48 hours, and she was hopeful Karen would get an operation date within 7 days.

Taking control of her own life again, making the call, and decisions helped Karen cope and feel more positive. She looked at the roses and freesia, they made her think about Brian and wondered what it would be like to talk to him about the breast cancer. She considered for a while. In a strange way, she missed him. The flowers had surprised and touched her. She opened her email and set about sending Brian a thank you message.

Her phone rang. 'Hello Karen, this is Jean at the Breast care unit, Dunfermline. Can you speak?'

'Hello Jean, yes, I can.'

'I have spoken to Mr Oldman, and he asked me to call you about a cancellation we had this morning. Could you be ready for the operation on Wednesday?'

'Err, yes. This Wednesday?'

'Yes. There's no pressure, if it is too soon there is no problem, you will get a date as originally planned.'

Karen called Bernie to ask if she would drop her off and pick her up from the hospital on Wednesday and stay with her for a couple of days.

She called the hospital back. All her plans fell into place, she would have the operation on Wednesday.

Karen carried on as normal. Cancer was an inconvenience but she was determined she would go into hospital on Wednesday without any distractions. It was important she was calm and able to deal with it all.

She didn't want to talk about it with anyone other than her close circle. She didn't want to manage their shock at her news or respond to their questions and curiosity. It wasn't about them.

The pre-op assessment took place on Tuesday morning at the hospital, so it was another drive back to Dunfermline. Karen sat with the nurse as she went through the questions. Ironically, she was well enough to have an operation.

Bernie dropped Karen off at the hospital for 7.40am on Wednesday morning. Karen made her way up to the ward and reported in. A nurse checked her blood pressure, took some blood, and put a plastic bracelet on her wrist. After a visit to radiology for an ultra-sound, she returned to the ward, changed into the operating gown, and waited. The Anaesthetist came up to the ward and introduced himself as Declan from Northern Ireland.

'I'm responsible for making sure you go to sleep and wake up again,' said Declan with a smile.

Karen laughed, 'pleased to hear it's a two-part process, can you arrange for some nice dreams of fairy tale lands and unicorns?'

'I don't do miracles, you know.' They laughed.

Declan left and Karen picked up her book, and thought it'd be a good to think about something else. Two pages in, a Nurse appeared by her bedside. 'Karen, we are taking you to the operating theatre in ten minutes.'

Keith Oldham came to see her, after a brief chat he marked her left shoulder with a large black marker pen with an arrow pointing down at her left breast. 'Simple but effective.' He said. Before she knew it, she was on the move and wheeled into the room next to the operating theatre. Declan told her what he was doing as he worked quickly putting the needle in the back of her hand and asked her to count down from 100.

'100, 99, 98, 97…96……9…'

A recovery room nurse woke Karen up. She asked how the operation went, heard the reply, and then dropped off back into an unnatural sleep. An hour later Karen woke up again back in the ward. She felt okay and wanted to drink water. By 1 pm she felt hungry, a nurse brought her two slices of hot buttered toast and a cup of tea. She texted Bernie. 'All done, trying to find out when I can escape.'

'When can I leave?' she asked the Nurse.

'We are waiting on the consultant coming up to the ward, once he's seen you, he'll let you know when you can leave.'

Karen was bored and disliked being in a ward of strange people. Thankfully, it was an all-female ward, but she didn't want to speak to people and started wishing her time away. She got up from her bed, pulled the curtains around and got dressed. It lessened her vulnerability and boosted her confidence.

Jean, the breast-care nurse peered around the curtain. 'Hello Karen, how are you feeling?'

'Very well, thank you, and keen to get home.'

'I've spoken to Mr Oldham and he said you are free to go home as soon as you feel able. He said the operation went to plan.'

'Great.'

'We will be in contact about the results, hopefully, you'll be back in 7 – 10 days.'

'Thanks, Jean.'

Karen called Bernie. 'Can you pick me up, please?'

'I'm leaving now, what ward are you in?'

'Ward 5, it's in the new part, just follow the signs to the operating theatre, I'm right next door.'

'Great, see you in forty-five minutes.'

Karen was back in Maryard by 4.30pm. I think I'll go lie down and have a nap. If you haven't seen me by 6 o'clock give me a shout?'

The girls had a relaxing evening. Annie called in with a bunch of flowers and a card. She hadn't planned on staying but they insisted. Karen was happy to see her, and Bernie hoped to ask a few probing questions about the murders. Faye called to see how Karen was feeling, they spoke for a while and Faye told her about her new art exhibition, Karen was pleased to talk about something other than herself and breast cancer. Two glasses of wine later, lots of laughter and Annie headed home. Bernie was had made no progress in her quest for more information.

The following day, Karen woke up and although a little sore she felt happy to the other side of the operation. She heard Bernie in the kitchen, and felt a warmth of appreciation of having her friends around her. The feeling of love and support touched her deeply. If she had a partner, he would have been responsible for creating these feelings in her. The happy feeling suddenly changed to feeling emotionally raw.

On Friday, Karen felt tearful, confused and down and as though a black cloud followed her around and weighed down on her shoulders. She couldn't shake it off, she cried and felt negative about everything. She knew she wasn't thinking straight and remembered it was how her body reacted to anaesthetic. Tears flowed, she felt drained, pathetic, stressed, worried, and unattractive. Her appetite had gone.

By Saturday she started to feel like her old self. Annie came around to the farmhouse and walked with her up to the horse fields. She loved getting out and feeling the breeze blowing her hair around. Her phone buzzed, it was an email from her Uncle Hamish.

Karen and Annie walked back towards the farmhouse through the woods. The sun had warmed the carpets of bluebells and their sweet scent filled the air, the birds sounded happy and for a moment it felt like paradise. Her brain came back to life, her body felt a new energy running through it and she was free from the black cloud.

'I have turned a corner, Annie. I feel so much more alive today.'

'That's great, you look brighter and happier.'

'I don't feel like a zombie anymore, and I'm actually feeling a little excited about getting back to work and my books.'

They parted company at the crossroads. Karen felt the air going into her lungs and strengthening her body. She was keen to get back and read Hamish's email.

'Call me if you need anything.' shouted Annie.

Karen read the email from Hamish and decided she'd call him instead of emailing a reply. 'Hello, Hamish!'

'Karen how are you, and a happy new year to you.'

She gave Hamish a summary of her year and her trip to the hospital. He suggested she recuperate on the west coast. Hamish's idea appealed, she loved his big house full of paintings and never-ending shelves of books.

She called Annie.

'Could you keep an eye on the farmhouse next week. I am thinking about going to my Uncle's on the West coast for a few days?'

'Yes, of course, don't worry about the house.'

One week and a day after her operation, Karen drove to the hospital to hear Keith Oldham give her the news. He confirmed she was free of the disease. She called Bernie from the hospital car-park. It was good news, she told herself, she was one of the lucky ones, again.

The release from the stress slowly washed over her like a warm wave. She phoned Hamish and shared her news. 'I'll drive over on Saturday morning.'

'That's great Karen, I'll book a table at Scotts for Saturday night. I'll drive, you can drink copious amounts of wine and fall over and I will ensure your safe return.'

Two emails sat unread in her inbox from Brian. Today, she felt she could read them. He was coming back to the UK in a week and wanted to meet her.

'Hi, Brian,

Thanks for your emails. I'm going away for a few days to recover from a small operation. I'll get in contact with you upon my return.

Karen.'

Within ten minutes, Brian had replied.

'Are you okay? I didn't know you were going into hospital. I am sorry. Can I call you?'

Brian x'

'No, please don't call me. I'm okay, I'll tell you about it when I get in contact.'

CHAPTER 20

K aren packed her bag, it felt good making plans for her trip over to the west coast. Hamish was the older brother of Karen's mother, and had been an artist since he left Glasgow School of Art in the late 1950s. He was 6ft 5", and loved his old cars. His twin sons and daughter, were successful actors and living in America.

Over his eighty-year lifespan Hamish had lived in Fife, Inverness, Italy, Chicago, Australia and returned to Scotland in the 1980s. He bought a large house with a half-moon driveway in Upper Skelmorlie.

Karen left Maryard early on Saturday morning, she texted Hamish. 'ETA 10.30am.'

The A92 was quiet as Karen turned off to join the M90 and took the Kincardine exit. She stopped at the petrol station on the west side of Rosyth to buy fuel and a coffee. She hadn't driven the route since last year and felt as though she was going on holiday.

The traffic flowed, and soon the M80 became the M8 through Glasgow. She loved driving. Dumbarton rock looked majestic as the morning light stretched across the Clyde. The A8 turned into the A78, and the roads became busier with Saturday shoppers around Port Glasgow. As she queued at the roundabout for the retail park, she decided to she'd stop off and pick up a few things. As she got out of her car, she felt the warmer west coast air on her skin. After a quick trip around M&S, she was back in the car and on the A78 through Greenock towards Skelmorlie.

It all looked familiar. At Wemyss Bay, cars queued to board the ferry to Rothesay. She turned left up the one-way steep narrow hill towards Skelmorlie. She crossed two junctions and continued to climb uphill into the green, wooded area of Upper Skelmorlie.

Skelmorlie had a castle, and lots of large red sandstone villas built into the hillside with long, wide streets and terraces.

Hamish's house stood out with its tower and mature trees. On The Crescent, she slowed down, and turned onto the driveway between the huge ornate red sandstone pillars. The grand house sat centrally in its grounds with a half-moon shaped driveway and formal lawns and circular flower and shrub beds. Wild animals often frequented the one-acre garden, and in the summer months Roe deer would show their offspring the way in and where to look for the tastiest shrubs and buds. Karen parked directly opposite the pillared front entrance with its ornate stained glass and tiled floor.

'KAREN!'

'Uncle Hamish!'

They hugged. 'Careful, don't squeeze me too tightly!' said Karen.

'Let me get your bags?' said Hamish as they stood at the back of the car. The light in the house was beautiful. The house was full of paintings hanging on the walls and many more pieces of work sat on the floors. Karen and Hamish sat in the front sitting room, drank coffee, ate carrot cake, and exchanged news.

'It feels so good to be here, your timing was impeccable you know.'

'Well, I had been thinking about you, I didn't know why but you kept coming into my mind, so I emailed you.'

'Do you fancy going over to Millport this afternoon. It's the first poetry meeting of 2018? You'll know a few of the guys.'

'Oh yes! I'd love to.'

'Great, I'll take my car, we'll drive to Largs, I leave the car there, and we can jump on the Cumbrae Ferry.'

They carried her bags up to one of the guest rooms. The wide staircase was an art gallery full of Hamish's paintings. Karen's room was at the front of the house, looking out over Clyde to the Kyles of Bute, Rothesay, and Port Bannatyne.

They took Hamish's dark blue Bristol 406 out of the garage. Karen swung open the heavy passenger door and sat on the cream leather seat. Hamish eased the car down the drive and out onto The Crescent, then downhill on Eglinton Terrace towards the A78. The tide was out and, in the distance, Seals sat on the rocks and watched the cars, occasionally they moved and curved their bodies up into half-moon shapes.

The Bristol wafted along the craggy coastline road to Largs. Hamish took a right turn before the railway station and parked on a side street, a few minutes' walk from the ferry terminal. Karen loved the short ferry trip over the Clyde to Great Cumbrae. They made their way onto the pedestrian walkway down the ramp and onto the slipway. The single-decker Island bus waited; its timetable matched the ferries and took people the four miles around the island to Millport.

The bus followed the righthand bend into Millport. Hamish and Karen got off the bus at The Garrison. The sun shone, and the air was warm. On the pavement, large tubs of daffodils swayed in the breeze. The notice board outside the Garrison was full of posters, Hamish pointed at The Cumbrae Modern Poets Society. 'That's who we are going to see.'

They walked through the old building towards the modern extension to the meeting rooms. 'Karen, hello! How's long has it been!' said Janice.

'Janice! Great to see you!'

'Kevin, look who is here with Hamish!' Karen heard Kevin's South African accent before she saw him. He hugged her. 'Let's catch up for a beer after we are finished here?'

Hamish and Karen sat down in the back row, and settled themselves in as Kevin organised himself to open the meeting and welcome everyone.

'How's your love life?' asked Hamish.

'That's a long story,' replied Karen.

CHAPTER 21

K aren stood in the window of the front bedroom of Waterson house and looked out over the Clyde. The light was good and the water calm as she watched the ferry return to Wemyss Bay from Rothesay. Her mind drifted to thoughts of Brian and to driving back to Fife. She had enjoyed her time in Skelmorlie.

She closed the bedroom door and made her way downstairs, she carefully placed her feet on the worn carpeted staircase to avoid the books stacked up on each step. In the hall, the morning light flooded through the etched glass door panel. Hamish was in the kitchen. 'Good morning Hamish, did you sleep well?'

He looked startled, 'morning Karen, it wasn't the best but that's an age thing, the old bones start to ache and you've got to get up and move around. I hope I didn't disturb you when I got up to make a cup of tea at 4 o'clock?'

'I didn't hear a thing.' Karen lied. Most nights, she heard Hamish as he wandered around. His nocturnal coughing and sneezing fits were usually followed by the full gamut of swearing. He'd often put the radio on in the kitchen, and sometimes the TV in the sitting room below Karen's bedroom. She guessed he had forgotten he had a house guest.

Hamish wore his dark blue pyjamas and colourful robe as he shuffled about the kitchen in his thick sheepskin slippers.

'I'm thinking about heading back to Fife, Hamish.'

'So soon? You arrived just the other day?'

'I've been here a week' Karen laughed. Hamish looked puzzled, he tried to count the days. 'Time flies when you are enjoying yourself,' replied Hamish.

He pushed his hair back away from his face and tucked it behind his ears. He had a puzzled expression as he looked around the kitchen.

'Are you looking for something?'

'Yes, my pills. I don't know where I left them? Damn things, they move around.' He scanned the cluttered worktops and the table. 'Oh look there they are.'

Hamish sat down at the table with his coffee and collection of pills. He tipped some cornflakes into his bowl, sliced up an over-ripe banana then submerged everything in milk. Suddenly, Hamish sneezed. His mouthful of breakfast splattered over the table and his false teeth clattered into the bowl. He grabbed the edge of the table to steady himself against the jolts of the sneezes. He cursed. Retrieved his teeth, and carried on with his breakfast.

'Are you okay, Hamish?'

'Damn it, something always sets me off!' He took a few mouthfuls of coffee, and adjusted his hair.

'Why don't I take you to lunch at Scotts? We can have a nice easy day before your drive back home tomorrow?'

'Thanks Hamish, what a lovely idea.'

'I'll get the old boy out of the garage for a run.'

Karen smiled, and looked forward to lunch at Scotts.

'I'll book a table for two at one. That'll give me a few hours to paint some more of that portrait I'm working on before we go out.' He pushed his chair back and grabbed the edge of the table and levered himself into an upright position. He looked stiff and sore. He shuffled over to the breadbin, took out two slices of bread and popped them into the toaster. 'It'll be productive morning and we'll have earned our time off for lunch.'

'Great, I'm going to catch up on some emails in the study so I'll leave you to it.' Karen took her coffee, walked across the hall, and opened the study room door. She manoeuvred around the piles of books and paintings to the huge desk by the window. The room was warm and bright as the sunlight stretched its long fingers in through the glass. She made a space in the centre of the desk and placed her laptop down and opened it up. In amongst the work related ones, were two emails from Brian.

'Dear Karen,

I hope you are well and things are improving after your operation? You said you'd get in contact in a few days. It's been more than a few days and I haven't heard from you. I hope you don't mind me getting in contact first? I haven't stopped thinking about you. I know things haven't exactly been brilliant for us and there have been a few obstacles, me taking off like that hasn't helped and I understand how stupid it makes me look. I really want us to sit down and talk about the future. I had to drop everything and fly over here, Debs was really in a corner and had no-one to help her. I'm not looking for sympathy or trying to give you an excuse but she had been badly injured and woke up from a coma as a widow (I didn't know she'd married Brad). I've done my bit, I have helped and I'm flying back tomorrow. I land at Heathrow 1am UK time, and should be back home sometime in the afternoon.

I need to see you, I need to talk to you.

Love,

Brian.'

There was a second email:

'Karen, please email me to let me know if you are open to us meeting and talking about the future. No matter what happens I don't want to leave it like this. I can drive down to your place, you can drive to mine or we can meet in the middle or anywhere. Please just give me a chance. I am sorry things have gotten in the way of 'us' but please, let's talk?

Brian xx'

Karen sat back in the chair and looked out the window at the blue sky, a distant plane, illuminated by the sunshine, caught her eye. Brian's email came at a good time, he had reached out and she liked that. She heard a loud crash and Hamish swearing.

'Hi Brian,

Thanks for your email and I'm sorry I didn't get in contact as planned. Yes, I'd like to meet up and talk. I'm happy to drive to you. Let me know what day and time suits you?

KKxx'

Brian replied: *'I can't wait to see you. How about 4pm on Wednesday?'*

Brian xx'

'Great I'll see you then, have a safe, comfortable flight.

KKxx'

Hamish knocked on the door of the study and weaved his way through the books into the centre of the room. There had to be enough books in Watterson House to stock a small town library. 'Ah! There it is, I've spent months looking for Alasdair's book!'

Hamish bent down and knocked three books off the pile to reveal Alasdair Gray's 'old men in love' novel. He smiled and flicked through the pages. 'What time do you want to head out?' He asked.

'I'm ready, well - almost ready. Karen smiled, 'I can be ready to go in ten minutes.'

'No rush, I need to pick up some more paint, so how about we leave at midday.' Hamish turned and walked towards the door, his right foot clipped a pile of books. They toppled into his pathway, he lunged forward, grabbed the door and managed to keep his balance. 'I swear they grab me by the bloody ankles!' He stomped out the room. Karen heard him swearing to himself as he walked across the hallway into the kitchen.

At midday they left Watterson House in Hamish's old Bristol. The engine sounded reluctant but as they reached the outskirts of Largs, the car felt smooth and warm. 'Bloody traffic wardens are everywhere today, I can't park here or I'll get a ticket. Can you drive the car around the corner and wait for me, and move if they appear?'

Hamish got out. His hand grabbed the door frame of the Bristol and he eased himself up and out onto the pavement. Karen settled herself into the driver's seat, 'I'll wait here, if I have to move then I'll drive around the block and hover until I see you.'

Hamish tried to walk upright but he had a bend in his back and his stride was short. Karen looked out down the main street and watched a traffic warden as he worked his way up towards where she was parked. Within minutes Hamish had returned. He opened the passenger door. 'Are you happy enough to drive the old boy and the car around to the marina?'

She smiled, 'yes, jump in!' Karen gingerly drove the Bristol to Scotts and carefully parked at the Marina.

Their table overlooked the water. Hamish told Karen the story of when he first saw the Bristol and how he had to buy it because it was made in 1958 and that was a special year for him because that's when his twins were born. Karen sat quietly and listened. She had heard the story so many times over the years.

'It's great to get out, Karen, it doesn't happen as much these days, everyone is dying off.'

'You're more active on the social scene than me, just look at your calendar, you have lots of things planned.' 'Yes, but many of the events, if you look closely, are appointments with the podiatrist, doctor, nurse, physio and hospital.' He laughed.

They left the restaurant, linked arms, and took a stroll along the seafront. A man walked two large Gordon Setters, the dogs made Karen smile and Hamish spoke in Gaelic to them. As they reached the Pencil Monument, Hamish leant on her for balance. She felt a twinge of sadness seeing how age had affected his mobility.

The early spring sunshine was low in the sky over Largs when they drove through the town on the way back to Skelmorlie. Hamish settled himself into his favourite chair, put the TV on and nodded off. Karen returned to her laptop in the study to read her emails.

Faye had sent a long email saying she'd had enough of the European art scene and wanted to return to Scotland to set up a permanent base and asked if she could stay at Karen's until she got herself sorted out.

'Of course you can, anything I can do to help just shout. It'll be great to have you back in Scotland. I'm at my Uncle Hamish's (he may be able to help with your art?) place on the West Coast, I'm heading back to Fife tomorrow. Let me know your plans and I can't wait to see you soon!'

KKxx'

Brian had emailed saying he was sitting in the JFK departure lounge, and on his way back to Scotland.

Both emails made Karen happy. It was time to go back to the east coast. Karen opened the sitting room door and asked Hamish if he'd like a cup of coffee. He pretended he hadn't been asleep but the words coming out of his mouth did not make sense.

'I think I've seen a ghost. It was an old man, he was dressed in tweeds and wearing a deerstalker's hat.'

'That's odd,' replied Karen, 'can you still see him?'

'No. He disappeared when you opened the door and spoke to me.'

'I'm going to make a fresh pot of coffee, would you like a cup? And, guess who is coming back to Scotland?' Karen's phone buzzed, she pulled the phone from her pocket and looked at the screen. 'More annoying news alerts.' muttered Karen.

'Okay, let me think about it – is it Faye?'

'Yes, I've just had an email from her asking if she can stay at mine until she gets herself and her belongings moved over and finds her own place. I suggested you may be able to help her with her art?'

'Yes, I'd be happy to do anything I can. That's great news, I like Faye, she's a great looking woman with loads of talent. Is she still single?'

'Down boy, give her a chance to get back and settled in Scotland!'

They both laughed.

Karen made coffee and sat with Hamish to watch the BBC News at 6pm.

'Oh dear, not another one,' said Hamish. 'There's been a plane crash, maybe that's what the news alerts on your phone have been about?'

'Where about?'

'I'm not sure,' said Hamish. 'You know what these reports are like, they're all over the place, determined to win the prize for breaking the news before any of the other channels. I think it's in America.'

A chill ran through Karen.

'This is Jasmine Woodcock reporting for the BBC, 'unconfirmed reports are coming in about USA Airlines plane exploding over the North Atlantic. We have yet to have confirmation of the details but we think it could be a flight from John F Kennedy Airport flying to Heathrow.'

'Oh my god. I don't believe this?' said Karen.

'What's wrong, Karen. You look like you've had a fright?'

'Please don't let it be him.... Brian, a friend of mine, emailed me earlier to say he was in the JFK departure lounge about to get on a plane back to Heathrow.'

'Do you know the flight number, there are hundreds of flights departing every day. I remember when I was flying back and forward with my art projects and lectures there were loads of flights. One in particular stands out for me because I was ....'

'Sorry Hamish, I can't listen to stories right now, I need to find out the details. Can you switch over to Sky News?'

Hamish changed the channels. Karen frantically searched online for news of the crash. All the reports were much the same, lots of general information. Karen couldn't think straight. She called Brian's mobile, it went straight to his voicemail. Of course it would, she thought.

'Who is Brian? A boyfriend?'

'He's a good friend and shaping up to be a potential boyfriend.'

Karen sat glued to the TV channels for the next 4 hours. At 10pm, it was confirmed a plane had been blown-up over the North Atlantic by a terrorist bomb.

Brian had been on the plane. Karen was numb with the shock and the realisation she would never see him again, they'd never get the opportunity to talk things through and make a future together.

'Here, drink this.'

Hamish handed Karen a large brandy and put his hand on her shoulder.

'I'm sorry Karen, he obviously meant a lot to you.'

CHAPTER 22

K aren sat in the car and listened to Radio Scotland news as the windscreen defrosted, the fans blasted warm air.

She drove to the clay shooting ground for a breakfast meeting with Warren. As the ate their breakfast, Warren told her about Tynetree estate, owned by Jane Blackstone-Steel, she inherited the East Lothian estate when her husband, Malcolm, died a few years ago.

'The estate is around 10,000 acres. Jane wants to develop it with small business units, accommodation and she wants me to install a clay shooting ground.'

'That's an interesting project.' Said Karen.

'Yes, it is. It'll be a huge challenge but a lot of the hard work has been done. Take the clay shooting ground, there are no clay shooting grounds in the region and look at the number of clay shooters driving over to Fife to shoot. I have a stake in it, and am partnering Jane in the building and development of the business.'

'So, where do I come in?' said Karen.

'Well, I'm not sure because there are so many opportunities. First of all, I'd like to introduce you to Jane and have a tour of the estate. Ideally, we'd go over early next week, can you do Monday or Tuesday?'

Karen stretched across to her bag on the next chair and pulled out her diary. 'Yes, I can do Monday.'

'Great, that's it settled. I shall pick you up at 0630, we could stop for breakfast en route, and I'll be able to share more information with you. Jane said she'd post more documents and plans to me so we can have a look over them before we arrive at the estate.'

'Does she have planning permission?'

'Yes, she has all the required planning permission, we have been working on it for the last two years. I wasn't sure it would ever come to fruition but it has. Jane is determined to see it all through.'

'It sounds costly?'

'Jane is happy to finance it herself, she is delighted to use her husband's money for something he was dead against. She wants to see the estate working at its full potential and do something that'll put East Lothian on the map for clay shooters.'

'Sounds like she has an axe to grind.'

Faye was at the farmhouse by the time Karen arrived home after her meeting with Warren.

'How was the meeting?' asked Faye.

'Good, thanks, and we're off to an Estate in East Lothian on Monday, Warren has loads of exciting plans in place to develop a new clay shooting ground.'

'Sounds intriguing. Damn! Sorry! Must run, meeting Annie at the stables in 10 minutes. I saw her earlier and said I'd like to get back on a horse. So I'm going to take a look at her horses. She's got them all in the stables as the blacksmith coming.'

'Oh that's good.' Said Karen, as she walked towards her office, 'look, I'll leave you to it, I need get on with some more writing.'

'Can I borrow your wellies?'

'Yes, feel free, there are a few pairs in the laundry room, and plenty jackets so help yourself.'

Faye pulled on Karen's Le Chameau wellies, they were a perfect fit but the jacket wasn't, she wasn't as tall as Karen and was a dress size or two smaller. She wrapped one of Karen's scarves around her neck and set off down the road, over the stile and along the muddy path towards Annie's stables. At the end of the path, she turned left and followed the old track leading towards the stables. A few hundred yards from the stables, a vehicle pulled up alongside her.

'Need a lift?'

'Ha, no I'll walk, thank you. Are you going to shoo Annie's horses?'

'I'm not going to shoo them today but I'm certainly going to take a look at them. My name is Tom, and you guessed it, I'm the Blacksmith.'

'Hi Tom, I'm Faye.'

'Nice to meet you, you have amazing eyes, Faye.'

Faye blushed.

'Jump in, let my chariot transport you to the stables in style.'

Faye smiled.

'Oh, go on then, Mr Smoothie.'

Tom's truck pulled up into the yard, he chatted to Faye for 5 minutes before they both got out.

Annie glowered at Tom. 'You're late!' she barked.

'Sorry, I got delayed picking up one of the local strays.' He looked at Faye and laughed.

'What do you mean?' snapped Annie.

'He was joking, Annie. He gave me a lift up the road, we met on the track.'

Annie's face was screwed up with annoyance. 'Do you know one another?'

'No, we've just met' said Faye.

'The horses are ready they're tied up over there.' She gave Tom a dirty look but he didn't see it because he was smiling at Faye.

'Can you hurry up, I have an appointment later.' Annie hissed. She lied. She had a new dislike for Tom.

Faye looked around at the horses. An older Cleveland Bay gelding caught her eye. Annie saw Faye looking at him. 'He's a gentleman, and a pleasure to ride.'

'He's gorgeous, can I take him out?'

'Yes, he'd love it. How about at the weekend? I can take Tilly out, and I can show you some of the routes?'

Tom walked over to the two women. 'If you give me a couple of minutes I'll give you a ride back into the village, Faye?'

'But I need to talk to you about my horses?' said Annie

'They're all good. Only the chestnut mare needs her back feet looking at.' He quickly turned away from Annie, and smiled at Faye.

'But I still need to talk to you about MY HORSES!'

Tom looked across at Annie, his face devoid of smiles. 'I've said what needs doing. There really isn't anything else I can help you with.'

'Jump in!' Tom pulled away from the stable yard at speed and left deep tyre tracks on the hard standing.

'God, she's a miserable old cow. How on earth do you get on with her?' asked Tom.

'I don't actually know her that well, only through Karen, my best friend. If your turn right at the bottom of the track, then the next right and follow the road and stop at the last house.'

'That's home then?'

'Nope, I've only just come back to the UK, I've been living out in France for decades.'

'What brought you back?'

'We're all getting older I thought it'd be nice to return to Scotland and get on with the next, and possibly, last phase of my work.'

'What do you do?' asked Tom, as he pulled up outside Karen's house.

'I'm an artist.'

'How long have you been shooing Annie's horses?'

'It must be a couple of years, I bought the business from one of my cousins, he took ill and never regained full health. I had helped him out when he needed a holiday over the years, so I knew most of his customer base. Can't say I enjoy working for old misery over the fields, my cousin couldn't stand her, but she always paid her bill without a grumble. We still laugh about her, she's the sort of woman you don't want to turn your back on. Pete's convinced she poisoned him.'

'Poisoned him? In what way?'

'It sounds daft, but he used to feel ill after he visited her. She always made him a drink of something. After each visit he'd be unwell. There's something about her, she tries to keep you there, she talks non-stop but all you want to do is get the horses shod and on your way. She has asked both of us if we could do some work around her house, we've both said no.'

'Oh, that's weird, maybe she is lonely. But as I said, I don't know her that well.'

'Thanks to you, I'm still alive and kicking. If you'd hadn't been there, who knows what could have happened. So, are you young, free and single?'

Faye smiled, 'I'm certainly free and single. Why do you ask?'

'Fancy coming out for a meal sometime soon?'

'Yes, that'd be nice, although I hardly know you.'

'Well, look at it another way, you are being presented with the opportunity of getting to know more about me. When are you free, the weekend?

'I'm pretty sure I'm free Friday, Saturday and Sunday, how sad is that.' Faye laughed.

'How about Friday night, I'll pick you up at 1845 and take you to one of my favourite restaurants?'

'Great, thanks, I'll look forward to that.'

He took Faye's hand, and kissed it. Here's my card with my mobile on it. If anything happens give me a call. Where can I see your art work?'

'Merci voici ma carte,' Faye smiled.

'Merci belle femme,' replied Tom.

'Oh, tu parles français? Asked Faye

'Un petit peu,' replied Tom.

Karen watched them from the kitchen.

'Bloody 'ell, you didn't hang about.' she laughed. 'Who's the hunk?'

'He's Annie's Blacksmith, and I have a date with him on Friday night.'

On Friday night Tom took Faye to a little restaurant in Cupar.

They clicked, and time flew, Faye felt relaxed and happy around Tom. He dropped her back at Maryard.

'It was a great night out, and I'd love to see you again.' Tom leaned forward into Faye's space and kissed her.

CHAPTER 23

On Saturday morning Faye was up early and ready to spend a few hours out riding with Annie. She looked forward to being back on a horse again.

'Morning Annie!'

'Morning Faye, are you ready for this? I've tacked up big George, and he's waiting in the stable. I'll bring him out and stand him by the mounting block at the end of the yard.'

Faye stood on the three stone steps of the mounting block, grabbed the reins, put her left foot in the stirrup, moved her weight forward and swung her right leg over George's back and gently sat in the saddle. Annie mounted Tilly and they set off down the track and into the woodland. Faye felt relaxed riding George, but Tilly was a handful. Faye was happy there hadn't been much conversation between her and Annie. On the way back, Annie suggested a canter up the old railway track and finish up by going across the fields back to the stables. 'Keep him under control, he'll set his own pace but keep a light tension in the reins.'

They set off up the old railway track, Faye eased George on, he responded and picked up his pace. Faye loved the wind on her face, and the feel of George's mane as it flowed and touched her hands. Annie struggled to control Tilly, suddenly, she flicked her head up, sprung to one side, bucked, and took off. Annie held on.

As they reached the end of the track, Annie yelled at Tilly and had managed to head her in the direction of the open gate to the field. Faye slowed George down as they crossed from the track into the field, and saw one of Tilly's horseshoes in the mud.

Annie finally got Tilly under control, slowed her down to a trot then a walk. 'Damn horse, you'll be the death of me!' She yelled. She lifted her riding crop up and brought it down hard on Tilly's rump. Tilly bucked and Annie cracked her again and again.

'ANNIE, are you okay?'

'Yes, I am NOW. I don't know why I don't sell that damn mare for horsemeat, she's evil!'

The women took the tack off the horses, brushed them down, rugged them up, fed them and put them out in the field. 'Do you know she's lost a shoe?'

'No, where?'

'There was a shoe in the mud down by the gate.'

'Thanks for letting me know, I'd better get it. I'll need to call the Blacksmith and get him out again.'

'He's a nice guy, I was out with him last night, we had a lovely dinner in Cupar.'

Annie scowled at Faye. 'Oh. You went out with him? On a date? Really?'

'Yes, he's a lovely guy, great company.'

Annie looked puzzled. 'Seeing him again?'

Faye smiled. 'Yes, and if I can still walk after that ride out on George, I'll see him tonight.'

'Oh. Right...' Annie turned her back, and made herself busy as Faye thanked her for the ride out on George.

Back at Karen's, Faye took off the borrowed boots and jacket. 'You smell of horse.'

'It was great fun but I'm not sure I'll be able to walk ever again!'

'I hope you're not planning a wild sex session with the hunky blacksmith?'

'I couldn't manage it.'

'Why don't you invite him around for dinner tonight? I can make myself scarce after we've eaten?'

'If I do invite him around you don't have to make yourself scarce. It'd be fun both of us getting to know him.' After a shower, Faye sat at the kitchen table with Karen, her phone buzzed. 'He said yes, he'll be over at 7pm?'

'That's great, it'll be a fun evening!' said Karen. 'And, I have dating news of my own. I'm going for coffee tomorrow.'

'Tell me more?'

'He's called Bill, he's in his late 50s, some sort of consultant, he's single, has three daughters and loves sailing.'

'Could be interesting. I hope you've studied all his photos and he's not a short-arse lying about his age.'

'He claims to be 6ft, with his own hair and teeth. He may not be right for me but I'm keeping an open mind and I'm happy to explore over a coffee on a Sunday afternoon.'

'Karen, you're always so sensible.'

Late afternoon, Karen's phone buzzed.

'Hi Karen, do you fancy an evening of wine and more wine?'

'Sorry Annie, I have plans tonight. How about tomorrow night? Annie read Karen's reply and threw her phone across the room.

She pulled on her wellies and old jacket and headed up to the stables to feed the horses and bed them down for the night. She closed the yard gate and walked down the track and wondered about another Saturday night on her own. A truck flashed its lights and blasted its horn, the beams blinded her and the horn startled her, she lost her footing and fell onto the grassy verge.

'*Fucking road hog!*' she shouted at the truck as it sped away in the darkness down the road towards Maryard.

Tom arrived at Faye and Karen's. He told them how he nearly flattened Annie. The three of them sat around the kitchen table, ate, shared stories and laughed. At ten o'clock Tom thanked the girls for a great evening so Karen made herself scarce.

'Thanks for inviting me around, I loved getting to know more about you and Karen. It's not often a bloke like me gets to spend the evening with an artist and an author, you know.'

Tom kissed Faye, and as he got in his truck, she shouted. 'Be careful, there are strange things on the roads around here!'

He waved and drove off into the darkness with the truck lights on main beam.

CHAPTER 24

On Sunday, Karen pulled up in the car park of the Farm shop. She scanned the area for a red Audi. A man got out of a car three rows in front of her and waved.

'Hi Karen.' He rushed over to greet her. 'Lovely to meet you, Karen. Gosh, you're tall.'

'Nice to meet you, and I'm exactly the height I typed into my profile.' Karen smiled. Bill opened the door to the café, as she walked through the gap she misjudged the opening and brushed against his protruding belly.

As he motioned to take her coat, she noticed his eyes rested on her breasts. 'I'll keep my coat on. Have you seen something, Bill?'

'Errr, no, your necklace caught my eye..'

'What necklace?'

'Oh, I thought you were wearing a necklace?'

Their coffee arrived. Bill liked to talk about his three favourite topics: his ex-wife, their daughters, and his boat.

'How old were the photos you uploaded to your profile, Bill?

'Oh, fairy recent. He lied. 'I love your hair.'

'Thanks.' Karen smiled.

'My ex-wife used to visit the hairdresser every week. She was high maintenance, but she was my wife and looked the part on my arm. That's why I was keen to meet you today, I wanted to see if we had any potential to look like an eye-catching couple because I do have a lot of social events to attend. I think it's only fair I am upfront about this.'

Karen replied, 'I don't have a problem with you being upfront.'

He continued, 'I think you have what it takes. I'd love to take you shopping to find a range of clothes to flatter your figure. The next time we meet I'd like you to dress up for me. It's not just the what's on the outside. Bill fidgeted in his seat. 'It's important you wear nice underwear. That's another thing, I am highly sexed and I need a younger woman to keep up with my demands in the bedroom.'

'You have bedroom demands?'

'I like to take control. Whatever I say goes. I think you would like me to dominate you. I can tell by the look in your eyes and your cool exterior.'

'You read me so well but please excuse me Bill, I need to go the ladies.' Karen picked up her bag, walked across the café, opened the door marked exit. She slung her bag over her shoulder, walked to her car, jumped in, and drove home.

The following morning Warren's Range Rover pulled up at Karen's at 0625, she was ready and waiting for him in the kitchen. Once they reached the south side of the Forth they stopped at the Dakota hotel for breakfast. Warren pulled out a load of architects drawings of the buildings planned for the Tynetree estate. Just before 0900 they drove through the entrance of the estate.

Meanwhile in Maryard, Annie had called the blacksmith and much to her annoyance her call went to his voicemail, she left a message asking him to make contact about another shooing job she needed doing urgently. He called back two hours later, saying he'd get over to her stables for 3pm the following day.

Jane met Karen and Warren at the main entrance of Tynetree house, a handsome Georgian mansion surrounded by mature trees and formal gardens. 'I'm so pleased you are here, Karen. Warren told me great things about you, and I'm sure I met your parents at a clay shooting competition decades ago. Your mum used to be a great shot, wasn't she?'

'Yes, she was, certainly picked up a few trophies in her heyday.'

They toured around the estate in Jane's Land Rover, and stopped at admire the views and discuss the plans for development. As they walked around the Mews, Karen asked Jane about the business people she ideally wanted to work on the estate. 'I'm open to everyone and have no fixed idea of the sort of businesses they could run from here.'

Jane walked over to the centre of the Mews, and pointed, 'see the unit over there? That's going to be the location of our farm shop and it'll stock a big range of free-range, organic food including our own home-grown venison. We will open our doors to a wide variety of businesses.'

'How about artists?' asked Karen.

'Yes, I'd be very agreeable to having artists on the estate,' said Jane. 'I love creative people.'

'Have you heard of Faye Robinsfield?'

'Yes, I have.'

'Faye is one of my oldest friends, and she's recently returned from thirty years in France and is looking to set up a base in Scotland.'

'I'd love to meet her. She could be our resident artist. Let me drive you over to a place that'd be perfect location for her, the light is superb. You can tell me what you think?'

At 1pm they returned to the big house, Jane took them in through the main entrance and down a corridor to the kitchen. It was huge space, complete with a large kitchen table, sofas, and comfy chairs. 'This is Clare, she is our head cook and knowledge base for everything and anything to do with food.'

'It's great having you here at Tynetree.' Said Clare.

'It's a stunning location, so much history and character, and beautiful ancient trees.' She laughed, 'I don't want to leave.' said Karen. 'How long have you been here?'

'Forty years, and the time has flown.'

'Wow, you must have started very young.'

Warren said, 'ah, don't be fooled, she's not as young as you think.'

'And he's as cheeky as ever!' laughed Clare.

After lunch Jane took Karen around the house. The large gallery, the formal rooms, the library stacked with thousands of books. The bedrooms with beautiful large windows flanked by shutters and dressed in swathes of fabric. There were many nooks and crannies in the house, hidden staircases and narrow corridors that led into other areas. 'I would need a map to find my way around.'

'You do get used to it, I think it's a happy house now.' Jane smiled.

'It's very welcoming and peaceful. Wasn't it a happy house previously?'

'It's a much happier place since Malcolm departed. Over the last decade he became the miserable monster of Tynetree. He was hard work, and not just for me. We're all a great big family at Tynetree, Clare is right, the times flies but we look out for one another, but Malcolm made things so difficult and tried to destroy it all. To this day, I still don't really know what happened to him, he appeared to want to grow old, lonely and disliked. We all breathed a sigh of relief when he died. I know it's not nice to speak ill of the dead, but he was a nasty old man. If he'd been an animal, he would have been put to sleep long ago.'

At the bottom of the stairs, Jane hugged Karen. 'I'm so pleased you are here, and I hope we can work out a plan so you can work here and make Tynetree your base. You'd be able to write here, wouldn't you?'

'Thank you, Jane, yes, I'd be able to write here. Gosh, I don't know what to say, I have fallen in love with Tynetree, it is so beautiful.'

'Karen, you are welcome to spend as much time here as you like. You have an open invitation to be my guest, the upstairs Blue Duck flat, as we call it, is yours whenever you want to use it or move into.'

'Jane, I really don't know what to say.'

'Don't say anything, have a think and come back next week. I'd love to have your energy around here and I'm sure it'd be a great place to write and to photograph the wildlife. I'm not trying to sell it to you. Come back over next week, stay over, we can have dinner and can map out a plan in the morning. How does that sound?'

'Perfect!'

'Oh, and maybe Faye would like to come over as well?'

Back home in Maryard, Karen gave Faye a rundown of the day's events and conversations. 'It sounds amazing and I can't wait to see it and meet Jane,' said Faye. 'I'll call her in the morning. I'm seeing Tom after he has finished shooing Annie's horses.'

'Aw, that's nice, where are you going?'

'I'm not sure, he's going to pick me up sometime between 4.30-5, he's hoping Annie won't delay him too much.'

CHAPTER 25

Tom arrived at Annie's stables, he moved quickly to the back of his the truck, keen to get the job done, leave and meet Faye.

Annie glowered at him, 'just before you start on the horses, can I ask you something?'

Tom looked puzzled, 'yes, I guess so.'

'Why are you dating one of my neighbours?'

'You are kidding, that's none of your business.'

'Well, I think it is my business. I thought your conduct here on Saturday was terrible, and I found it highly unacceptable.'

'What the hell are you talking about?'

'You were flirting with Faye and right in front of me, have you no decency or manners?'

'Lady, I think you need to get a life and keep your nose out of mine.'

'So you are not denying it?' snapped Annie.

'Look, I am here to shoo your horses and I either get on with it right now or I get in my truck and go.'

Annie's eyes narrowed, her lips were white and pulled tightly together. 'They're in the stables,' she hissed.

Tom strapped on his farrier apron, grabbed his tools, and headed over to the stables. His head was full of thoughts about Annie, and maybe her business was no longer worth the hassle. He was determined he'd get the job finished and leave as quickly as possible.

Annie was about to follow him but remembered she hadn't sedated Tilly. 'Tom, hold on!' shouted Annie.

Tom carried on to the stables, he didn't want to listen to anymore from her. She had stepped over the line this time.

'Tom! Damn you!' Annie ran to the store room on the other side of the yard. She opened a small cupboard hidden in a crevice in the wall, and took a key from her pocket and unlocked the padlock. She took out a needle and a large vial of Ketamine.

As she Annie ran across the yard, she heard a commotion coming from the stables. 'What the hell are you doing?' yelled Annie. 'Get out!'

'That mare is bloody dangerous, she reared up and tried to kill me!'

'You fucking useless idiot, you shouldn't be in beside her!'

'What the hell are you talking about? You told me the horses were in the stables!'

'GET OUT!'

The mare snorted, reared up, then kicked out at the stable partition. Annie pushed Tom out of her path, she shouted, 'get out of my fucking way, she's going to wreck my stables because of you!'

Tom grabbed her arm. 'Don't go in there, she'll kill you!'

Annie spun round, and shrieked at Tom, 'get your fucking hands off me!' and stuck the needle into his forearm. The Ketamine flowed into Tom's arm and quickly around his body.

Annie screamed and flew at him with her hands out-stretched like claws. Instinctively, his arm came up to protect his face and he knocked her off her feet. His head was spinning, and he lost the sensation in his legs and his arms felt rubbery. Tilly kicked the stable door open, she bolted through it, trampled over Annie, and knocked Tom clean off his feet.

Tom lost consciousness. He came round lying on the cold, wet, stone floor. Annie was sitting propped up against the closed stable door. 'You fucking idiot, this is all your fault!' she snarled.

Tom tried to get to his feet, but he couldn't get his legs and arms to work, his vision was blurred.

'I hope you fucking die, you stupid bastard!'

He tried to speak but his mouth couldn't form the words and his throat made a rasping sound. He started to vomit.

Karen was in the kitchen making a pot of coffee, as she waited on the kettle boiling, she gazed out of the window across the fields. 'Faye, come and look at this mad horse running about the fields?'

Faye walked over to the kitchen window and looked out, 'that looks like Tilly, the nutter Annie rode out on Saturday. Tom is supposed to be shooing her because she lost a shoe in the mud when she took off.'

'He must have finished, and Annie put her out in the field.'

'Karen, have you got a pair of binoculars?'

'Why? They're over there by the door.'

'I'm not sure about this...'

Faye looked though the binoculars, a chill ran down her spine. 'Something isn't right, Tilly isn't in the field she's galloping down the track to the main road.' Faye looked at Karen, 'I really do not like the look of this.'

'Okay, get your boots on, we'll take the car up and see what's going on.' The girls got into Karen's car. Before they reached the turning for the road to the stables, they saw Tilly grazing on the roadside verge with only a headcollar on. She was covered in mud and sweat.

'This definitely isn't right, Faye.'

'Let's leave the horse and get up to the stables, I'm worried about Tom.'

Karen drove up the track and parked the Merc at the back of Tom's truck. 'Have you got your phone?' asked Faye.

Faye called out across the yard. They heard a noise in the stables, and ran over.

'Oh my god, Tom!' Faye cried out, and ran to him. He lay on the stone floor covered in vomit and groaning.

'What happened, Annie? Are you alright?'

'That fucking idiot spooked my horse, I hope he fucking dies. Fucking waste of space. His cousin was just as bad, fucking men, they're all fucking useless.'

The broken needle and vial were lying on the floor near Tom.

'Tom, Tom, say something...!' Tom's breathing was laboured and uneven, his eyes kept closing. 'She went for me, she stabbed me with the needle..'

'I'm phoning for an Ambulance,' said Karen. 'Annie what happened?'

'Oh, fuck off Karen, you're not bothered about me so don't start asking now!'

'What are you on about?'

Annie sat by the door, covered in dung, wide-eyed and mad looking. 'Get out of my fucking yard, I never want to see you every again and take that trashy bitch and that cocksucker with you!'

Annie tried to get up, she screamed in pain, and banged her fists on the floor and on the stable door.

'Fuck you, get out of my yard!' she screamed.

Within ten minutes two ambulances had arrived in the village. The driver spotted an old man leading a horse. They slowed down, switched off the lights and the sirens. 'Excuse me, can you tell me where Maryard livery stables are?' shouted the Paramedic. The old man turned around.

'What was that?' the old man asked.

'Do you know where Maryard livery stables are?'

'I do. Go down the road, then turn left up yon stony track, you'll see the buildings at the end, that's the stable block. What's happened?'

'Thanks, mate. There's been an incident. Thanks for your help.'

The old man asked again, 'is someone hurt?' The ambulance pulled away slowly, and gave the old man and horse a wide berth. He held onto the horse's headcollar and tried to quieten her down.

The Ambulance parked close to the stables. Karen took them into the stable block. The paramedics rushed in. Faye came out of the stables, tears ran down her face. 'They are attending to Tom and need to get him to the hospital quickly.' Karen hugged Faye.

'He'll be okay, he's in good hands now,' said Karen

Faye wiped her face, 'they're trying to find out what was in the needle she stabbed him with. It could be poison.'

The old man turned up to the stables. 'I found the horse on the road, I'll put her in the field.'

He walked back into the yard. 'What's happened?'

'Err, I don't know.' said Karen.

'What has she done?'

'What do you mean, what has she done? Who?'

'I heard you say poison.' Said the old man.

'Who are you?' asked Faye.

'Rob, I'm Ron's twin.'

Faye looked puzzled. 'Who's Ron?' Karen remembered she'd met him at the local theatre. replied, 'Ron was Annie's second husband.'

'I think I know what she had in that needle. I'll go and speak to the paramedics.'

'The Police are coming, she's threatening to kill everyone and they can't get near her.'

'Annie?' asked Rob.

'Yes, she's completely lost the plot,' said Karen.

'It's not the first time,' he said. Rob stepped inside the stable block, looked at Tom lying on the floor and spoke to the Paramedic, 'excuse me, I know we can't touch anything but...' Before he could finish, Annie screamed him. She tried to stand up but fell down hard against the stable door. 'Get out of my fucking yard!'

One of the Paramedics told her to calm down and took two strides towards her. 'Don't come near me, don't you fucking touch me!'

Tom lay still on the stone floor, surrounded by lots of equipment.

Rob stepped back outside and out of sight of Annie. 'She's done this before. If he's been stabbed with her needle, I think its Ketamine, she used it a lot.'

The paramedic replied, 'tell the Police that, they're on their way. I need to get back in.'

The Police took statements from Karen, Faye, and Rob. Tom was rushed to the Western General in Edinburgh and Annie was taken in the second ambulance to the Victoria Hospital in Kirkcaldy.

Faye and Karen drove back to the house. They hardly spoke. They sat in the kitchen and tried to come to terms with what had happened. 'Had she poisoned him?'

'I'll never get that scene out of my head. Sitting there screaming her head off, and Tom lying on the floor.' Faye started to cry again. 'God, it was awful, it was unreal, like a scene from a horror film.' Karen hugged her.

Over the next few days the police asked lots of questions about Annie. The Police were reluctant to give out any information to Karen and Faye, apart from letting them know Annie was in hospital with a broken hip and ribs and helping with their inquiries. The police asked them not to talk about the incident and not to respond to any enquiries from the local newspaper. Tom was in intensive care.

By the end of the week the local area had been invaded by a swarm of forensics officers. The stables were torn apart after multiple human remains had been found underneath the dung heap. Reporters appeared in the village, knocked on doors and asked questions. TV crews invaded Fife to report on Fife's only serial killer. They nick-named Annie the 'petite serial killer' on account of the body tally being in double figures.

Karen and Faye were woken up at 0300 on Friday morning by sirens and flashing blue lights. Annie's empty stable block and yard were on fire. By daylight, only charred stumps of wood and twisted metal remained. Thin strands of dark grey smoke rose upwards from the fire site. Karen's view had been changed forever.

On Friday at midday, the Police visited Karen and Faye to inform them Tom had died, and they were investigating his murder and many others.

CHAPTER 26

The following week, Karen and Faye drove to Tynetree. 'This traffic is a bore, isn't it?'

Faye smiled, 'yeah, it is but you know what, I don't mind sitting in it. I like looking at Scotland as a passenger, I get to see so much and don't have to think about anything. I like your driving, I always feel safe.'

'That's good. I can't say I felt the same when I was over in the west with Hamish. His driving and parking were nightmarish.'

'I forgot to tell you, I saw his profile on a dating site a couple of weeks ago. I logged in to deactivate my profile because Tom was on the scene. Anyway, Hamish had sent me a message, he introduced himself, don't think he knew it was me.'

Karen laughed, 'Imagine that! I think it's great he is putting himself out there on the dating scene at his age.'

'Yes, it's positive and he was highly creative about his age. He's 80, isn't he?'

'Let me guess,' said Karen, 'he's shaved a few years off?'

'He said he was 68.'

'That's priceless. At least he won't have to lie about his height.'

Karen drove around the Craighall roundabout and uphill onto

the slip road for the A1. 'I'm pleased to get away from Maryard. After everything that's happened, I'm not sure how I feel about the place now.'

Faye looked over a Karen, 'I know what you mean, it's sort of tainted, isn't it?'

'Yes, each time I think about the farmhouse, I think of Annie. We sat around that kitchen table countless times, we laughed and joked about all sorts and now I find myself going over everything she said in case there's information about another murder. I feel bad that I sat there and laughed at her jokes. Christ, she confessed about her ex-husband, the professor... how many were there?'

'We were all conned by her, but that was her intention and not our failing.'

'I can see it now, how oddly she reacted to the things we spoke about and how she was towards people. She never missed a trick. She would know what time I arrived home, and who had visited, what time they left. I never thought anything of it, I just assumed, she was like a personal neighbourhood watch.'

'I think we will all go over every interaction we had with her for a long time,' said Faye.

'Look at that view.' said Karen as they drove over the hill on the A1 towards Dunbar, 'that's Tyninghame Bay.'

After a guided tour of the estate, buildings, cottages and farmhouses, Karen and Faye relaxed in the flat in the big house. 'Isn't Jane so easy to be around?' Said Karen.

'She has amazing zest for life, I'd love some of it.'

'Me too. I'm exhausted after all that. What time do we have to be ready for dinner?'

'I think we meet in the hall at 7pm, for pre-dinner drinkies!'

A few hours later, the girls made their way downstairs to the hall where drinks were being served. Clare brought a tray of drinks over to Faye and Karen. 'Ladies, this is Jeff, my husband. He also works here, he's my second in command in the kitchen, head butler, chauffeur and chief dog-walker.'

Jeff stepped forward, he shook Karen's hand. 'It's a pleasure to have you're here at Tynetree.'

Karen smiled at Jeff, 'thank you, Jeff this is Faye.'

'Good evening Faye, it's a pleasure to have you here at Tynetree. I am familiar with your work especially your early work with The Brodie Collective. I remember the huge exhibition at the Academy decades ago, it was a street away from my office when I worked in Edinburgh. I think it must have been the late eighties?' Faye smiled, 'what a great memory you have, it was 1988.'

'Do you give painting lessons?' asked Jeff. Clare prodded him in the back. Jeff ignored Clare.

Clare said, 'he's a great help around here.' She lied. She smiled, and tried to lose her irritation. 'He used to work in finance in Edinburgh but enjoyed helping me out evenings and weekends, so he jacked it all in, and made himself useful here.' She lied.

Jane appeared, 'I couldn't imagine Tynetree without both of you here.'

'Are you ready to sit down for dinner? Asked Clare.

'Yes, I think so. I'll ask everyone to take their seats,' replied Jane. 'Ladies and gentlemen, please take a seat at the table, dinner is about to be served.'

Clare shot a look at Jeff, he moved away from Faye, and helped serve the dinner guests. Around the table sat Jane, Warren, Karen, Faye, Simon, Taylor, Jennifer, and Gregor. Jane stood up. 'Thank you all very much for coming to Tynetree House this evening, I am delighted you are all here. I hope our discussions are the start of a long and fruitful working relationship with the Tynetree Estate.' Jane raised her crystal champagne flute, 'here's to the A team of Tynetree and a wonderful future for us all!'

'Here, here!' said Warren.

The dining room was filled with laughter as they ate and drank. Karen noticed Jeff constantly watched Faye.

'We had fun, didn't we Taylor?'

Taylor replied, 'we certainly did, Jane. I just wish I could remember it all!'

How do you and Taylor know one another?' asked Karen.

'Taylor is my dear friend and ex-boyfriend. We met at University and he has followed me around ever since.'

'That's not strictly true, Jane.' Taylor smiled, 'I did have a period of thirty years when I was married to Maria and we lived in Milan.' They laughed.

'Anyone special in your life, Karen?' asked Taylor.

'No-one yet, I am on a quest to find a good man, I have used online dating sites, and have endured a few dates.'

'Endured?' questioned Jane.

'It's proved difficult finding an intelligent man with manners and one able to accurately record his height and age.'

'Oh?' said Taylor.

'Most men claim to be over 6ft. It is an industry-standard-lie in the over 50s dating scene, but they're usually much, much shorter.'

Jane reached over the table and squeezed Karen's hand, she smiled, 'maybe you'll find the man of your dreams here at Tynetree? There are plenty to choose from.'

Taylor coughed, 'I'm youngish, free and single.'

'I can recommend him,' said Jane.

'Thanks, Jane, you make me sound like a restaurant. Do I get a five star rating as well?' They laughed.

Karen looked across the table at Faye, she was deep in conversation with Simon, Jane's Architect. At the end of the table Warren chatted with Jennifer and Gregor. Jeff lurked in the corner of the room and watched Faye's every move. After the meal, he served coffee and cognac, and quietly offered Faye a nightcap in the library.

By eleven o'clock everyone had said goodnight and retired to bed leaving Clare and Jeff to tidy up. 'You are an embarrassment!' hissed Clare.

'What the hell are you on about? I did my job, I kept everyone happy.'

'Yes, you kept everyone happy alright, especially the artist!'

'Get over yourself, you're just jealous your so-called art career never took off.'

Upstairs in the Blue Duck flat, the girls flopped on the sofas. 'Wasn't that a nice evening?'

'It was so relaxing and a tableful of interesting people to chat with is such a treat,' replied Karen.

'Everyone is so nice. Simon was fun,' said Faye.

'I think Jeff has the hots for you.'

'Don't be daft, of course he hasn't.'

'I gave him a card, if he is serious about art lessons I could have a teaching studio here.'

At the other side of the house, Jane and Warren made their way up the small staircase to Jane's bedroom. He grabbed her by the hips and turned her around on the small landing between the staircases. They kissed.

They carefully avoided the 17th century oil painting of Lord Tynetree the 4th, as Warren unbuttoned her shirt and kissed her. Jane whispered in Warren's ear, 'I need you now.'

'I'll get you safely to your room, m'lady'

'Here. Now!' She demanded and unbuttoned Warren's trousers and belt, and put her hand inside. 'Just the way I like you, no underwear and hard.'

Jeff scanned the security cameras, he looked out across the formal gardens then checked the rooms and the staircase. A movement caught his attention on the back staircase to Jane's apartment. He pressed record on the security camera app then sat back and watched Warren and Jane having sex up against the staircase wall. He heard their flat door open, and Clare moving around. 'Are you going to bed?' she asked.

'Yes, I'll be finished in a few minutes, I'm doing the last security sweep of the house.'

Jeff made a copy of the recording onto his cloud storage, then got into his bed in the room next to Clare's.

CHAPTER 27

The following morning the girls awoke refreshed. 'I slept so well,' said Faye. 'Yes, I went into a deep sleep and the next thing I knew was the sun rising over the trees. It was bliss.'

An hour after breakfast, the group met and talked about the plans for Tynetree.

'I forgot to tell you about the Daffodil Ball! You must come, it's on Saturday 13th April in the ballroom.'

'Will you both come to the Daffodil Ball?'

'Yes, we'd love to!'

'Excellent, I'll ask the party planner to make room at the top table, do you think your friend Bernie would like to join us?'

'Yes, I'm sure she would love it.'

'Great, that's it settled, Karen you have the Blue Duck flat at your disposal, there's plenty room for Bernie and Faye. In fact, why don't you all come over on Friday and stay until Monday? It's a fabulous weekend and the Ball has been a Tynetree tradition for sixty years. Tickets go on sale on the summer solstice and sell out within hours. I donate the money to a local charity, and various companies donate stuff we raffle as prizes.'

'It's a big event on everyone's calendar,' said Clare, as she put fresh coffee on the table. 'We get loads of agency staff in, catering people, organisers, security, photographers, bus and taxi firms, you name it, they're here.'

'Is it fancy dress?' asked Faye.

'No, it's casual evening wear and you must wear something yellow', said Jane. 'Some guests go for the full yellow outfit, and others wear a yellow shirt, yellow shoes, yellow dress - whatever works for you.'

Jane got up from the table, 'I have a couple of things I need to sort out, why don't you all enjoy Tynetree? Go for a walk around the grounds, relax in the library. If you go out around the estate take the Land Rover sitting at the stables, the keys are in it. Shall we regroup at 12.45pm for lunch in the conservatory?'

'Karen, would you like to accompany me on a tour of the estate in the Land Rover?' asked Taylor. 'Yes, I'd love to.'

Warren disappeared with Jane, and Faye went to the library with the others. Karen met Taylor at the back entrance next to the conservatory. 'I don't think I've driven a Land Rover so this could be interesting!' exclaimed Taylor.

'Would you like me to drive?

'Do you know these big beasts?'

Karen smiled, 'actually I do, I have owned a few over the years but now-a-days I prefer the comfort, speed and mod cons of a Mercedes Benz.' They climbed into the blue 110 Land Rover, 'you can be my co-driver,' said Karen.

Driving down the main access road to the house, Taylor said, 'let's turn left up here, it'll take us up to the moorland, high above the estate. It's a long climb up to the top and if we're lucky we'll see some grouse.'

Driving back to Fife, Karen said, 'going to the ball will be a great way to get to know some of the locals?'

Faye wriggled her nose. 'I can't wait but I'm not looking forward to finding something to wear. It's not as if yellow is my colour.' Faye pulled her notebook out from her bag, flicked through the pages until she reached her notes and sketches about the Daffodil Ball. 'It doesn't have to be a complete outfit, just something yellow, actually, I'm not sure what I'll wear, I don't think I own anything yellow.'

'Think we'll need to go clothes shopping, and you know how much I detest that.' Said Karen.

'Let's talk to Bernie, she will have some suggestions?'

'Good idea, but I have an image of three of us traipsing around Edinburgh looking for yellow clothes, finding nothing but a cocktail bar.'

'Ha, I've had an idea! Wear any outfit in any colour but buy yellow underwear – problem solved!'

'Huh, that's funny but if someone asks you about your yellow item of clothing, what are you going to do? Show them your knickers?'

They laughed.

As Karen turned the car off the A92, she felt a sadness. 'I feel different about Maryard,' she said. 'Getting away from the house and forgetting about Annie and what she did has given me time to digest how I feel.'

'At least we don't have to worry about her being around, she's still in hospital on her way to prison. Murdering bitch, I hope she is locked up for life.'

Karen turned the car into her driveway at the farmhouse, they carried their bags into the house. 'I'll put the kettle on, do you fancy a cup of tea?'

'Yes, please then I want to clear my thoughts and come up with a plan for moving forward with Tynetree. I think it'll be a great base for me and my work,' said Faye.

'Maybe I will do the same. Being away from here has made me release I don't want to live here anymore. I doubt I'll be able to sell this house considering what's gone on and the pending court case.'

Faye took their bags upstairs.

'I'm going to do a few sheets of automatic writing. It'll clear my head and maybe give me some ideas,' said Karen.

'Jane made it clear there is a place for all of us at Tynetree.'

'I'm not sure Bernie would want to move,' said Karen, 'but, who knows, it could be the start of a new chapter.'

'While you are writing, I'll call Bernie, tell her about the Ball. Shall I ask her over tonight for dinner so we can all put our heads together?'

'What a great idea.'

Faye sat in the chair by the sitting room window.

'Bernie, how are you?'

'I wondered how you two were getting on?' said Bernie, 'when did you get back?'

'About an hour ago. Listen, instead of nattering on the phone why don't you come over, we have a few ideas, and things we need to share with you. It's all rather exciting.' said Faye.

'Great, I'll get over about 6pm, I need to finish writing up my proposal for a documentary – it's profiling our local, friendly serial killer.'

'Oh my god, can you do that?'

'Yes, but I need to wait for a few things to happen but I can profile her and have it in the bag when she is sentenced. Plus being local means I can fill in the gaps with my local knowledge.

Whats-her-face from the central Newsroom is hardly on the doorstep but she is itching to get involved on the story, she has told everyone she had the biggest range of experience with serial killers. We had the big conference call yesterday, I have been given the nod from the powers at be.'

'That's good news, well done. I'll leave you to it. See you tonight.'

Karen shut herself in the office. She looked out over the fields for the horses then reminded herself Annie was no longer there

Bernie's car pulled onto the driveway just after 6pm. Faye opened the kitchen door and gave Bernie a big hug. She took her coat off, opened a large bag, the contents clattered together. 'No guesses what you've got in there.' said Faye.

Bernie smiled, and lifted three bottles of wine from her bag and put them in the fridge.

'Hi Bernie!' Karen hugged her. 'Faye told me about your next assignment, that's going to be an interesting one.'

That evening the woman sat around the kitchen table, they drank wine, ordered a take-away and talked about their ideas. 'Jane is looking for a completely new community on the estate, people who can live and work there, and appreciate what it has to offer. She made it clear the three of us are welcome to make it our home,' said Karen.

'Maybe it could be the fresh start we all need?' said Bernie. 'I'd be happy to rent out Jute House.' Bernie looked across the table at Karen. 'Why don't you rent out this place?'

'Hmmm, I wonder what I'd get for it?' pondered Karen.

'Look at it another way, you can hand it over to an agent and let them do all the work for an agreed fee?'

CHAPTER 28

On Friday 12th April, the three girls travelled over to the estate for the Ball in Bernie's Land Cruiser. 'You bought a great dress, the navy and yellow combination suits you,' said Faye.

'Yeah but I will be so out of my comfort zone wearing a dress, especially a long one. And, I'll have to pretend to be lady-like while I'm wearing it.' laughed Karen.

'Wonder if I'll meet a man this weekend?' said Faye, 'there's no denying I could do with one.'

'Can't we all.'

'Gawd, just look at the three of us, all single.' said Karen.

'What about you and Taylor? You seem to be getting on well?'

'He's a nice guy but something is missing, not sure what it is. I think he's still recovering from the divorce and the change of scenery.'

'There's certainly a few differences between an Italian vineyard and a Scottish Estate.'

'Karen, have you heard any updates from the police about Annie?'

'No, it's all gone quite this week, I think they're interviewing everyone.'

The Friday morning drive to Tynetree was an easy journey with no hold-ups. 'Look at the huge sign they've put up.' said Bernie.

A security guard stopped them as they turned up the private drive towards the big house.

'Can I have your names please?' asked a guard with a clipboard.

Bernie replied, 'Bernie Flynn, Faye Robinsfield and Karen Knighton.'

Karen wondered why his voice sounded familiar.

'Thank you,' said the guard.

'David! How are you getting on?'

'Heeelllllo Kaaaaaren,' stuttered David Soutar. 'I'm great thanks. How are you?'

'I'm very well thank you, and looking forward to the Ball.'

'How is your friend getting on?' he asked. 'Did she recover from the attack at the local theatre?'

Karen shook her head, 'it's a long story but she's not doing very well, and I am not able to talk about it.'

'Oh, sorry, I didddddddddddddn't mean to pry...,' said David, his face was bright red. 'You can drive up to the main house, and park at the back next to the stable block.'

'Okay, thank you,' said Bernie.

'Bye David,' said Karen. 'Lovely to see you again.'

'He was with his mother at the Theatre when Annie had a fight with her ex-step daughter. I'll bet the police will want to talk to him about that night.'

'Don't think about it,' said Bernie, 'we're here to have fun.'

Bernie parked the car in the marked out bays by the stable

block. Two security guards patrolled the area around the stables and cars. They talked into their radios and took photos of the car registration. 'Good afternoon ladies, if you use this entrance into the house.' The taller security guard guided them to the rear door.

Inside they heard lots of movement down the hall. 'Girls! Fantastic to see you all!' said Jane. 'Bernie it's great to meet you at last. I'll ask Jeff to take your bags up to the flat and I'll show you around the ballroom.'

'Here's my donation to the auction, Jane.' Faye handed over a large bubble-wrapped painting.

'Thank you very much Faye, there will be a bidding war for it, I'm sure.' said Jane.

They walked down the great hall. 'We have closed off all areas in the house apart from the Ballroom and the adjoining kitchen. It's amazing what you have to do to satisfy the insurance firms these days.' said Jane. 'We only have two doorways to access the private area of the house, and we have security guards on them with a list of names. They will be on duty until midday on Monday, so don't be surprised if you get asked for your names countless times. I did think about an identity bracelet but they're not exactly in keeping with evening wear.'

They all laughed.

Jane took them through the private hallway to the huge double doors, a security guard stood in front of the doors. 'James, I'd like you to meet Karen, Bernie and Faye, they will be staying in the house this weekend.'

'Good afternoon ladies, it is a pleasure to meet you all.' James shook everyone's hand.

'James Tilbury is head of security at Tynetree, he's been here for many years.... How many years?'

'This is my fifteenth Daffodil Ball,' said James.

'Time flies.' replied Jane.

James unlocked the righthand door into the Ballroom. 'It looks amazing! Jane, what a magical place you've created.' said Faye.

'Thank you, I didn't really do anything. I gave Simon the Architect a brief outline of what I'd like so he and his team got on with it. They have done an amazing job. We have outdoor canopies, posh toilets, first aid area, parking, buses, taxis, – in fact, you name, he's organised it.'

'It's all beautifully finished and with a lovely creative flourish.' Said Faye.

Jane and the girls spent the next hour looking around. 'Let's get back into the main house, I could do with a stiff drink or a strong coffee, or both.' said Jane. 'Tonight, we're having a dinner in the small dining room, well, it's not so much dinner as a buffet. I thought it would be easier since Clare is having the weekend off to enjoy the Ball. I insisted she enjoy it rather than fret, worry and miss out on all the fun.' They sat in the kitchen, drank coffee, and ate sandwiches.

'What are you wearing, Jane?' asked Karen.

'I'm not really sure, I have a few outfits to consider. I think I'll pick one tomorrow. What about you?'

'I have a long dress with a navy and yellow pattern. It's a new addition to my wardrobe.'

'It looks fabulous!' said Faye.

'I can't wait to see it, Karen. Faye what about you? Have you made up your mind?

'Yes, I have. Miraculous really, as soon as I saw a black and mustard trouser suit, I thought, that's the one.'

'Ooh, lovely!' said Jane.

'Bernie what are you going to wear?'

'Well, as the mistress of indecision, I have three outfits with me, and a few accessories. It's what we are always told when you're in front of the TV camera, 'Accessorise, Accessorise, Accessorise!'

They laughed.

The girls retired to the flat to prepare for a quite evening before the Ball. 'Great, our bags are here,' said Karen.

'Ooh look, the fridge is stocked with wine and champagne!' exclaimed Bernie. 'That'll help calm the excitement. What do you think?'

'Pour me one, please!' said Faye.

'Coming up!'

'Karen?'

'Yes, please!'

At 7pm, they all went down to the dining room, Jeff met them at the door and served them more champagne. 'Help yourselves ladies,' he said, pointing to the huge spread of food.

'Thanks Jeff,' said Faye, she smiled at him and walked away.

'Faye,' Jeff called out after her.

'Can I have a quick chat with you?'

'Yes, certainly, what can I do for you?'

'Mmm, I wish you could do a few things for me,' said Jeff.

'Jeff, that sounds a little pervy, was that your intention?' Faye asked.

'Oh sorry, no, I didn't mean to offend you.' Jeff went red, 'it must be the excitement about tomorrow, it's clouding my judgement.' He lied. 'Please accept my apologies.'

Faye curled her lip. 'Thanks. Apology accepted. What do you want to talk to me about?'

'I'd like to have art lessons from you and wanted to find out when we could start and how much you charge?'

'Okay, let's catch up on Monday before I head back to Fife, we can chat about it then?'

'I could meet you in the library later on?'

'Why would we do that, Jeff?'

'Okay, Monday works….I'll…' Faye walked away.

'Have you got your outfit for the Ball, Karen?' asked Taylor.

'Yes, I found an outfit.' Karen smiled. 'Me wearing a dress is a big occasion.'

'Oh, can't wait to see you in your dress, it will be a very special occasion.' said Taylor, he smiled back at her.

'Very, very special. And it may never be repeated.' laughed Karen. 'What are you wearing?'

'Well, I'm not very adventurous so I'm going to wear some yellow accessories and have some yellow detailing.'

Jane stood up. 'Goodnight all, I'm going to retire early in the hope I'll be able to sleep. Before I forget, breakfast will be served from 7 – 9am, and lunch will be sandwiches.'

'Night Jane, thank you for another lovely evening, sleep well, and see you tomorrow,' said Karen. 'I think I'll do the same and retire early.'

'Not a bad idea,' said Taylor, 'I need my beauty sleep.' He smiled, leant over and kissed Karen on the cheek and whispered in her ear, 'sleep well, and I look forward to having a dance with you tomorrow.'

The girls were pleasantly merry as they headed back to the flat.

'I could get used to this lifestyle,' said Faye. 'Why did I spend so much time in France when I could have this much fun in Scotland?'

CHAPTER 29

'Okay, be honest gals, how do I look?' asked Faye. She stood in the sitting room of the flat in front of the Georgian Fireplace. Her dark long hair gleamed.

'Wow!' said Bernie, 'you look great, and very sophisticated.'

Faye laughed, 'we all know that's not true!'

'What about me?' said Bernie, 'do you think this looks better than my first outfit I tried on?' Bernie did a twirl. Her blonde hair sat neatly on her shoulders. The canary yellow 1950s style dress with the sweetheart neckline flattered her shape.

'Amazing, that's so you!' said Faye.

Bernie smiled, 'thanks, it fits me really well, and it's a lovely feeling wearing my mum's jewellery. She would have loved to have been here for the Ball.'

Karen peered around the sitting room door frame. 'She would have been the Belle of the Ball,' said Karen. 'You look amazing.'

'You have an amazing figure, I am so envious,' said Faye. 'The dress is perfect, it's so you. Come on Karen, out you come!' she shouted.

'We're waiting!' said Bernie.

'I'm coming, don't nag me!' Karen, laughed. She picked up her long dress and walked carefully into the sitting room.

'Wow, look at you, a picture of womankind in full bloom,' said Faye, 'you look beautiful, it is a perfect fit and look at your curves. Karen, in all the years we have known one another I've never seen you so beautifully dressed. You look fabulous darrrr-rling.'

'I feel nervous…' said Karen.

'Me too!' said Faye.

'And me three,' said Bernie.

'We don't have to worry, we have each other. It's going to be a great evening!' said Bernie.

'Yes, you are right!'

The girls completed their final checks on their make-up, zips, and bag contents. They opened a bottle of champagne, stood in a circle and raised their glasses, 'Onwards and Upwards!'

They walked down the small staircase through a doorway then down a huge flight of stairs to the first floor of Tynetree House. At the end of the hall they met James the security guard.

'You all look amazing. Enjoy your evening ladies, and if you need me, I'll be right here.' James opened the right hand side door leading into the ballroom.

Karen lead the way, followed by Bernie then Faye.

'Good evening ladies, may I have your names?' asked an attendant. 'If you would like to go to Bar one to your left for drinks, then you will be escorted you to your table shortly after 7.30pm.'

'Oh look, Jane, Warren, and Clare are over by the bar,' said Karen. The girls were served glasses of champagne and canapes.

'Wow, ladies! What can I say, you all look stunning! And, I'm almost speechless, is that glamorous gal in the yellow dress really my dear friend Karen?' said Warren.

'Isn't it going to be an amazing night?' said Jane, wide-eyed with excitement, and looking very regal in her couture gown and glistening diamonds. A small band played Scottish music on the stage as other equipment was being set up around them.

Bernie looked over to the stage. 'Are you having a number of bands playing tonight?' she asked, 'it looks like they're still setting up their gear?'

'It's one of the musical guests, he's a local lad,' said Clare. 'He had a number of hits years ago. You'll know him.' Warren leaned in close between Bernie and Clare, 'and he turned up late!'

'It'll be okay, he looks as though he's nearly finished.' said Clare.

'Who is it, Clare?' asked Bernie.

'It's Fletch, from Vermillion,' said Clare, proudly.

Bernie looked puzzled.

'Oh, you'll know him,' said Warren, 'remember the song, Hayley?'

'Oh god, yes!' said Bernie.

'He is the main event and he is doing the auction before he sings. Followed by Stefano Verdano Bianchi, the DJ,' said Clare. 'Excuse me.' She walked across the main floor of the Ballroom towards the stage, and spoke to a security guard. He went up the stage steps and tapped Fletch on the shoulder and said something to him. Fletch turned around, smiled, and climbed off the stage and embraced Clare.

'I haven't seen you in years!' said Fletch.

'It's been too long.' said Clare.

'You are looking well, and as sexy as ever.' said Fletch. 'Are you still married to the city nerd?'

'Ha, well, yes, although he's no longer working in town, he works here on the estate with me.'

'I should kidnap you and take you away to my highland lair where he'd never find you,' said Fletch.

They hugged and kissed. 'Let's catch up after my set?' said Fletch. 'Where can I find you?'

'Great, I'll be over there by the big table arrangement,' said Clare. They kissed and Fletch hugged her tightly, he enjoyed feeling the warmth and contours of Clare's body against his.

The Daffodil Ball was a huge success, everything worked to plan, raffle tickets were sold out, and the auction, hosted by Fletch, brought in thousands. Afterwards, he sang a couple of his recent songs, no-one knew, but when he sang his biggest hit, 'Hayley' everyone joined in. Fletch was swiftly followed by the DJ, and the Ball had turned into a party with a dancefloor bursting full of people.

'Don't great ladies loos make all the difference,' said Bernie to a woman washing her hands.

'You are so right, they're essential.' She replied, as she dried her hands. 'Are you enjoying the Ball?'

'Yes, it's my first one, and hopefully one of many. Have you been to them before?'

'I think this is my seventh Daffodil Ball, I started coming here when I met my partner and moved over from Fife.'

'Oh, Fife! That's where I'm from. What part are you from?'

'I was born in Cupar but most of my family live on farms around the county.'

'Small world,' said Bernie. 'I'm in Kirkcaldy.'

'I like Fife but haven't been back for a few years. I was talking to one of my cousins about the serial killer.'

'Shocking, isn't it?' said Bernie.

'All those men she killed. I'm not really at that surprised though, she was married to a distant uncle of mine. The family have always claimed she murdered him.'

Back in the Ballroom. 'That was fun but I need a seat. Fancy a drink?' said Simon.

'Thanks, I think I need some fresh air,' said Faye. 'I don't think I've danced like that since I was in my twenties.'

'Fancy getting out of here? I have a bottle of champers under the table.'

'Sounds like a plan, where shall we go?'

Faye smiled, 'if you can discreetly grab the bottle I know where we can go. Follow me.' At the huge double doors at the end of the Ballroom, Faye knocked on the right hand door.

'Good evening Faye. Good evening Simon,' said James.

'Thank you James, we need to escape the Ballroom for a while, you can't hear yourself think in there.'

'No problem. Come through.'

Faye and Simon walked down the long hallway, she stopped at the library door. 'How about in here?'

They walked into the library and closed the door behind them, the soft lighting and the stillness amongst the books was a haven away from the noise and energy of the Ballroom. Faye kissed Simon. He slipped her jacket off and pulled her into him. 'I've waited all night to do this,' Faye said.

Simon replied, 'actually, I've waited since we met at dinner a few weeks ago.' Simon took his jacket off, deftly opened the champagne, 'you'll need to take a swig from the bottle as we don't have glasses.'

Faye took a swig from the bottle, the fizz exploded over her face and down her top and the front of her trousers. 'Oh dear, I'll have to get you out of those wet clothes.'

'Really, why?' said Faye, smiling.

He took Faye's mustard silk shirt off over her head and placed it over a chair, he unbuttoned and unzipped her trousers, she stepped out of them and he hung them over another chair. Faye stood by the huge book shelves in her yellow underwear. Simon led her by the hand towards the shelves of books. 'Climb up there,' he said, and pointed at the vintage oak spiral library steps.

Faye smiled and climbed up the steps. 'How far do I go?'

Simon watched her, 'stop on the third step, and carefully turn around, and hold onto the handrail.'

Faye stood on the third step and turned around. 'Perfect.' said Simon. He kissed her left thigh, and then the right. He slipped his hands behind her and pushed his fingers under her yellow lace knickers stretched across her bum. His teeth gripped the ties on the side of knickers, he slowly pulled them off. His hands moved across her hips and over her stomach, and down. He opened her legs wide. 'This is why.'

Jeff's security phone alerted him to movement in the closed off part of the house. He opened the security camera App on his screen and scanned through the rooms. He looked around the library and saw a man with his face buried between Faye's legs as she balanced on the library steps. He hoped it would be his turn once he started his private art lessons. He pressed record and watched them. His viewing was interrupted by a second security alert. He glanced through the rooms of the house then checked the garage alarm. He scanned around the cars and spotted a couple having sex on the bonnet of the estate Jaguar. He zoomed in. It was Fletch with his trousers at his ankles. Jeff smiled, pressed record, and thought it would be a good video to add to his private collection. Fletch kissed the woman passionately, he stopped thrusting, and turned her over on the bonnet of the Jag. Jeff blinked. They hadn't had sex in years yet his wife was willingly being screwed by Fletch over the bonnet of a car.

Karen and Taylor sat in the summer house in a secluded corner of the formal gardens. 'What are you looking for in man?' asked Taylor.

'Why do you ask?' said Karen.

He smiled and looked at her. 'I recall at dinner a few weeks ago you mentioned a few of your dating experiences and they didn't sound too positive.'

'I've had a couple of tough years, and getting through them has helped me discover who I am. I want to find a man who makes me happy, and I make him happy.'

Taylor hugged her. Karen smiled, 'I guess that's the thing with age and experience, it gives you an opportunity to take stock. I don't mean it to sound dramatic and sad, but I have experienced almost every emotion apart from true love. For some reason, a loving relationship has evaded me.'

'Until now...' said Taylor.

CHAPTER 30

'Sharon is coming over tomorrow morning to photograph the farmhouse. She is confident I'll get a steady rental income from it,' said Karen.

'Can you text me her number?' said Bernie.

'Yes, will do. I did say to her you'd be in contact because you had thought about doing the same thing with Jute House.'

'When are you planning to move to Tynetree?' asked Bernie.

'I'd love to go tomorrow but I am so exhausted with all the court appearances and the harassment. I'll see how quickly Sharon thinks she'll get it rented out and take it from there.'

'Is the harassment still bad?'

Karen sighed, 'yes, a journalist from some New York paper called me early this morning. I'm so sick of them. I know it's been a big story but why can't they just move on to something else.'

'Can't anything be done to stop it?'

'I asked Justine but she said there's very little she could do apart from get another number. She said because I'm out there in the public domain, I'm deemed fair game.'

Sorry Karen, it's not fair on you. It was a sensational, shocking, and tragic, she killed more than 10 people but it's all out there now.'

'The sooner I can move away from Maryard the better.' said Karen.

She put her phone down on the kitchen table, switched on the kettle, and caught sight of herself in the mirror. She looked closer, and saw a few grey hairs had appeared in her hairline. Karen's phone rang, she looked at the screen but didn't recognise the number and let it go to voicemail.

The following day, Sharon arrived. 'I'll show you around first then we could have a coffee,' said Karen as she took Sharon's coat and hung it on the coat stand in the kitchen.

'How are you coping?' asked Sharon.

'Honestly, I don't know. I think I'm okay then I've felt shocked, and thankful it wasn't me she targeted and then downright stupid I didn't pick up on any of it.'

'You shouldn't beat yourself up, she was clever and conniving,' said Sharon.

'It is hard to comprehend, isn't it?'

'Do you think she killed more than the ones she was charged with?'

Karen raised her eyebrows and nodded. 'The Police think they'll uncover more but they don't know how many. They said she used drugs, many of the poisons she grew in the garden.'

Sharon signed. 'She was very clever. Didn't she have some kind of background or training in the drugs industry?'

'Yes, she was a pharmaceutical toxicologist before she retired,' replied Karen.

'Bloody hell, you should write a book about it!'

'Bernie has been commissioned to do a documentary about it so we shall see what the response is but I don't know if I could write it, it feels too close and personal.'

'Maybe you'll feel different in a year's time?' asked Sharon.

Karen poured the coffee into mugs, 'I wish I could just flick a switch to turn off the harassment from the Press though.'

'They'll move on.' Said Sharon.

'Yes, that's exactly what Bernie said. Did she call you?'

'I'm going over to Jute house when I leave you, she said she was working from home and keen to see me.'

'There's a lady coming over from America, she's an Art history lecturer. She is starting a three or five year secondment at Edinburgh University, this could be the perfect house for her.'

Karen laughed, 'she can move in straight away, I'll move out tonight!'

'Are you serious?' Sharon's eyes opened wide. 'Do you want to rent it out as furnished?'

'What do you think?'

'You'll get more for it as a furnished house.'

'I bought most of this stuff when I moved in, more or less everything you have seen in the rooms can stay. What do you think I could get for it?'

Sharon looked around, then walked into the kitchen and looked out the window.

'Off road, private parking for two cars, detached, a garden, two bedrooms, study and all this space downstairs.'

She walked back to the kitchen table, looked at her phone, 'I think you could be looking at least £1,200 -1,500 a month.'

'Really?'

243

'Yes, really!'

'I didn't think it'd be that much.'

'Realistically, what sort of timescale are you thinking about, Karen?'

'I was serious, I don't want to be here and would be happy to move out tomorrow if it were possible.'

'That's excellent. I'll talk to Lily Steinbugler-Leigh this evening and come back to you.'

'That's a wonderful name. Do you know her well?' asked Karen.

'Nico worked for her first husband back in the 80s when he was still modelling. I think he helped them move house and did some driving for her. I think she used to call herself Lilianna Lestrange in the 80s, she was married to a very wealthy man who owned large areas of England.'

'Shall I give you a set of keys? I'm going over to Tynetree this afternoon.'

'I think it'll all happen quickly so keys would be handy if you're away.'

'Thanks Sharon, I appreciate you coming over. Call me as soon as you have an update. If you're going to Bernie's can you give this, it's one I borrowed from her.'

'Topical.' said Sharon as she looked at the front cover of the book Karen handed to her, 'Inside the Mind of a Serial Killer.'

'I wish I had read it years ago, but there again, I'm not sure it would have done any good. Imagine knowing you were having coffee with a serial killer, and she only lived a few fields away.'

'You couldn't make it up,' replied Sharon.

Karen sat on the chair and looked out over the formal lawns towards the lake. Tynetree estate was beautiful. She took a deep breath, and allowed her eyes to focus on a distant oak tree. She opened the large, heavy art book she had taken from the shelf in the library section close to the window. The smell of the old paper made her sneeze.

'Bless you!' came a voice from the doorway.

Karen smiled, 'thank you Jane.'

'I thought I'd find you in the library, it's one of my favourite rooms to sit and enjoy the peace.'

'I love being surrounded by all your beautiful books,' said Karen as she gazed around the room at the tall shelves full of books covering all the walls.

'I'm pleased you have settled in, Karen,' said Jane, 'it is great to have you here. You have added to the happiness of Tynetree.'

'I feel so much better, and happier now I'm miles from all the Annie stuff.'

'I can understand getting away from the all the stress, but do you miss Fife?'

'It's odd, years ago, I moved back to Fife because of my ex-husband's job offer. I hadn't thought about it before and I never imaged I'd live back in Scotland, never mind Fife. I left in my early twenties because I was searching for a better life elsewhere.'

Jane nodded, 'I can understand that. I also left Scotland but it wasn't my decision, I was sent away to boarding school, came back for the summer then was packed off to University and never returned apart from family visits, funerals, and weddings. I had a great life in London and the home counties, we all did. I met Malcolm on his family's Buckinghamshire estate. They used to hold a country fair at the end of May, everyone I knew had the date logged in their diaries. We would make the pilgrimage from London to Amersham for the day. Malcolm was the safety officer at the clay shooting competition. That was when I discovered I could shoot,' Jane smiled.

'What a lovely memory,' said Karen. 'It sounds fairy-tale like.'

'The early years were great, we travelled all over the world but Malcolm started to get bogged down with the family business. We moved to Tynetree when his Uncle died and Malcolm inherited the Scottish country pile. Plans were made before the funeral and we moved up within a month.'

'Did you talk about the move?'

'It was simple. We were married and he made the decisions. I was his wife and wasn't part of the decision making process.' Jane sighed.

'It was a big life-chaning decision.'

'Yes, it was. It took me years to realise I was married to a bully. He seemed to get a pleasure from shocking people. At the end of one harvest suppers, he stood up from the table and thanked everyone for turning up, then said, make the most of the food and wine because this is the last Tynetree harvest supper and there would be no more farming. He laughed, downed his wine, and left. He wanted to rewild the estate so he sacked the farmers and staff. Thankfully, I was able to keep them employed on the estate so they kept their homes, they all had families but Malcolm didn't give a hoot.'

'What a horrible thing to do.'

'It was awful, he even gave people money to leave Tynetree.'

'Money?'

'Yes, thousands of pounds in cash. Malcolm gave them all envelopes with a letter saying they were sacked and had to leave immediately. Their belongings would be sent on. He told them they would get an addition bonus of five thousand if they left within 12 hours and kept quiet.'

'Utter madness!'

'He was mad. It just goes to show how loyal they all were because everyone returned the cash to me. I said nothing to him and carried on as normal, so did the staff. It was never mentioned again.'

'How could you live with him?'

'He became fixated about his routines, and double and triple checked everything. When he came to bed at night, he'd go around the house switching lights off and on and off. It was infuriating.'

'Isn't that an obsessive compulsive condition?'

'He wouldn't see a doctor but we all knew there was something happening to him but we couldn't get him to leave Tynetree to see a specialist. He was awful to everyone. He lived on his own in one wing of the house, we wouldn't see him for weeks on end.'

'What about you?'

'Well, I carried on living my life. I travelled as often as I could.'

'Did you think about divorce?'

'Yes, daily. I couldn't see how I could do it, he would have cut me out of everything and goodness knows what he would have done to the estate staff. I carried on though and we had completely separate lives. I managed to glide through life for weeks without seeing or speaking to him.'

Karen smiled, 'thank goodness this place is so big.'

'He thought I hated the place, and it was a hassle for me but it was him I disliked and not Tynetree.

'I admire your staying power, Jane.'

Jane stood by the huge Georgian window, she turned around and slipped her hands into her trouser pockets, walked around the table, and leant against the back of the chair. 'When Malcolm died in 2015, it took me a while to realise I was no longer in limbo. I was free and Tynetree was not the millstone around my neck that Malcolm hoped it would be. He left everything to me with specific instructions of how he wanted the estate managed and rewilded. However, he hadn't taken into account a couple of important updates and failed to lodge them through the proper legal channels, so the entire estate was legally mine, I could do what I wanted as his instructions were null and void.'

'Thank goodness, Tynetree wouldn't have been the place it is today without you, it's like a love story, Jane.'

'Yes, I guess it is. I am making big decisions for the estate and it feels great and there's no Malcolm controlling us.'

Karen's phone rang, she pulled it out of her pocket and looked at the screen. 'Number unknown! I'll give you two guesses what that is likely to be about? Annie Bloody Northwood!'

'It must be so tiresome for you, hopefully they will move on and find another story.'

'The sooner the better. I never realised the ramifications of the trial. Some of the magazines I worked for asked me to take a break because the interest in the trial didn't do their circulation figures any favours. I had a book event cancelled because the organisers feared a gang of journos would turn up and hijack it.'

Jane smiled, 'at least they can't harass you here. If I find any of them on the estate I'll have them shot and fed to the hounds.'

They laughed.

'I am going to carry on with life and refuse to let it get in the way. Tomorrow, I'm going to explore.'

'You should take a look in North Berwick, there are some interesting shops and quirky cafes.'

'I think I'll call Faye and see if she fancies a trip out, would you

248

like to join us?

'You and Faye enjoy exploring, I've got a load of estate business to deal with so I'll join you another time.'

CHAPTER 31

In the morning, Karen phoned Faye, 'Fancy a trip to North Berwick?'

'Yes, I could do with a break from painting. I'll get myself ready.'

'Fab, see you in an hour-ish!' said Karen.

Karen drove down the main drive, turned left at the T-junction by the ancient wood and followed the bend in the road. Faye locked the big glass doors of the gallery as Karen pulled up.

'How's things?'

'I'm good thanks, how about you? Still enjoying a wild sex life with the man of your dreams?'

'Hmmm, he is getting boring.'

'In what way?'

'Let me buy him a pipe and a pair of those dark brown tartan slippers with the fake furry turnovers and then I'll tell you.'

As they joined the A1, Karen asked, 'why do you say he is boring?'

'Well, when we first met we used to do lots of different things all the time. He made a big effort.'

Karen drove towards Tyninghame village. 'Isn't he just getting comfortable? You know, he's done all the hard work attracting a mate?'

'There's something else going on, and I can't put my finger on it. He says all the right things, it's all timed to perfection. I think we'd call him a patter merchant.'

'A patter merchant!' Karen laughed, 'I haven't heard that term in years.'

'It's like he's memorised the latest version of the awardwinning patter and chat-up guide. He was full of compliments, considerate, kind, and thoughtful. But I think they were all fake and shallow. I am getting to see the real person behind the screen of charm. Oh, and don't get in a car with him. He's hell behind the wheel, so bad tempered.'

'I detest angry drivers. Sounds like the shine has worn off.'

'You know what we always say about gut instinct, you have to listen to it.'

They arrived in North Berwick.'Let's get a coffee before our mooch around?' said Karen as she turned left into the car-park.

As they left the carpark, Faye smiled then linked her arm through Karen's as they walked down the narrow pavement of the main street. 'I haven't had my daily 3 gallons fix of strong coffee yet.'

They found a small coffee bar within a bakery. 'You grab a seat, I'll get the coffees ordered,' said Faye.

Karen perched herself on one of the two bar stools near the window. Faye returned from the counter and tried and failed to get on the bar stool. She laughed, 'I'm not as tall as you, I need a different technique.'

'Oh, come on, when did you last struggle to clamber on top of something?' Karen giggled.

Faye laughed all the more as she tried to lever herself onto the tall seat using the table. 'There! Finally made it! I hope they bring the coffee over because I'm not getting off this again.'

'Two coffees and two Danish pastries,' said a voice from behind them.

'Oh lovely, thank you.' said Karen.

A tall woman with her hair in a ponytail smiled at them. She placed the coffee and pastries on the table, 'I love your books.'

'Thank you very much for saying so.' Karen smiled back at the woman.

'I saw you at the Daffodil Ball a couple of months ago.'

'Wasn't it great fun, we're still talking about it.' Said Karen.

'Sorry, I should have introduced myself, I'm Anita Layton, this is my bakery and coffee bar.'

'Nice to meet you Anita.' Karen shook Anita's hand. 'This is Faye Robinsfield.'

'Hello Faye, lovely to meet you, I also love your work and a pleasure to meet you. Enjoy your coffee and pastries, ladies,' said Anita, she walked back to the counter, and disappeared into the kitchen at the back of the shop.

'That's nice,' said Faye, 'and so is this coffee.'

When the girls left the bakery, they turned right and crossed the narrow main street.

'How gawdy, just look at all the sparky stuff in the window, I mean, no one with creative talents smoothers everything in glittery things.' Faye half-laughed, half-sneered. 'Let's go in for a look!'

'Hello darlings, do come in!' boomed an operatic style voice in the doorway. A short black-haired woman with long, pointed blood red nails held the large wood edged, glass door open.

'Do take a look around, if you have any questions please ask, I am here to help you with your purchases.'

'Err, thank you,' said Karen.

'Can I ask if you are seeking a particular statement piece?' The woman looked at Faye.

'No, we are just browsing,' said Faye.

The woman looked back at Faye, as though she had a question for her. Faye smiled and walked further into the shop. Faye nudged Karen, 'darling let's take a look!'

As they walked around the shop and looked at the pre-loved designer coats, hats, and bags they heard the familiar Facebook ping coming from the front of the shop. Karen glanced back at the shop owner. She was crouched low behind her sales counter, making a call, and trying to talk in a whisper.

Karen turned around and looked through the displays of bags on a large round table. 'Some nice things in here.'

'Yes, a few but it's not really my thing. Can you see me using this?' Faye held up a huge Mulberry handbag to her chest, pushed her chin out and fluttered her eyelashes, 'do you think it's me, darling?'

They laughed.

'Are you Faye Robinsfield?' asked the shop owner. Her posh accent had disappeared and swapped for something more re-gional.

Faye turned around, smiled. 'Yes I am.'

The woman had one hand on her hip, she sneered, and curled her lip. 'I thought it was you!'

'Yes, and what?' said Faye, her voice had quickened. 'Do you want to buy a painting?'

The shop owner spat out words in a broad Fife accent, 'I hope you're enjoying screwing ma husband?'

'What the hell are you talking about?'

'You've been fuckin' ma husband since you met him up on that estate.'

Faye looked down her nose at the woman, 'who is your husband?'

The woman sneered again. 'You don't know? Are you screwing so many local men you don't know their names? If I told you ma name was Glassington I'd hope it'd ring a few bells?' The woman tilted her head and looked Faye up and down. 'WELL, DOES IT?'

'Come on Faye, let's leave, we didn't come here to get harassed,' said Karen. She reached out and put her hand on Faye's forearm.

'Aww, yes.' Faye laughed. 'Simon told me you ran off with the local builder's mate.'

'He's still my husband and you need to stay away from him!'

The girls walked towards the front door, the woman flew after them. 'You need to fuck off back to France, you slut!'

Karen grabbed the brass handle and pulled the door open, and made sure Faye was right behind her. The woman snatched the door from her grip. As they stepped down to the pavement, there was an almighty crash and shards of glass fell at their feet. Through the door frame minus the large glass panel, the red-faced woman foamed at the mouth, 'you slut, just fuck off!'

'Wow, welcome to North Berwick!' said Faye.

They walked quickly away from the shop 'Did you know about her?' asked Karen.

'Simon told me he had a pending ex-wife but I wasn't sufficiently interested to find out more.'

'Let's go in here.' They turned left, and walked into a small, converted building with bare brick walls, chalk board menus and quirky seating. They ordered coffee and sat at the back of the seating area.

'What the hell was that about?' asked Karen.

'Your guess is as good as mine?'

'Are they still married?'

'Yes, technically married but officially separated.'

'I wonder if she knows that.'

'Ha, yes she knows alright. They've split up and got back together many times. He told me she returned on one occasion to give the marriage another go, and gave him a STD.'

Karen screwed up her face.

'I haven't seen him that much, his moany, miserable face isn't exactly what I looked forward to. I used my painting as an excuse to shut myself away. No-one wants to be around a misery guts.'

'Did he warn you about her being unhinged?'

'No, he was always so matter of fact and how he pleased he was to see the exit door at the end of the two year separation.'

'It's odd, why act like a screaming banshee and smash your shop door? I doesn't take Freud to work out she still has feelings for him or is jealous he has moved on.'

Faye smiled, 'do you think she'll calm down if I go back and buy that Mulberry bag?'

CHAPTER 32

Faye studied her painting. There was something about it she liked but there was also something she disliked. It was time to take a break. She would revisit it later. Her phone vibrated in her pocket.

'Hi Karen, I'm good thanks. No, I've just finished painting. How are you?'

'Do you fancy a coffee?' asked Karen 'I'll come down and we can go somewhere, or you can come up to the house?'

'Getting out is a good idea, I need to get away from a painting, it is still in the development stage and I need to update you about Simon.'

'Oh, sounds ominous! I'll come down and pick you up in 20 mins?'

'Great, I'll be looking a little like the wild artist but I don't care.' Faye laughed.

'I'm hardly the epitome of high fashion, Darling!'

They both laughed.

Faye washed her hands, took off her painting shirt and pulled on her one of her favourite Hobbs tops. A Land Rover pulled up outside the art studio, it took Faye a moment to see it was Karen behind the wheel. 'Jump in!'

'Oooh, this is fun!'

'I met Jane in the back kitchen, she said it needed to be used and I could take it as often as I needed it.'

'Great, I can see over hedges!'

'Jane said she'll be down to see you later today, she wants to speak to you about a commission for the house.'

'She mentioned something about it a while ago, I thought she'd forgotten about it.'

'I think she's had a lot on her plate, there's been countless meetings in town for the planning permission of the clay shooting ground. She has the go ahead but they're dragging their heels on some of the details.'

'Do you fancy going to the little tearoom in Tyninghame?'

'Yes, sounds great, and as long as it doesn't have any mental ex-wives lurking in the dark corners.'

The girls settled into the snug tearoom, with coffee and scones. 'So, come on, I have waited long enough, tell me about Simon?'

'Okay, I have cut all ties with him.'

'Was it straightforward?'

'Nope, this is where it gets interesting.' Faye laughed.

'He was still very intertwined with her, what's her name, Christie or something?'

'You were right.'

'He called me three or four days after we'd been in her shop, tried to say he'd been busy with this thing and the next. I played it cool, and remarked about his increased workload. He said part of it was connected with his ex-wife. My ears pricked up. He went to the shop to sort out the door she smashed but that wasn't the story she told him. Apparently, she was all over him saying she'd had rowdy customers in the shop and they had upset her displays and thrown something at the door on their way out, and broken the glass.'

'That's a joke.'

'So, I asked about how it happened, and when he finished giving me the sob story of how tough it is for her I told him you and I had gone into the shop, she had gotten aggressive and warned me off, slammed the door and broke the glass herself.'

'Good for you for telling him.'

'He hung up on me then he called me back about an hour later, and told me we had no right going into HIS shop and harassing HIS wife!'

'Ha! What planet is he on?'

Faye shrugged. 'I told him to look at the internal CCTV, and he'd see what really happened.'

'He ranted down the phone we had harassed her and we shouldn't have gone to North Berwick, apparently, l had no right to be there.'

'What?'

'I couldn't believe it but I couldn't stop myself from laughing. He is as unhinged as she is.'

'What happened next?'

'I couldn't stop laughing so he hung up on me, again. He called back 10 minutes later to ask if I found harassment funny, so I took the opportunity to suggest he shoves his head up his ass and not to bother me ever again. Fancy another coffee?'

When Faye returned with more coffee, 'how are you and Taylor getting on?'

'Okay, he's a nice guy but I haven't progressed anything with him.'

'Aww, that's a shame.'

'I asked Jane about him, she diplomatically said he's worth a body swerve.'

The girls returned to the estate, Karen dropped Faye off at the studio. Jane was getting into her car as Karen pulled up in the Land Rover.

'Hi Jane, it was great being back in the LR again. Faye and I had a girlie catch-up over coffee in Tyninghame.'

'Has she ditched Simon?'

'How did you guess?'

'There's always some drama following Simon around.'

'I didn't tell you, but Faye and I had a strange experience in North Berwick. We went to his on/off wife's shop, we had no idea it was her. She started having a go at Faye for having an affair with her husband, she was spitting feathers. She slammed the doors behind us so hard she shattered the huge glass panel.'

'I'm not surprised, that sounds like her.' said Jane

'Really?'

'I had to ban her from here, Simon is welcome but only if he leaves her at home. He was a great architect but she is a nightmare. She came to the Daffodil Ball a few years back, and started a fight in the ladies loos with another female guest because she wore the same outfit as her, then she had a go at the door steward.'

'Sounds as though she's still on form,' said Karen.

Back at the flat, Karen made some tea and sat at her desk. Her phone rang. 'Hi Bernie, how are you?'

'Pretty rubbish, I need to talk, something has happened at work and I'd appreciate your wisdom, a shoulder and some wine therapy.'

'Sure, come over. Are you okay?'

'Yes, I am okay but I just need to talk.'

'See you when you get here, safe drive.'

Her phone buzzed with a text message, *'Meant to ask, do you need anything picking up? I'm stopping at Morrisons. Berniexx'*

'Got everything, if you don't fancy spicy pizza and wine pick something else up Kxx.'

At 6.05pm, the door of the flat swung open, Bernie had her overnight bag over her shoulder and three Morrison's shopping bags. She looked tense.

'Let me sort the bags out, do you want a shower or bath before you eat?'

'How much time do I have?'

'As long as you want?'

Within 20 minutes, Bernie was showered and sitting at the kitchen table in her multi-coloured leggings and a Robbie Williams tour t-shirt, with a large glass of wine in her hand. 'I have been sacked from work.'

'What?'

'A made complaint was made against me. It claimed I harassed a man in the work environment. It turned out it was that prick I went to Penrith with.'

'The guy who wore women's knickers and you left him there to get the train home?'

'Yes, that's the one.'

'What happened?'

'There was a big department party last month, loads of people attended. Dave spoke to me later on in the evening, and as he walked away, I playfully grabbed his bum and asked if he still wore his mum's knickers, and did they turn him on. You know the sort of thing, it was always called banter, and we've all had it done to us over the years. Janine, Susan, and Helen were there, we all laughed. The following day he reported the incident to HR, the case was reviewed, we were all interviewed and he said he didn't feel comfortable being around me because I had belittled and bullied him in the work environment. After countless official meetings, I was sacked for sexual harassment.'

'Oh bloody hell, I am so sorry. What a complete joke!'

'HR quoted the 2010 Equality Act at me about sexual harassment and told me I was guilty of violating his dignity, and my behaviour had been unwanted, inappropriate and intimidating.'

'That's unreal!'

'Yup, I thought the same,' said Bernie.

'Can you get legal advice, and appeal?' asked Karen.

'I had specialist legal advice, and they said I shouldn't fight it as my chances of getting it overturned were almost non-existent. The girls were called to give evidence, and of course they told the truth, why wouldn't they. As women we lived with this sort of behaviour our entire lives. They were as shocked as I was, they all said it was fun, he didn't look offended, and had joined in with the laughter. The legal specialist said what I had done was deemed as sexual harassment, I had touched him inappropriately, and degraded him in the work place in front of colleagues.'

'I think of the times over the years we have been groped by men, propositioned and had to listen to vile comments about our bodies. We had to grow thick skin and a sense of humour because we were subjected to male letches, perverts, men who ogled us. We've been sexually harassed our entire lives. We've all had experiences of serious sexual harassment, and didn't have the protection of the Equalities Act. It was always shrugged off because it was men being men.'

'I'm so sorry, Bernie, it's like a bad joke!'

'A tiny part of me is trying to laugh at the ridiculousness of it all.'

'Try to put it out of your thoughts,' said Karen, as she struggled to find the right thing to say.

'I'll try to put it out of my mind but I need to think of work. I can carry on freelancing but maybe go for something more local – like UK based, or Scotland based.'

'Why the hell not? It could be the change you need, a new direction, a new challenge?'

'Maybe…. But.. oh god, I'm not sure. I'm still in shock.'

'I'm not surprised. Look, why don't you stay here for a few days, or longer?'

'Thanks Karen, that's probably good idea. I wouldn't mind catching up with Faye and seeing how her new project is developing.'

'Great, that's it settled, stay as long as you want.'

Karen walked across the kitchen, and took out the two pizzas from the top oven and placed them onto a huge wooden chopping board. She sliced them up and put them onto a large colourful serving dish.

'They smell, and look great!' said Bernie.

'Get stuck in, then we can drink more wine and plan your new career path.'

CHAPTER 33

'We're picking up Faye in a few minutes, are you ready?' asked Karen.

'Yes, I'm ready to go now,' said Bernie

'Getting out will do you the power of good, you have been sulking around Tynetree for too long.'

'I know, I know. I'm aware my few days have turned into a few weeks...'

Karen cut her off before she could finish. 'You are welcome to stay as long as you like but I don't like seeing you so down. I know it has been a shock but you have picked yourself up from much worse.'

'I know. But I'm older, and my options are very limited.'

Faye skipped across the carpark when the Land Rover pulled up. She flicked back her long dark hair. 'Ladies, how lovely to see you!'

'Gosh, have you been on the happy pills?'

'I have been in talks about a new exhibition, and it may be held in Edinburgh and not London later this year.'

'Well done!' said Karen.

'That's great news, Faye!' said Bernie.

'You don't fancy being my PR guru, Bernie?'

Bernie smiled.

Faye leaned forward across the footwell between the front and middle seats of the Land Rover. 'I'm serious, I need some help. I can't do it, well, apart from the fact I don't know what I'm doing, I have to paint and stay in my creative zone. AND, you have loads of experience in the media!'

'True, it sounds interesting. Let's talk about it over the next few days and see if we can thrash something out?'

It took just thirty minutes to drive to Gullane. The long main street stretched out ahead of them as they slowed down to look for the pub. Karen reverse-parked the long-wheel base of the Land Rover on the main street into a space between two small cars. 'Most blokes couldn't do that,' said Bernie.

They walked into the reception area of The Bonny Brock, the latest celebrity chef pub and boutique hotel to open in trendy Gullane. 'I likey!' said Faye, looking around and appreciating the design details and the art on the walls.

'Your stuff would look good in here,' said Karen.

'I agree.' said Faye.

A tall, slim waiter took the girls to a table in the main dining area. 'Order what you'd like, and drink what you want, I'm paying and also the head chauffeur today, no arguments!' said Karen.

'On one condition, I get to pick up the bill.' said Faye.

'Aww, no, really..!' said Karen, shaking her head.

'I'll get it!' said Faye.

'Nope!' said Karen.

'Yup!' said Faye.

'For god's sake, listen to you two.' said Bernie, she rolled her eyes and resumed studying the menu. 'Well, I'm not paying!'

They laughed.

'It's my treat, I'm paying,' said Karen. 'And it was my idea, so there.' She stuck her tongue out.

'Okay, it's yours but the next one is on me,' said Faye.

'And the next one, possibly a few light years from now, will be on me.' said Bernie.

They enjoyed the food, and shared their dishes. 'I can't say I'm stuffed after that but it was, unquestionably delicious.' said Karen.

Bernie nodded, 'I agree, but I'd rather feel this way and be comfortable. I don't want to burst out of my clothes and get done for more sexual harassment.'

They laughed.

The waiter brought coffee to the table. He smiled at Karen, 'it's a pleasure to have you dine with us, Ms Knighton.'

'Thank you,' Karen replied. A distant version of the William Tell Overture could be heard. They all looked at one another, trying to figure out where the sound was coming from. 'Oh Christ! Sorry, it's my phone,' said Bernie, as she fumbled in her bag for the phone.

The waiter said. 'Tim has asked me to invite you and your two friends to our game menu launch evening? May I have your address to send out your invitation?'

'Thank you, that's very kind of Tim. Here is my address.'

'Thank you very much, Ms Knighton. Tim would like to say hello before you leave.'

'Lovely, I look forward to meeting him.' said Karen, with a big smile.

The waiter walked across the restaurant floor and out of sight, both Faye and Bernie pulled a face at Karen, and Faye said, 'Oooh, get you!'

Karen faked a look of smug satisfaction, 'well, you know, I can't help it.'

'So, who are the two friends you are taking with you? Come on, you can tell us, and we won't be jealous?' said Bernie.

'Did you sleep well?' asked Karen.

'Yes, I did, thanks, and you know what, I have made a decision,' replied Bernie. 'You know the phone call I got when we were at lunch? Well, it was from Fergus.'

'Fergus?'

'You met him years ago, he was mum's oldest friend.'

'He lives in Cumbria?'

'We had a long chat, he's not in the best of health, and he wants me to go to visit him soon.'

'Are you going to go?'

'I slept on it. This morning I phoned him back and told him I'd be down tomorrow.'

'Fantastic! A complete change of scenery will be good for you, and you used to love it there.'

'You are right, Karen. It's not as if I have any pressing business meetings or filming deadlines.'

'You did say you were going to help Faye out?'

'Yes, I haven't forgotten about that and I won't let her down.'

'How long are you going to stay in Cumbria?'

'I don't know. Fergus was keen to see me sooner rather than later.'

'Do you need any help with anything?'

'No, I'm good.'

'Are you okay for money?' Because if you are not, you know I'll happily help you in any way I can.'

Bernie hugged Karen, 'thanks Karen, I am okay but that's not to say I may need your help in the future.'

'Anytime, and never forget that.'

The girls sat at the kitchen table with large mugs of coffee and gazed out across the formal lawns. 'I still think about Annie, and how we sat at the kitchen table in Maryard, and chatted about everything.'

'You must miss her? You are probably still mourning the loss of the friendship.'

'I think about all the chats we had, and it still sends a shudder down my spine when I recall most them were about men and she killed them.'

'I still have the rights to make, produce and screen the documentary about her but I am not sure if I really want to do it anymore.'

'Things can change at the flick of a switch.'

'You're not wrong. Look at me now. Do you think Jane would mind if I took the Land Rover down to Faye's studio?'

'No, of course not, she wants us to use it on and off the estate.'

'Good, I'm thinking of getting rid of the Land Cruiser and maybe get something smaller or just different.'

'Enjoy the drive. It'd easily carry all your gear around, and you get them in more interesting colours than blue and green.'

'I'm going to have a chat with Faye about the promotional work she wants doing, and I'll let her know about my trip to Cumbria.'

'Okay, could you ask her if she has made any plans for tonight, and if she hasn't ask her if she wants to come up for food and wine?'

'Yeah, good idea, Karen. Onwards and Upwards!'

'The LR keys are on the desk in the hallway, see you later.'

Simon's car was parked outside Faye's studio when Bernie turned up in the Land Rover. Faye stood close to the doorway as she spoke to Simon. 'Hi Bernie, come in, Simon is just leaving.' She looked at Bernie and made a face.

'Yes, yes, I'm leaving but look, I just want us to be friends, carry on where we left off. It was a complete mis-understanding, I'm sorry!' Truly sorry!' pleased Simon.

'Is everything okay, Faye?' asked Bernie, as she tried to put together what was going on.

'Yes, it is.'

Faye turned and looked at Simon, 'go away, and leave me alone.'

'But Faye, we were good together....'

'Simon, don't be so ridiculous!'

'Look Faye, we had fun...and.....'

'GO AWAY and leave me alone or I'll tell your wife you are pestering me for sex.' Simon's eyes widened as Faye's words filtered through to him, he inhaled, turned on his heels and walked to his car. He stopped to look back at Faye but she had closed the door.

'Prick!' said Faye, shaking her head.

'Is he that bad?'

'Gawd, yes!

'You know he came here hoping we could be friends and still have sex.'

'God, that's some nerve.'

'I quote his exact words, "we enjoyed great sex so we should carry on just fucking one another" unquote.'

'Only a man could come up with that logic.'

'Do you fancy a coffee?' Faye and Bernie sat on the old sofa in the corner of the studio.

'All the promotion work can wait, you know. The corporate wheels are slow to turn. It's a change in venue from London to Edinburgh so it shouldn't be a big project.'

'I don't know how long I'll be in Cumbria, I'm keeping an open mind about it because I'm not really sure what the state of his health is.'

'Do you think Fergus is going to sell up and retire?'

'Maybe, he's getting on a bit. I was trying to work out how old he'll be.'

'You'll get the full picture once you're down there, maybe Karen and I will come down for a short break?'

'I hope he has modernised the place, my childhood memories are of dark rooms, flock wallpaper and candlewick bedspreads, cheese toasties and pork scratchings.'

'Eeew...' Faye pulled a face.

'Right, I'd better get back to the house.'

'Are you going back to Kirkcaldy?'

'No, I have decided to leave tomorrow and head south. Sharon has a set of keys to Jute House, and is showing people around it. She has a couple of very interested parties looking for a long term let, they're connected to some new building work that's going on in the town.'

Faye hugged Bernie tightly, and kissed her on the cheek. 'Have a safe drive tomorrow, Onwards and Upwards!'

'DAMN! I forgot! Karen asked if you fancied coming up to the house for food and wine tonight?'

'Sorry, I can't tonight, I've been invited as a guest speaker at a local art club in West Barns. If I can get them all on my side they can travel by the bus-load to my big exhibition in Edinburgh at the end of the year.'

'Good thinking Ms famous artist!'

CHAPTER 34

Bernie left the estate just after ten o' clock. South of Edinburgh, the landscape opened up. The rich green tones and patchwork fields filled her vision. She remembered the café at the foot of Soutra hill, her eyes searched the road ahead for a sign, after a left-hand bend in the road she spotted the café carpark next to a collection of buildings. She indicated left, and pulled in. Drops of rain dotted her windscreen as she switched the engine off.

She climbed the short staircase up to the entrance, and pushed open the heavy glass door. The café was quiet. Bernie sat at a table by the large window, sipped her coffee, looked out across the landscape, and watched as a raincloud passed through.

Her phone vibrated in her bag, *'What is your ETA? Fergus.'*

'Hi Fergus, I should be with you mid-afternoon, Bernie X'

Then she listened to her voicemail message, 'Hi Bernie, it's George Richardson, can you call me please, it is rather urgent.' Bernie felt her happy mood slip away. She finished her breakfast, visited the ladies, and went back to her car to make the call. 'Hi George, it's Bernie Flynn.'

'Thank you very much for calling me back so promptly. I had a call a short while ago regarding the sexual harassment case. I am sorry to have to tell you this but David Wilkinson is taking out a private prosecution against you and is suing for sexual harassment and is seeking personal damages and court costs.'

'Whaaaaaaaaaaaaat? He can't do this? I thought it was all finished. I've been sacked, I've left!'

'He's taken further advice to pursue for personal damages.'

'I don't believe this, why is he doing this to me?'

'I am afraid I am unable to answer that. Do you have your diary to hand? We must make an appointment for next week?'

'Err, yes. Let me see.' Bernie looked into her handbag for her diary and a pen. She dropped the pen in the passenger footwell. 'Fuck it!' she muttered. 'Sorry, George, you were not meant to hear that.'

'What day?

'I suggest Thursday morning, I will have spoken to his representative by then and should have a forward plan.'

'Okay, Thursday morning. What time?'

'Shall we say 10am in my Edinburgh office?'

Bernie sat back in the car and felt the knot of stress tightening up in between her shoulders. She opened the car door, jumped out and walked around the perimeter of the car park. She tried to clear her head. She reminded herself she was going to help an old family friend and it would take her mind of it. She kept repeating, 'stay positive, stay positive, stay positive.' The drive down the A68 and through the Kielder Forest had taken her mind off everything. She had pulled in by one of the clearings, and went for a short walk down by the side of a small lake. 'Onwards and upwards!' she said, as she got back in the car.

The drive along the B road took her close to Hadrian's Wall, and the vast open views pushed her worries away out of sight. On the A69, as she crossed the border between Northumberland

and Cumbria, she had a strange feeling, a warm, welcoming sensation, the sort she had to when she arrived home after a long drive.

The M6 traffic moved well, she took the Hutton-in-the-Forest turning, and headed west for Lamonthwaite. She could see the hotel in the distance. The Lake District opened up to her left, with Blencathra standing proud on the skyline.

The Oak and Bell didn't look any different. The carpark was uneven, and the ancient oak stretched it's huge bows out across the beer garden. Bernie suddenly felt nervous, she hadn't seen Fergus in years. She recalled the last time was at her mum's funeral. She followed the path between the car park and the pub garden to the main entrance, and pushed the heavy wooden Tudor door open into the main reception area.

'Darling, you made it!'

Fergus moved slowly out from behind the large, curved reception desk. He supported himself on the desk as he made his way to the side opening, stopping to pick up his elbow crutches before he made it out onto the carpet.

'Fergus, what has happened?'

'Give me a hug!' They hugged awkwardly. His body felt thin and bony, his clothes offered no padding.

'Come with me, I'll get the coffee made and tell you all about it! It's so good to see you. How was your drive?'

'I took my time, and enjoyed the scenic route down the A68 and A69, it brought back lots of memories travelling with my mum.'

'She'd like that, she was a wonderful old girl, everything was done with style and aplomb, she never missed a beat, did she?'

'She didn't!' His comment filled Bernie with warmth. She smiled at Fergus but he has his head down, focussed on getting across the hall into the lounge on his crutches. His face looked tight and his body misshapen.

'Could you live here?'

'Err, live here?'

'Yes, could you live here?' asked Fergus as he made a pot of coffee.

'I don't know, I've never thought about it.'

'Would you want to live here, and run the hotel?'

'Fergus, what is wrong?'

'I'm getting old, and need to know the hotel will carry on with a new face at the helm. Age does terrible things to you, and I don't have the same enthusiasm for it.'

'I'm sorry to hear that.'

'Don't give me sympathy, instead, seriously think about taking this place over? It does well, I can show you the accounts, and there's money in the bank.'

Fergus looked around the empty lounge distracted by something. 'How are your friends getting along?'

Bernie sipped her coffee, 'Faye left France, and moved back to Scotland and Karen has moved to East Lothian to escape the aftermath of the serial killer.'

'Terrible business,' said Fergus. 'It was on the news, in the papera, on the radio, everywhere!' He took two pills from his shirt pocket, popped them into his mouth and swallowed them with a mouthful of coffee. 'Why don't we invite them down?'

He struggled up from his chair, and shuffled towards a large box file sitting on the table by the fireplace. 'Ah, here it is.'

'They're both busy with work stuff, Faye has a new Edinburgh exhibition planned later this year. It'll be her first Scottish one.'

'I don't miss that world at all, my art gallery on George street was good fun but it took over my life. Can't imagine the Edinburgh lifestyle would be as much fun these days.'

Fergus put the box file on the table and returned to his seat next to Bernie. 'Tell me what happened with your work? It sounds bizarre. Were you being flippant about the sexual harassment?'

Bernie sighed. 'No. I was sacked for sexual harassment. I still don't believe what happened. All the years I had put up with sexism and macho bullying and I make a comment and pinch someone's bum at a work's party and I'm reported and sacked.'

Fergus pulled out two envelopes from the box file, 'these are for you,' and handed them to Bernie.

'Open them.'

'This can't be right?'

'Yes, it is. Now, please open the other one.'

'You've left me everything in your will?'

'Everything. You are my daughter, and this is all yours.'

ABOUT THE AUTHOR

L inda Mellor is a columnist, feature writer, and photographer. She grew up in Fife, Scotland then moved to London in her early twenties to further her career in Search & Selection. In her mid-30s, after years of city life, she returned to the countryside and established herself as a photographer and began writing. She regularly writes for countryside magazines and enjoys wildlife photography.

Over the last 25 years, Linda beat cancer three times, and, now at 55, is living a happy life in the Scottish Highlands.

www.lindamellor.co.uk

Printed in Great Britain
by Amazon